Desert Vengeance

Books by Betty Webb

The Lena Jones Mysteries
Desert Noir
Desert Wives
Desert Shadows
Desert Run
Desert Cut
Desert Lost
Desert Wind
Desert Rage

The Gunn Zoo Mysteries
The Anteater of Death
The Koala of Death
The Llama of Death
The Puffin of Death

Desert Vengeance

A Lena Jones Mystery

Betty Webb

Poisoned Pen Press

Poisoned Pen
PRESS

Copyright © 2017 by Betty Webb

First Edition 2017

10 9 8 7 6 5 4 3 2 1

Library of Congress Catalog Card Number: 2016952020

ISBN: 9781464205934   Hardcover
9781464205958   Trade Paperback

Poisoned Pen Press
6962 E. First Ave., Ste. 103
Scottsdale, AZ 85251
www.poisonedpenpress.com
info@poisonedpenpress.com

Printed in the United States of America

Dedicated to Louise Signorelli, 1941-2016

Acknowledgments

Many thanks to the people who helped make this book possible. Attorney Rachel Mitchell, sex crimes bureau chief for the Maricopa County Attorney's Office, and her staff provided immense help in helping me understand the dynamics between child molesters and their domestic partners. Stepping up to the plate (as usual) were the Sheridan Street Irregulars—especially Louise Signorelli. Also, Kathy Wasserlein's help was invaluable. Smiles and thanks go to Nancy Miller-Borg and Linda McCracken, both of whom I met at Birmingham, Alabama's Murder In the Magic City; these kind ladies agreed to lend their names to characters in this book. I hope they enjoy it.

"In everyone's life, at some time, our inner fire goes out. It is then burst into flame by an encounter with another human being. We should all be thankful for those people who rekindle the inner spirit."

—Albert Schweitzer

Chapter One

I was waiting for him when he stepped out of the prison van. The man who had raped me when I was nine years old squinted against the savage August sun and took a hesitant step toward the beat-up Honda Civic. The driver's side door opened.

"Get in here, quick!" the rapist's wife yelled. "She's here, too!"

And so I was. Instead of parking my tricked-out 1945 Jeep at the far side of the lot to escape notice, I had parked right behind the Civic. I wanted them both to see me, to take note, to realize that after almost thirty years, I still remembered.

As the rapist shuffled toward his wife, I stepped out of my Jeep. Smiled. Waved. Flashed my Vindicator. Made certain the rapist noticed the gleam of the sun along the knife's ten-inch-long, tempered steel blade. Made certain the rapist knew it was nothing like the cheap kitchen knife I had defended myself with the last day I'd spent under his roof.

My Vindicator wouldn't break.

Neither had I.

Chapter Two

It's easy to follow a car once you've affixed a GPS tracker onto its passenger-side wheel-well, so I could have slipped several cars back while following the Civic north along State Route 79 to Apache Junction, but what would be the fun in that? I wanted the Wycoffs to know they weren't done with me, nor I with them.

During the trial, two of the Wycoffs' former foster children came forward to testify against him, with five more kids waiting their turn. But knowing what I now know, I guessed there had been even more victims during the couple's years working with Child Protective Services.

Child Protective Services? What a joke.

When the Civic sped up, I sped up. When the Civic slowed down, I slowed down. When the Civic pulled into a rest area at the side of the road, I pulled in. Neither Wycoff got out of the car, but I saw Norma take out a cell phone and punch in a number. I was close enough to see her lips moving, but I didn't need to be a lip-reader to know she was on the phone with the Pinal County Sheriff's Office, begging for help. After a few minutes' wait and not one squad car in sight, the Arizona heat finally got to the Wycoffs and they took off again with me right behind them.

I've always loved this stretch of desert. Miles and miles of low flat land forested with saguaro, cholla, and prickly pear cacti. A hard landscape, but if you knew its moods, a sustaining one. Had Brian Wycoff recognized its beauty as he paced the exercise yard at the Florence Correctional Facility? I doubted it, since his eye was more attuned to the defenseless beauty of nine-year-old girls.

The Wycoff house, on the eastern edge of Apache Junction, wasn't much. To pay the trial's expenses, Norma had vacated their Scottsdale house and moved to this cheapo neighborhood. It hadn't looked too bad at first, but over the years I watched it deteriorate to the point where most people would have torn the house down and built a new one. I doubted Norma Wycoff, that Mistress of Denial, could see it as it was: an unkempt faux-stucco with blistered blue paint defacing the window and door sills. As if determined to keep up with all that ugliness, the dying grass in the front yard was littered with empty soda cans, plastic Circle K bags, and freebie newspapers rolled into rotting cylinders.

Welcome home, perv.

Yet the house sat at the base of one of the most spectacular sights in Arizona—the Superstition Mountains. Lit by the morning sun, the mountains' red, gold, and purple cliffs rose straight up behind the Wycoff hovel, as if trying to shame it into beauty. Fat chance. Once my former foster father had been outed for the monster he was, Norma stopped trying to keep up appearances and let everything slide. If it had been within her power, like all good passive-aggressives, she would have allowed the mountains themselves to crumble.

The Civic pulled into what was left of an asphalt driveway. I parked at the curb and watched them exit the car. Before they reached the door, I caught up with them.

"No balloons, Papa Brian? No party favors?"

He said nothing.

"You can't harass us like this," Norma said, her chin jutting out from her fleshy face. "It's against the law."

"So's child rape."

"You were a liar then, and you're a liar now. My husband never touched you."

Behind her, as if taking refuge in her bulk, Wycoff plucked at her dress. "Norma. Please. Let's just get in the house."

The jowls on Norma's face wobbled as she jerked her head around. "She needs to be told a thing or two!"

Oh, I loved the way this was going. I flashed my knife again. "Pretty, isn't it, Papa Brian? You wouldn't believe how much it cost me."

Wycoff's complexion, already prison-white, paled even further.

"It's called a Vindicator. Correct terminology is important, don't you think?"

Norma jerked her head back toward me. "I'm calling the police right now!"

"Be my guest."

"I'm going to tell them all about you!"

"I've always been a fan of freedom of speech."

By now several neighbors had emerged from their houses to see what was going on. Exactly what I'd intended.

"Hey, everyone, look who's home!" I shouted, as Norma messed with her iPhone. "Brian Wycoff! Isn't that great?"

The pregnant woman in the well-tended house next door was too young to have followed the trial so I briefly summarized it for her. Loud enough for everyone to hear.

"Mr. Wycoff here was convicted of thirty-eight counts of child rape and sodomy, got sentenced to twenty-five to life but hit the jackpot in his last parole hearing. Prison over-crowding, good behavior, the usual excuses. No children for him to rape in prison, right? Mr. Wycoff is what they call a Level Three sex offender, a perp most likely to re-offend. Anyone up for a Welcome Home party?"

After a horrified look at her new next-door neighbor, the pregnant woman ran back into her house and slammed the door. Several other neighbors did the same, but a few stragglers remained. One of them, a grizzled oldster, listened intently.

"You bitch," Norma huffed.

"Takes one to know one. Hey, Papa Brian! I can hardly see you there, hidden behind your wife. Get fitted for your ankle bracelet yet? You're supposed to wear one for the rest of your life, I hear, and not live within one thousand feet of any school or child care facility. But unless I'm wrong…" I pointed down the street "…that's a nursery school on the corner."

"It's just some slut had more brats than she can handle!"

"Hmm. I see two toddlers on a swing set, three on the slide, and the woman watching them doesn't look like their baby mama. Even if it's an unlicensed day-care facility, the law would still apply."

Norma looked like her eyes were about to explode. "The police are on their way!"

The oldster went back into his house but left the door open, which I found interesting since Arizonans are usually careful to block the heat out and keep the air conditioning in. Seconds later he returned with a Mossberg shotgun almost as big as he was. After delivering a fuck-you look at Wycoff, he flourished the shotgun in the same manner I'd flourished my Vindicator. A warning, not yet a promise, but considering it, considering it…

My work here finished, I drove away as the music of sirens filled the air.

When I reached Desert Investigations, it was just after eleven, time for an early lunch if I felt so inclined. But the faces of the two Scottsdale PD detectives waiting for me would put anyone off their feed.

I forced a smile. "If it isn't my good friends Sylvie and Bob!"

Bob smiled back. Sylvie, the pit bull of the two, snarled.

At separate times, Bob Grossman and Sylvie Perrins had been my partners while I was still with the Department, but that was many years and many loyalties ago. Their visit today would show if any of those old loyalties remained.

"You just had to go and do it, didn't you?" Sylvie snapped. Last week she'd been a blonde; today she was a brunette. Woman never could make up her mind who she wanted to be. A scowl marring her otherwise model-perfect face, she sat behind my desk, leafing through my papers while Bob watched, aghast.

"Go and do what?"

"Pester the Wycoffs. Sumbitch did his time, now leave him alone." She looked down. "Jesus, your handwriting's as bad as my gynecologist's."

Jimmy, my business partner at Desert Investigations, wore an I-told-you-so look on his face. He shook his head sadly, then went back to his computer.

Knowing Sylvie wouldn't move until she was ready, I sat down in the client's chair across from her. Like everything else in the office, it was new, purchased after arson had forced a redo of the entire office. This time I'd let Jimmy choose the furnishings. Thus the décor was a hymn to his Pima ancestors, with a sand-colored carpet, chairs upholstered in hand-worked Pima Indian designs, and petroglyph-style paintings by one of his artist cousins that featured Earth Doctor, Spider Woman, and Night Singing Bird. I waited for Sylvie to say something nice about it. She didn't.

Annoyed, I said, "Don't keep me in suspense. What did the Wycoffs claim I did?"

"Threatened them with bodily harm."

"What kind of bodily harm?"

"The standard, I imagine. Loss of life, loss of limb, et cetera." She flipped another page. "You can actually read this shit?"

"On occasion. Which one of the Wycoffs told you this? Norma? Brian? Or do you just sit around listening to rumors these days?"

"Apache Junction PD reached out."

"So it was AJPD who told you I threatened the Wycoffs with bodily harm, not the Wycoffs themselves."

A slight smile. Sylvie wasn't as cranky as usual, which I found interesting.

"Say, it's hotter than hell outside. You guys want some Tab? Ice tea?"

"Tea, no sugar, I'm sweet enough." The smile broadened.

Bob spoke for the first time. "I'll go for the Tab. God knows where you find it." Judging from his incipient pot belly, he drank Classic Coke, calories and all.

"I have my sources." I got up and went to the office refrigerator. "Jimmy, how about you?"

"Tea for me, too." He stopped typing.

For the next few minutes the four of us sat around sipping beverages and discussing the weather. We came to the conclusion that it was hot.

"Already one-eighteen at the airport." Bob.

"Made it to one-twenty-one in Scottsdale yesterday." Sylvie, leafing through my papers.

"Only one-fifteen on the Rez." Jimmy. "More brush, less asphalt."

"Rain's forecast for tomorrow. Should cool us off some." Me.

"Monsoon season's starting early." Sylvie.

"Sure hate them haboobs." Bob.

"Handwriting like this, I can't see how you made it through college." Sylvie. In one big gulp, she drained her glass.

"Same way your gynecologist did, probably." Me.

Sylvie put my papers back down, squared them off in a neat pile, and stood up. "Bob, we better get our asses back in gear. Places to go, creeps to see."

Without another word, they left.

But they didn't drive off right away. They sat there in their unmarked black Dodge, studying our storefront while sweating early-bird tourists passed by them on their way to the nearest Main Street souvenir shop or art gallery. Some might even make it before collapsing from heat stroke. August in Scottsdale should come with a warning label.

Fully ten minutes later, Sylvie and Bob drove away. Slowly, making certain we noticed.

After a few moments, Jimmy said, "That was weird."

"Sylvie has a nine-year-old daughter. Bob's got two girls. One's eleven, the other's eight. They had to put up a front, not that they wanted to."

"Oh."

"Yeah, oh."

But I wasn't kidding myself. The detectives had delivered an official warning, and whatever I did from here on out needed to be less publically confrontational than the airing of grievances, so I spent the next hour designing and printing two hundred flyers on Day-Glo yellow paper. Over the photo I'd taken of him in the Florence Correctional Facility's parking plot, the headline read: BRIAN WYCOFF, CONVICTED MULTIPLE CHILD RAPIST NOW RESIDING AT 70325 E. SARSAPARILLA LANE, A.J. Below his picture, it said: LEVEL THREE SEX OFFENDER—LIKELY TO RE-OFFEND. The lettering was large enough for a blind man to read.

The day slid into routine. One phone call after another requested our assistance in tracking down deadbeat parents and runaway children. The high spot was when Evelyn Morris, a four-times-married sixty-something woman who walked in without an appointment, told us she was about to tie the knot again but first wanted to make certain her pool-boy boyfriend was marrying her for love, not her considerable fortune

"Make sure there's nothing unseemly in his past," she said.

"Like cattle-rustling?"

She cracked a dentured grin. "I just want to make certain he's never done this before. Marriage, I mean. I don't want any trouble with jealous exes."

I told her she'd come to the right place, had her pay a retainer, and sent her happily out the door.

Fifteen minutes later, Jimmy's computer check came up with the name of the pool boy's current (his second) wife; he was still living in her twelve-room mini-mansion overlooking some scrub land up north. She, too, was in her sixties.

Another check showed that the love-struck Evelyn Morris owned a twenty-two-room mansion—nothing mini about it—overlooking Paradise Valley Country Club.

"Boy's moving up in the world," Jimmy said.

"Not once I call her."

At five, we closed up shop for the day. I took the flyers and a heavy-duty stapler to my Jeep, then drove back to Apache Junction.

Two hours later, all the supermarket bulletin boards and utility poles closest to the Wycoffs' house were papered with flyers. I had saved the best for last—the telephone pole right in front of their house. The Civic was still parked in the driveway, and as I stapled the Day-Glo yellow sheet to the pole, I saw Norma watching open-mouthed from her window. Good. I wanted her to see me, to think about me. I smiled and gave her a wave.

I have a memory...

I was nine years old. It was Thursday morning, the day Norma always volunteered at her church, the day Papa Brian always came home early from work, the day he always raped me. It had been going on for weeks and I couldn't stand it anymore. This time I would tell, no matter what he threatened to do to me or to my dog Sandy.

Norma was in the kitchen, where several loaves of banana bread sat cooling on the counter. She was adding an egg to a large bowl of what looked like cookie dough. As I watched her, Sandy leaned against my leg, giving me the courage I needed.

"Mama Norma, I have to tell you something."

"Make it quick, Lena. I still have four dozen cookies left to bake. Those homeless families, these might be the only treats they get all month."

I took a deep breath. "Papa Brian's been doing things to me, bad things."

Norma dipped a finger into the cookie batter. Tested it. "Needs more sugar."

"Bad things."

She looked up. "You're late for school."

Last week one of the girls at school, another foster child, had used the word so now I knew how to say it.

"He raped me, Mama Norma. Papa Brian raped me."

She added sugar to the bowl. Tasted the batter again. "I said you're late for school!"

"He raped me lots of times. The first time he was hiding in my closet when I got home from school and he told me that if I ever told anyone he would kill Sandy."

She didn't look up. "Little liars go to Hell."

"He hurts me a lot. Every Thursday because you get home from church late."

She still didn't look at me or raise her voice in the slightest, but she said, "Get out of my kitchen you lying little bitch before I knock you from here to wherever. And if you ever say anything about this to anyone, I'll cut out Sandy's heart with a knife."

I got out of her kitchen.

Papa Brian raped me twice later that day, but Mama Norma had given me an idea.

Pleased to see Brian Wycoff join his wife at the window, I reached into my tote, and pulled out the Vindicator. When I was nine, he had looked so big. Now, wizened by decades in prison, he looked little taller than me. Norma, however, had fattened to twice his size.

Hoping they could hear me or at least read my lips, I shouted, "Maybe my Vindicator isn't as long as the knife I gutted you with years ago, Papa Brian, but it won't break like that one did!"

I sat there for another hour until the AJ cops pulled up and ran me off.

Chapter Three

Monsoon rain and thunder woke me at one in the morning. I never got back to sleep, so by six I was again parked in front of 70325 E. Sarsaparilla Lane. The Wycoffs must have had trouble sleeping through the monsoon, too, because through the living room window I could see someone moving. He or she—it turned out to be Norma—looked out, noticed my Jeep, shook her fist at me, and closed the curtains. Smiling with satisfaction, I settled in for the long wait.

When you've been a cop, then a PI, as long as I have, you learn a lot about stalking. The average stalker is an intelligent but underemployed male in his thirties who has trouble maintaining relationships. He often suffers from a borderline personality disorder, magnified by a fear of abandonment. His only goal in life is to make his victim pay attention to him.

Simple as that.

His victim—usually female—being unaware of the stalker's true motivation, unknowingly encourages him. She answers the phone when he calls. She doesn't turn away from him when she runs into him on the street. Instead, she repeatedly pleads with him to stay away. Sometimes she even initiates a contact herself, thinking that if she can only find *just the right words* or present a *good enough reason* why any relationship between them is impossible, he'll finally get the message and leave her alone. In reality, she has accomplished the exact opposite of what she wanted.

She gave him a food pellet.

In 1953, Psychologist B.F. Skinner ran his classic conditioning experiment on lab rats. At the beginning of the experiment, every time the rats pushed a lever, they received a food pellet. After a while, they only received a food pellet every other time. The rats quickly adapted and would give the lever two quick pushes. Then the pellets came only randomly, seemingly unconnected to the lever pushes. Toward the end of the study, the rats could push the lever as many times as they wanted, but wouldn't get any pellets. Oddly enough, this didn't make them give up. They kept pushing the lever again and again and again, in an obsessed frenzy.

Stalkers are like rats. When you reward them with any kind of attention, negative or not, you've given them a food pellet. Like the food pellet Norma just gave me.

By seven, and one more fist shake and an upwards thrust middle finger—two more food pellets!—I pulled away from the curb and headed to L.A. Fitness. Sitting on your butt all day isn't good for your muscle tone.

As usual for this hour, the gym was crowded with the standard desk jockeys, attorneys, accountants, and upwardly-mobile IT nerds attempting to vanquish their broadening rear ends on the Nautilus machines. I ignored them and went straight to the treadmill area, where I pounded through five miles. Loosened up, I hit the free weights for a while, then the leg press, and finally returned to the treadmills for a leisurely cool-down. While jogging along next to Terri Richter, an attorney friend of mine, I planned my next assault on Casa Wycoff.

Given the après-rain humidity and rising temps, I decided a dead fish on their doorstep should be good for a few more food pellets. God knows the timing was right. Safeway was having a sale on mackerel, a particularly smelly fish, so sometime today I would stop by and purchase one. Or two. Or three. Humming happily, I shut off the treadmill, said goodbye to Terri, and headed for the shower.

I arrived at Desert Investigations mere minutes ahead of Sylvie and Bob, which surprised me. Since when did non-violent stalking garner an early morning visit from the cops? Jimmy had that I-told-you-so look on his face again.

"So what's Apache Junction PD's complaint now?" I asked, heaving a sigh. "Littering? I'll save you some time and plead guilty. We might have enough in our petty cash to cover the fine."

"Lena Jones, we need you to accompany us to the police station, and, uh, you'd better call your attorney." I had never heard Sylvie sound so formal, yet so hesitant.

I looked at Bob. He wouldn't meet my eyes.

"What happened, Bob? Wind blow one of my flyers into some litigious asswipe's face?"

Bob cleared his throat as if he was getting ready to speak, but said nothing.

"Sylvie?"

Damned if the woman didn't have trouble meeting my eyes, too.

"Look, Detectives, unless you have an arrest warrant I don't need to go anywhere with you."

"Lena's right, Detective Perrin," Jimmy said. "Without a warrant, you can't force her to go anywhere."

Sylvie glared at him. The glare softened when she turned it on me. "Call your attorney, Lena. This could take some time."

Her very softness made up my mind. "Come to think about it, I'd kinda like to see what this is all about, so just give me a sec." I picked up my phone and dialed Terri Richter, who—judging from the background noise—was still on the treadmill at L.A. Fitness.

"Can you meet me at the cop shop in ten?" I asked.

"Which one?" Thud, thud, pant. Thud, thud, pant.

"Scottsdale Headquarters, Indian School Road."

"Ah, your old stomping grounds. Be there in a half hour, gotta shower first."

Dial tone.

My old stomping grounds being mere blocks from Desert Investigations, we beat Terri Richter to the cop shop by twenty minutes. Up until she arrived, I continued yesterday's conversation about the weather, careful to avoid all mention of the temps in Apache Junction.

"It'll rain by noon." Me.

"One can only hope." Bob.

"Where were you between six and nine this morning?" Sylvie.

"I like the way the rain makes everything smell so fresh." Me.

"Makes the flowers bloom, too." Bob.

"Wrong season for flowers, they're all dead by now," Sylvie groused. "Just like…Well, we'll get to that later. Anyway, what's the problem with telling us where you were this morning, Lena?"

The interview room door opened and my attorney rushed in, her hair still wet. With her sun-streaked blond hair and hazel eyes, the former Miss Arizona was still beautiful, but she could turn ugly on you in an instant. She was looking pretty ugly now as she narrowed her eyes at the two detectives.

"Are you charging my client with something? If not, she's out of here."

Sylvie, who had faced down many an attorney in her years on the job, said, "We just want to ask her a few questions, that's all."

"Questions about what?"

Sylvie flicked a quick look at me. "Her whereabouts this morning. Maybe even what she did after papering Apache Junction with a million flyers." She handed one to Terri, who gave the flyer a brief glance, then handed it back.

"It was only two hundred," I said. Oops.

"Don't say another word, Lena." Then, to Sylvie, Terri said, "What makes you so interested in my client's movements this morning? You have nothing else to do with your life other than harass my client? Get a boyfriend, for Christ's sake!" The way those two talked to each other, you'd never guess they'd been friends since childhood.

"Just trying to map out a timeline, Terri."

"Again, for what reason?"

Sylvie looked at Bob.

Bob looked at Sylvie. Shrugged. "Might as well tell her now. It'll be on the noon news anyway, so what's a couple of hours?"

With no expression on her face and no inflection whatsoever in her voice, Sylvie said, "A UPS driver found Norma Wycoff dead at her Apache Junction home at eight-thirty-six this morning, and there are indications the death wasn't, ah, natural."

I resisted the urge to jump up and cheer.

Terri, attuned to the lightening of my mood, placed her hands on my shoulders and pressed down hard. "And you dragged my client down here why?"

"There was no dragging involved. She came voluntarily. But to answer your question, we want to interview Ms. Jones because several witnesses saw her Jeep parked in front of the Wycoff house this morning from six until seven."

Terri laughed. "So? It's a free country, and there are plenty of Jeeps around here."

"Not sandstone-colored 1945 Jeeps decorated with Pima Indian designs. There's only one like that I know of, and it belongs to your client. Mention was also made that a blonde was sitting in it."

Terri thought for a moment, then said, "Even if my client was seen parked outside a convicted pedophile's house from sunrise 'til friggin' midnight, so what? The Superstitions are a well-known scenic area, prone to spectacular sunsets, and if I remember correctly, we had a wowser of one last night before the monsoon hit. Pink, purple, orange, it looked like an orgy in a Crayola box. This morning's sunrise was a copycat. Anyway, a little fresh air does a gal good, and as for the blonde bit, get real. Last I heard, bleach is still legal in this state." She flipped her own dyed locks for emphasis, then lifted her hand off my shoulders. "C'mon, Lena. We're out of here."

I followed her out the door.

Neither of us said a word until we reached the parking lot, then she snapped, "Stay away from Apache Junction, you idiot."

I looked up at a gray-and-white sky. A thin layer of clouds blocked the scalding sun but hiked up the humidity. "I thought you said it's a free country."

"Yeah, but attorneys aren't, and unless you stay far, far away from Brian Wycoff—don't give me that surprised look, I read the newspapers, too—you'll be paying me enough to add onto my house that new sunroom I've been thinking about."

"Nobody in Arizona needs a sunroom."

"You don't listen, do you?"

I imagined the murder scene. I hoped it was messy and that her death had been slow and painful, because I hadn't been the only little girl Brian had raped while Norma looked the other way. From the trial transcript, I knew that at least two of the other children had told her what he was doing to them, but she'd ignored their accusations in the same manner she'd ignored mine.

"I wonder how she died. Shot? Stabbed? Strangled?"

"Lena! Shut up and listen to me!"

"I also can't help but wonder where Brian was when she got offed, either."

"Oh, dear God, you're hopeless. Look, I'll say it again. Stay. Out. Of. Apache. Junction."

"Huh?"

"Stay out of Apache Junction!"

"You don't have to shout."

Looking ugly again, Terri climbed into her pearl white Cadillac and sped away, leaving me to walk fifteen blocks back through the heat to Desert Investigations.

An hour later I was parked a quarter mile away from the Wycoffs' house on Sarsaparilla Lane. The street had been cordoned off, with what looked like the entire Apache Junction Police Force attending the festivities. Several yards away, a couple of plainclothes guys were talking to a UPS driver—I made note of his truck's license plate—but the moment the detectives spotted my Jeep, they sauntered over.

"Something tells me you're Lena Jones," said the one who introduced himself as Detective Guillermo Arrize. He was in his mid-forties, Hispanic, and in terrific shape. No hanging around Dunkin' Donuts for him.

"Pleased to meet you, Detective."

His partner, at least a decade and a half older and considerably wider, said, "We should take her down to headquarters." A Mississippi drawl. Light blue eyes. Frown lines bracketing his mouth. Two chins. Close-cut brown hair in the process of graying.

"And you are?" I asked.

His quick smile surprised me. "Detective Bruce Cole. Pleased ta meetcha, too, but y'all still need to come down to headquarters with us. Just a little interview, nothin' serious."

Now, I could have played the same game I'd played with Scottsdale PD, but I had no history with either of these guys. While letting them take me in for "a little interview" was my best chance of getting more info on Norma's murder, what with the video cameras and all in the interview room, it was too risky.

"Sorry, Detectives. To save you the trip, I'll tell you what my attorney told Scottsdale PD—I'm not going anywhere with you."

"We could always just arrest you," Arrize said.

I conceded the point. "Maybe. Pat me down, stuff like that. Whatever."

Still smiling, Cole said, "You're packin', right?"

I smiled back. "Always."

"Handgun? Rifle?"

Cole's blue eyes narrowed slightly when I answered "handgun," so I took a chance and gestured toward my tote sitting on the Jeep's passenger seat. "Colt .38, snub-nose revolver." I hadn't been to the firing range for two weeks, and had cleaned the revolver since, so I figured I was in good shape there.

"Might we see it?" Arrize looked almost bored, which was also interesting.

Instead of drawing out my handgun myself—no point in taking needless risks with the long arm of the law—I handed the bag over to Arrize. He pawed through it. "Jesus, what else you got hidden in here? Mickey Rourke?" He finally cleared away enough debris that he was able to pull out the Colt. He unsnapped the holster, looked at the Colt, sniffed at it once, then put it back.

"Norma was shot, right?"

The two detectives looked at each other. "What makes you say that?" Cole asked, squinting at me.

"Because you didn't ask about my knife. But you can take a look at that, too, if you wish. It's called The Vindicator. I keep it in the glove compartment, along with the faux leopard-skin concealed-carry pocket holster I bought last month."

"We'll pass."

"So where was she shot?"

I meant in which room—foyer, living room, secret torture dungeon—but Cole surprised me again. "Both eyes, double-tap. Probably died instantaneously."

What a disappointment. I had hoped for a belly wound, because it usually takes people a while to die from those and the dying time hurts like hell.

"Anybody hear the gunshots?"

Cole laughed. "In this neighborhood? Half of them are deaf and the other half mind their own business."

Since he was on an information roll, I asked, "Then may I ask where Brian Wycoff was between six until nine this morning? And where he is now?"

The two looked at each other again before Arrize answered my question with another question. "What makes you ask about that particular timeline?"

"Because Scottsdale PD did."

Cole sighed. "See, Guillermo, what'd I tell ya? That's always the problem with these mixed jurisdiction messes. Somebody's always sayin' too much to the wrong somebody."

Arrize snorted. "True, that."

This whole thing felt off, as if neither of them gave a damn about Norma Wycoff's demise and were just going through the motions. But maybe one or both had read the trial transcript in anticipation of Brian's release from the Florence Correctional Facility. Come to think about it, Mississippi accent or not, Cole was old enough to have been a rookie cop in AJ or Scottsdale when the whole ugly thing went down.

"Where's Mr. Wycoff now?" I asked.

Arrize handed me back my tote. "Waiting for us down at the station, gonna help with our inquiries. You know the drill."

"Does he look good for it?"

"You'll find out when we do, Ms. Jones. In the meantime, you have a nice day."

Cole snapped me a little salute. "And why don't y'all give us a break and stay out of Apache Junction for the next few days?"

In a neatly synchronized half-turn, the two detectives walked back to rejoin the others.

I drove two blocks down the street, where I pulled into a Circle K parking lot and checked my cell phone. The GPS tracker on the Wycoffs' Honda Civic told me it was parked in his driveway. Unless the car was impounded I would still be able to keep an eye on him. If he turned out to be the killer, no problem. He would go back to prison and that would be the end of that.

If someone else had killed Norma, though…

Hot as it was, I remained in the Circle K lot for another half hour until I spotted the same UPS truck emerge from Sarsaparilla Lane and head north on Apache Trail. I followed behind it until the driver turned onto Old Dutchman Boulevard, then a couple of blocks later, hooked a left into a sprawling retirement community. As soon as he pulled up to the recreation center, I parked behind him and waited until he got out.

I walked over, flashing my PI license. "Just like to ask you a couple of questions, if you don't mind."

Jim, which is what his nametag called him, gave my license a deer-in-the-headlights look. He was in his early twenties and good-looking in a bland way. His arms had a deep tan, but the shock of his discovery had drained the color from his face.

"The police told me not to discuss it with anyone." His voice sounded wobbly, although he did his manly best to hide it.

"Oh, they just meant anyone not *officially* involved in the investigation, Jim." I gave him an encouraging smile. "How'd you wind up finding the body?"

He cleared his throat. "The, uh, the door was open and I had this package, and, uh, the minute I walked up the steps I could see her. She was, uh, lying face-up in the hall and she, uh, she'd been shot. I think." He swallowed. "She didn't have eyes anymore."

"Her eyes were shot out?"

"I'm thinkin' yeah. Oh, they was drippin' and I don't feel too good."

"Her eyes. How big were the holes? Nickle-size? Quarter-size? Part of the forehead or cheek missing?"

"I didn't exactly measure, you know? They were just bloody holes and that woman was dead as shit." Then he gulped and added, "I, uh, I don't think any other, uh, parts of, uh, of her face or, uh, her head were missing."

Arrize and Cole had shown little interest in my .38 revolver, so I suspected that whatever had taken Norma down was something smaller. Still, with shots to both eyes, she was dead before her brain had time to register the impact.

"Did you see anyone around? Hear any strange noises?"

"Just the screen door in the rear. I could, uh, from the front door, I could see all the way down the hall to the back, and it was flapping back and forth."

During an earlier prowl-around the Wycoff property, I had discovered a Dumpster-lined alleyway cutting through their block. Odds were, the killer had come in from the back.

"You're sure, then, that both doors were open? Front *and* back?"

He nodded. "What I said, isn't it? And I, uh, I gotta get back to work."

"One more question. The delivery you were about to drop off. What was it?"

At my mention of "delivery," he began sounding more confident. "Single small package. DVD-sized. Cops took it."

Pornographic videos of children, maybe, the better to welcome Wycoff home with? "Was anyone supposed to sign for it?"

"A Mrs. Norma Wycoff. Now get away from me. I'm done."

With that, he turned his back on me, hauled out a large box, and hustled up the walk to the rec center.

On the way to my office, I sifted through the reasons Wycoff might want to kill his wife.

He felt betrayed.

She'd demanded a divorce.

He got drunk or drugged and fried what was left of his perverted mind.

None of those reasons worked for me. For starters, Norma had never betrayed her husband—just every foster child who had ever walked through their front door. As for asking for a divorce, if she'd wanted one she would never have waited thirty years to file. Like most women who knowingly live with child molesters, she loved playing the loyal martyr too much to give it up. And as far as the booze and/or drugs motive went, mood-enhancing chemicals had never been Brian Wycoff's thing. In those terrible months I'd lived with them, I had never seen him take a drink, let alone indulge in pharmaceuticals. He played the part of an upstanding, church-going man, and showed up in the pew every Sunday. Wycoff's only addiction was little girls.

My suspicion was that someone else killed Norma. The question was—did I care?

By the time I pulled into my private parking slot at Desert Investigations, I had decided to leave Norma's demise on the back burner and concentrate on Wycoff himself. He might have served his time, but there was no way the man wouldn't re-offend, and soon. Popular belief notwithstanding, there was no sure-fire treatment for pedophiles, not even aversion therapy. Once pedophiles started molesting children, they continued right into infirm old age, never stopping until their wheelchairs rolled down the ramp to Hell.

My mission was to make certain Wycoff did not hurt another child. How I could accomplish that I wasn't certain, but the research I had done on his extended family, aided by the GPS tracker slipped under the Civic, would help. I'd programmed the tracker to download the car's position to my smartphone every fifteen minutes, and a glance at my Jeep's own retro-fitted Nav screen confirmed that the Civic remained in the driveway at the Wycoff house. It wouldn't stay there forever. Without his conscienceless wife to run interference for him, Wycoff would soon be on the move, and I doubted he would let a little thing like an ankle bracelet stop him.

"Still haven't been arrested, eh?" Jimmy looked up as I entered the office. It was blessedly cool after my long, hot drive on State Route 60.

"Me or Wycoff?"

"You, Lena. You've been asking for it ever since they let him out."

Jimmy and I have been in business together for years and have grown so close that my nickname for him is Almost Brother. Although we don't look anything alike—he's a dark, full-blooded Pima Indian, and I'm a green-eyed blonde of probable Caucasian heritage—we both share backgrounds in foster care. Jimmy lucked out, being adopted by a loving family, while I…well, I wasn't so lucky.

Although Jimmy and I can squabble like siblings, we understand each other, which is why his criticism hurt. "What do you expect me to do, Jimmy, sit back and watch passively while he starts up with kids again?"

"Wycoff had years of therapy in prison. That's why he was cleared for release by the Arizona Protection and Treatment Center."

When I laughed, I could see the beginnings of a flush underneath his dark skin. "The only thing sex offenders learn in therapy is to say 'I recognize that I've done wrong, and now that Jesus is my own personal lord and savior, I see the error of my ways and I'll never do it again. Hallelujah! Hell, Almost Brother, you know as well as I do that he's been counting the days when he could get to the nearest park and the nearest unsupervised child."

He gave me a perplexed look. "You can't save the world, Lena."

"But I can try." I sat down at my desk and began checking my phone messages.

Two were from clients, each wanting to know the status of their cases. The first was from Yolanda Blanco, who was trying to find her missing eighteen-year-old daughter, Inez. Two months earlier she had gone to the store for a pack of cigarettes and never returned. After a short investigation, the police learned from the daughter's best friend that Inez had talked about her unhappiness at home with her too-strict mother, and was planning to run off and start a new life with her boyfriend. Since Inez was of age, there was little else the authorities could do, so they dropped the case. Ergo, Yolanda's reach out to Desert Investigations.

The second message, from Frank Gunnerston, was similar, except he was looking for his wife. Early into the investigation, I could see what the end game was going to be, so I wasn't looking forward to calling him back, but I did anyway. I suggested he give up his search, adding that since his wife had vanished four years ago and no one had seen neither hide nor hair of her since, finding her was next to impossible.

Which was a lie. A week after taking the case, a talk with Mrs. Gunnerston's closest friend revealed that Mr. Gunnerston was an abusive husband. The friend's story was backed up by a sister and two cousins. Later that day, Mrs. Gunnerston herself had called my office and confirmed what they'd told me. She had just been released from an out-of-state hospital after undergoing reconstructive surgery on her face, revising the scars put there by Mr. Gunnerston's loving attentions. After seeing the before-and-after pictures she faxed me, I made my decision.

Gunnerston wasn't happy when I told him I would send Desert Investigations' bill—a small one—the next day, but hey, you can't please everyone, can you?

The third message was from Brian Wycoff.

He wanted to meet with me.

Chapter Four

I have a memory…

I was nine years old and Brian Wycoff was hiding in my closet when I arrived home from school. I had gone upstairs to change from my pretty dress into jeans and a tee shirt. The moment I opened the sliding closet doors, he jumped out.

"Surprise!"

While I was still screaming, he dragged me over to my bed and…

No point in getting clinical. Suffice it to say I was never the same again. I never screamed during the daytime again, either—not when I was shot in the hip during a drug raid gone bad with Scottsdale PD, nor the time I took a bullet in the shoulder while working a private case. If there was one thing Brian Wycoff had taught me, it was how to keep my mouth shut. Now, irony of ironies, he wanted to talk.

I thought about the wisdom of a sit-down for a while, then returned his call. "When and where?"

"Lena, Honey…" His voice quavered. Whether from age or fear, I couldn't tell.

"Don't 'honey' me, you child-raping son of a bitch. You want to talk, tell me when and where and never call me 'honey' again."

"You don't have to…"

"When and where or I'm hanging up."

"Someplace private."

"Bullshit on *private*, you creep. It's public or nothing."

"Please, I'm not a cre—"

"When and where?"

"Tomorrow?"

"What time?"

"Nine-ish? In the morning?"

"Nine on the dot. Where?"

"The Denny's on Apache Boulevard? They've got a quiet area in the back where…"

"See you at nine tomorrow." I slammed the phone down.

Then I ran into the bathroom and threw up.

Jimmy was waiting for me at my desk when I emerged. "I was on the verge of breaking down the door."

"Good thing you didn't. I'd hate to have more repair bills around here."

"Please tell me that wasn't Brian Wycoff on the phone."

"Okay. That wasn't Brian Wycoff on the phone."

The tribal tattoo on Jimmy's temple always darkened when he was angry and it was beyond pitch-black now. "Sit down, Lena. We have to talk."

I've never had a conversation worth having when the other person started it by saying, "We have to talk," so I did the only thing possible.

I left.

By the time I got back from Scottsdale Fight Pro—yes, I belong to two different gyms—Jimmy had gone home for the day. It was, after all, eight-thirty p.m. God knows how long he'd waited for me, but I was good at the waiting game, too, only my waiting tends to be more active. I had begun taking Krav Maga classes at Fight Pro a few months earlier, and the Israeli martial arts classes had already come in handy on a couple of occasions. Still, when I met with Wycoff tomorrow, I would be armed to the teeth. Memory is a great teacher.

As soon as I reached my apartment upstairs from Desert Investigations I went through my weapons cabinet and reloaded my tote with the necessaries: my faithful Colt .38, a can of wasp spray, a Taser, a Fury Tactical Leather SAP, and my beloved Vindicator. Confronting Wycoff in a prison parking lot was one thing, sitting across from him was something else.

I didn't sleep at all that night, but in the morning I was so hopped-up on adrenaline it didn't make any difference. Borrowing Jimmy's Toyota pickup—this was a good time for vehicle anonymity—I arrived at the AJ Denny's a half hour early. It was right down the street from the Apache Junction Public Library, which I found interesting. A few family sedans, a couple of minivans, three pickup trucks, and a Harley sat in the parking lot. The hidden GPS tracker on the Wycoff's Honda Civic assured me the Civic remained parked at the Motel 6 near his house, but by beating Wycoff to the restaurant, I would be able to scout out the perfect seat for our encounter. The front of the restaurant was filled, but only one booth had been taken in the overflow section at the back. Perfect. I headed for the booth closest to the rear exit, taking a seat that faced the entrance so I could see Wycoff before he saw me. I kept my right hand on the can of wasp spray in my tote. If necessary, I would work my way up the munitions ladder, finalizing our conversation with a statement from the Vindicator.

No shooting, though. There were too many families in the restaurant enjoying a late breakfast, and I especially didn't want to hurt the little girl sitting with her parents eight booths away from me. Blue eyes, red hair done up in pigtails, pale face accented by a faint dusting of freckles. Adorable. She appeared to be about nine, the age I'd been when CPS placed me with the Wycoffs.

An elderly waitress who looked like her feet hurt took my order for coffee and Danish, then limped toward the kitchen. She returned almost immediately with the Danish and a full carafe of coffee.

"Enjoy, Hon."

I never mind when waitresses call me Hon; it makes me feel less alone. This would be a short meeting, so I took a twenty-dollar bill out of my billfold and left it under the carafe. Then I settled back to wait.

Wycoff walked through the door promptly at nine. Saw me. Froze.

He gave me a wobbly smile. His steps were hesitant as he walked toward me, but I noticed how his eyes kept flicking to the child at the other table. So much for years of court-mandated "treatment." He was still the same old Papa Brian. As he neared, I could see how red his eyes were. Mourning his wife? Or mourning his enabler?

"Take a seat," I ordered.

He slid into the other side of the booth.

"Now, Lena, Honey…"

I took my hand out of my tote and spread my fingers so he could read the label: WASP KILLER. "Call me 'Honey' one more time and you get this in your face. Now, why'd you want to see me? And by the way, put your hands on the table so I can see them."

Prison being a great place to learn how to take orders, he complied.

He cleared his throat. "I asked to see you because I wanted to tell you that you, uh, you need to stop doing this."

"Stop doing what?"

"Stop harassing me."

He flinched as the waitress limped up to take his order. If she saw the wasp spray, she didn't let on.

I waved her away. "Nothing for him. He's just passing through."

As she limped off, I added another twenty to the one underneath the carafe. Discretion should always be rewarded.

With his jailhouse pallor and red eyes, Brian Wycoff looked a decade older than sixty-five, but multiple experiences with ex-cons, many of them elderly, had taught me to never assume anything. Wycoff's arms may have been thin, but the ropey muscles proved he was no stranger to the prison's weight room.

He waited until the waitress was out of earshot, then said, "Harassment's against the law."

"Cry me a river."

"You don't have to be so…"

"Where were you when Norma was killed?"

He blinked. "Huh?"

"You heard me. Where were you?"

A child's giggle from the only other occupied booth made him turn around. A smile crept across Wycoff's face as he stared at the little redhead. Taking him for nothing more than a friendly old guy, she grinned. When he waggled his fingers at her, she giggled and waggled back. People who believe children can tell good from evil had never seen a pedophile work a room or playground.

"Stop grooming the kid, Brian, and answer my question."

He whipped his head back around, put on an injured air. "I was just…"

"I know what you were 'just' doing. Where were you when Norma was killed?"

He clasped his hands into such tight fists the knuckles turned white. "Why is that your business?"

I took the cap off the wasp spray, pointed the nozzle toward him, and put my forefinger on the firing button. "One more time. Where were you when Norma was killed?"

"At the Pinal County Sheriff's Office, getting fitted for my ankle bracelet!" Catching himself, he lowered his voice to a near-whisper. "Several sheriffs' deputies will back me up."

"No kiddies around to keep you company?"

Color rushed to his cheeks. "You…you…"

"Bitch. Yeah, I know. Before you left for there, did you walk past that *sub-rosa* child-care center at the end of your block? Did you pause for a while?"

He pulled an aggrieved face. "Why do you always have to think the worst of people?"

"Because you taught me to."

"Hon…" He caught himself just in time. "Lena, I never meant you any harm, and I'm sorry if I…"

"Shut. Your. Mouth." I put the wasp spray back in my tote, and after making certain no one at the other booth was watching, pulled out the Vindicator and laid it next to my coffee cup. "I played with the idea of a gelding knife, but finally decided on this. It'll do the job just fine, don't you think?"

"I've changed!" When his voice rose to a near-shriek, the family in the other booth turned around to see what was going on. The little redhead's smile vanished.

I raised my own voice. "If you want this discussion at top volume, I'm happy to accommodate you."

Wycoff's eyes widened in panic, but somehow he managed to force his words back into a whisper. "You know what? You're crazy!"

"No argument there." I rustled through my tote and one by one put the rest of my weapons on the table. Taser. Fury Tactical Leather SAP. Colt .38. "I'm undecided as to which I should start with, SAP or Taser. Or maybe the knife? Help me out here."

He couldn't take his eyes off the Vindicator.

"Good choice," I said. "I admire your taste."

"I'm calling the police." Still in a whisper.

I raised my voice further. "I'm sure the police will be delighted to hear from their friendly neighborhood pedophile."

The father in the other booth, a bulky man who could have passed for a professional wrestler, turned around again and narrowed his eyes at Wycoff.

"Hmm, I forget. How many children were you convicted of raping?" My voice volume even higher.

"I wasn't convicted. I took a plea!" This time he forgot to whisper.

"Yeah, after the first two kids had testified about what you did to them. Five more were waiting their turn, including me." I said it so loudly they could probably hear me in Vancouver.

The father gestured toward the elderly waitress, who had been hovering near the overflow section. He asked for the check, which gave me another idea. After sweeping my arsenal back into the tote, I hauled it and myself out of the booth and approached their table.

I handed the father several flyers. "Mr. Wycoff's house is only four blocks from here. Maybe you'd like to give these out to your neighbors, especially those who have children."

Nodding, the man took the flyers. Read one. Got up. Started walking toward Wycoff. With a squeak, Wycoff tumbled out of the booth and ran out the back exit.

As he fled across the parking lot, I realized I was shaking.

And I felt about nine years old.

Thursdays were horrific when I was nine years old and living with the Wycoffs, but in a way, Wednesdays were almost as bad. On Wednesday, I spent all day dreading what would happen the next afternoon, as soon as Norma left for her church activities and Papa Brian came home early, and…

One Wednesday morning, my teacher asked me why I was crying, but I couldn't tell her because Papa Brian had threatened to kill Sandy if I ever told on him, and I loved Sandy more than I loved life. Life? Is that what you called it when your every day was filled with pain, but Thursdays brought the kind of pain that paled all others? And when Wednesday, oh Wednesday, delivered the awareness that tomorrow I would be praying for death so the pain would end? The teacher, so well-meaning but not knowing what to do, ~~escorted~~ sent me to the nurse's office. The nurse, also not knowing what to do, called Norma to come and pick me up.

The minute I climbed into Norma's car, she slapped me.

But this was a Wednesday filled with triumph, not dread. I had faced-down the dragon and won. After Wycoff fled out the back door of Denny's, I made a quick swing by the Apache Junction Library. There, I gave some of my flyers to Bess Graves, a librarian friend of mine since our college days at Arizona State University.

Then I headed back to Scottsdale, where Jimmy was waiting at Desert Investigations, wanting to talk.

"I don't get it, Lena. You tell me you're going to shrug off a woman's murder? Aren't you at least curious?"

"At best, Norma Wycoff was an enabler. At worse, she colluded in her husband's crimes."

"Still…"

"There is no 'still,' Jimmy." How could he ever understand when he'd spent his whole life being loved?

"You're going to get yourself arrested for stalking, and we don't have enough in petty cash to bail you out."

"Then write a check on the company account." I sat down at my desk and picked up the phone to retrieve my messages.

"Bail bondsmen don't take checks."

I had missed fourteen calls, six of them from Frank Gunnerston, who apparently didn't take no for an answer. Was he dumb enough to think I would turn over his runaway wife's address after what I'd learned about him? In a just and wise world, I'd be able to bill him extra for wasting my time.

As I erased his messages, Jimmy rose from his desk and went over to the coffee machine. A coffee snob, he had tired of Jamaican Blue Mountain and moved on to Graffeo Dark. Next week we would be drinking something picked by a virgin on the north slope of Kilimanjaro at midnight during a lunar eclipse.

The Graffeo smelled good, though. "You could always bail me out using our company Visa." I held up my cup. "Hit me."

"We're already at our credit limit. Sugar?"

"Surely you jest."

"About the Visa limit or the sugar?"

"Both."

He poured me a cup, sans sugar. "No on both."

The coffee tasted as good as it smelled. "They won't arrest me for stalking if I get Wycoff arrested first." I remembered the little girl at the restaurant and Wycoff's inability to ignore her.

"That's all you're trying to do—get him arrested?"

"Yes," I lied.

Jimmy always knew when I was lying, but there being nothing he could do about it, he went back to his desk and lost himself in his computer.

I was about to do the same when my cell phone beeped. Glancing at the screen, I saw an update from the GPS system installed on Wycoff's car. After a short stop at his motel, he was on the move again, headed west on I-60 in the direction of the Superstition Springs Mall. A shopping excursion, perhaps? Even child molesters need clothes. Or, while rotting away in prison, he had read about modern malls' ability to attract free-range children and was trying his luck.

Wrong. The Civic passed the Superstition Springs exit and continued west until it arrived at the 101 interchange, where it turned north. For the next half hour I sat at my desk and watched as the little red dot on my screen left Scottsdale, crawled west across the outskirts of Phoenix, then skated onto the I-17 interchange where it swung north again, picking up speed. Wycoff was leaving town.

Monkey see, monkey do.

I told Jimmy I might be gone for a few hours, or days, grabbed the emergency backpack I always kept supplied, and rushed to my Jeep.

The official outskirts of the Valley of the Sun ended soon after I passed Anthem, a relatively new bedroom community of north Phoenix. From there, I-17 began a long upgrade into hill country. Years earlier, in anticipation of Wycoff's eventual release, I had put together a file of his known contacts. Although he had been active in various church activities, the parishioners who had once been vocal in his defense dropped him like a used Kleenex when his confession aired live on FOX-10 News. Most of his relatives dropped him, too. In fact, during his entire incarceration, his only regular correspondent had been Norma, but a couple of years ago one of my contacts at the prison alerted me that Wycoff had begun receiving letters and visits from someone named Grace Genovese, a resident of Black Canyon

City. Further research revealed that Grace Genovese's maiden name was Wycoff. She was Brian's only sibling, a younger sister.

Grace and her husband, Mario, had a thirty-something daughter named Shana, mother of Luke, thirteen, and Bethany, eight. Due to a split a year ago from her husband and the ongoing financial squabbling, Shana and her children had temporarily moved into Casa Genovese. Surely Wycoff wasn't heading there! Another stipulation of his probation was that he never live under the same roof as minors. Yet as I tracked the GPS signal up I-17, my worst fears were confirmed. The Civic exited the freeway on Old Black Canyon Highway.

Black Canyon City, population four thousand-something, once served as a stagecoach stop, but was now home to a combination of ranchers, farmers, hard-core commuters, and a trickle of exhausted retirees eager to escape the Valley's hustle and bustle. Other than its interesting Old West history, the town's major claim to fame was the Rock Springs Café, where the pie list alone drew customers all the way from Phoenix and Flagstaff. But I doubted Wycoff made the trip here for a slice of its famed Bourbon Pecan.

I took the same turnoff and followed the GPS signal along the main drag, past a small strip mall designed to look like a stage stop, a thrift store, a couple of saloon-styled bars, a combination psychic readings/souvenir shop, a beauty parlor, a Quik Snax, a general store, and a fry bread shack. While the town couldn't exactly be called bustling, judging from the pickup trucks and motorcycles parked in front of the stores, business was steady. The bad news was that some of the businesses, especially the Quik Snax, attracted children.

Deciding not to confront Wycoff until he reached his sister's house, I doubled back to the fry bread stand and stood in line to buy myself an extra-large, slathered with cinnamon and honey. To wash it down, I had a regular Coke since they were out of Diet, and had never heard of Tab. The combined sweetness left my teeth aching. After a brief glance at my Timex, which had taken many a licking but kept on ticking, I realized my lunch break had lasted little more than ten minutes. To kill more time, I walked over to the supermarket and started reading the notices on the bulletin board.

Bulletin boards give you a snapshot of a community. Hiking and fishing were a big thing up here, as were horseback riding at Red Rock Ranch, and mud-bogging with a group named the Dirty Dozen. People were selling trailers, pickup trucks, backhoes, wood-burning stoves, and roosters. I wasn't interested in roosters or trailers, but the index card advertising Debbie's Desert Oasis, a local B&B, caught my eye. There was no telling how long I'd be up here, so I scribbled the number down in my notebook.

Then I checked my Timex again. If Wycoff hadn't settled in by now, it wasn't going to happen, so I walked back to my Jeep and took off.

Despite naming itself a "city," the town was small enough that I didn't need the GPS tracker's signal to guide me to 17034 Moonbeam Lane, but when my Jeep topped the hill leading down to the long, narrow valley carved out by Black Canyon Creek, I had to pull off to the side of the road to calm myself. Even after a series of deep breaths, I had trouble holding my binoculars steady as I checked out the scene below.

On a slight rise overlooking the mostly dry creekbed sat a cottonwood-shaded ranch house at the northern end of a property large enough to run several head of cattle, four horses, and a Shetland pony. Parked in the house's wide driveway were a crew cab Chevy pickup, a Jeep Cherokee so new it still bore dealer's tags, and an elderly Volvo missing one of its hubcaps. Behind the Volvo sat the beige Honda Civic. On a cement pad on the other side of the house sat a well-travelled Winnebago camper with a Pink Princess bicycle leaning against it.

The craft of manipulation being a pedophile's *pièce de résistance,* I could imagine the conversation taking place inside the house, but as it turned out, I was wrong.

Several minutes later, just as I had decided to drive down to the house and educate the adult inhabitants of the illegality of allowing convicted pedophiles to live under the same roof as minor children, the front door flew open and Brian Wycoff emerged. Rather clumsily, at that. Squinting my eyes against the early afternoon sun, I saw the reason for his staggers. He was being pushed forward by a burly, fifty-ish man with olive skin and slightly graying black hair. Mario Genovese, Wycoff's brother-in-law. Since the wind was right, I could catch snatches of their conversation.

"…see you anywhere near her and…"

"…got me all wrong, I…"

"…if not for my wife I'd kill…"

"…wanted to get to know my niece…"

"…don't you even mention her name…"

"…I did my time so…"

"…fuck's the matter with…?"

This intriguing exchange ended when Genovese opened the Winnebago's passenger's door and shoved the still-protesting Wycoff in. Puffing with rage, Genovese bent over his granddaughter's Pink Princess bicycle, tossed it into the yard, then went around to the driver's side of the RV and climbed in. Seconds later the engine roared to life and the RV backed out of the driveway and rumbled down a dirt track that led up to a livestock gate. Genovese got out, opened the gate, drove the RV through, then got out again and closed the gate behind him. He drove the Winnebago toward the far end of the pasture, then slowed as it neared a long stand of cottonwoods. Steering carefully between the trees, he parked it in the shade.

A few seconds later Genovese re-emerged. Wycoff didn't.

The horses' ears pricked up as Genovese left the Winnebago behind and jogged across the pasture back toward the house. The cattle, less curious, kept on grazing.

I had been so busy watching the Winnebago drama I hardly noticed the door to the house open again, but my own ears pricked up when a middle-aged woman came out wailing. She was joined in her distress by a young blond girl. Genovese's eight-year-old granddaughter, Bethany.

She looked a lot like me at that age.

Chapter Five

Because of Madeline, I knew what I looked like before the worst happened.

The memories of the first few years of my life were wiped away by the bullet that almost took my life. Once I learned to walk again, I made my way through several foster homes until CPS placed me with Madeline. She was, and still is, an artist. Images were important to her. From the day the social worker walked me through Madeline's front door with my garbage bag "suitcase," she began taking pictures of me. She drew me, she painted me, she delighted in me. If only…

What's the old saying? *If wishes were horses, beggars would ride?*

Madeline developed breast cancer and became too ill to care for me, although God knows she tried. When the social worker learned about her condition, he moved me to the Wycoffs, and the only thing I was able to salvage was the scrapbook Madeline and I had put together. In the pictures, I was always smiling.

Pictures lie.

Years later, when my therapist decided I was ready to face the past, I had gone to the library and looked up old editions of the *Arizona Republic*, and read the coverage of Wycoff's trial. In the photographs accompanying the articles, he looked like your typical clean-cut, church-going suburbanite, a man no sane person would suspect of harboring sexual fantasies about children. Norma didn't look like a monster, either. In photographs taken as she entered the courthouse, she appeared to be just another attractive Scottsdale housewife, although a bit camera-shy. The social worker who had placed children with those two monsters appeared bored, but I later learned he had attempted suicide.

Pictures lie. A lot.

In response to his wife's pleas, Mario Genovese had not turned her brother away, but for safety's sake, he'd moved the pedophile as far from his house as possible. As long as Wycoff remained on the property, however, Wycoff was in defiance of his court-ordered probation, and conceivably, Genovese could be charged for endangering his granddaughter. He needed talking to, and I was just the person to do it. For now, though, the Genovese family needed some time to themselves.

Cognizant of the day's rising temperatures—Black Canyon City wasn't far enough north of Phoenix to completely escape the August heat—I steered the Jeep off the shoulder and into a copse of acacias for some shade and settled down for a long wait.

By five, Wycoff still hadn't poked his nose outside the RV, but I had been treated to the view of the muscular Mario Genovese as he tinkered with a tractor motor, replaced loose boards on the barn, and—aided by his grandson—hauled bales of hay out to the livestock. The sight of all those animals chowing down reminded me that the only thing I'd eaten all day had been one helping of fry bread and two stale granola bars out of my emergency backpack. My stomach growled so loudly it was a miracle the Genoveses couldn't hear it, and I was sweating so heavily it was another miracle they couldn't smell me, too. I needed food and a shower, in reverse order.

Debbie's Desert Oasis was located on the same road that led over the hill and down to the Genoveses' spread. In fact, the B&B was close enough I could have walked the distance in less than ten minutes.

The bed and breakfast came as a surprise.

At the front of a small gravel parking lot near a small yellow house sat a turquoise 1956 Ford F100 pickup truck. Script writing on its side promised that at Debbie's Desert Oasis, the fish were always biting.

The house itself sat in a mini-forest of gnarled mesquite and acacia, looking cute enough to be featured in *Arizona Highways,* but it wasn't a B&B in the usual sense. Instead of bedrooms, Debbie Margules rented out single-wide trailers, each tucked separately among the mesquite and brush for maximum privacy. In accordance with the latest Southwestern travel trailer rage, they were painted to illustrate differing themes. The exterior of mine, aptly named "Monarch," was buttercup-yellow, and sported hand-painted pictures of butterflies all over the sides. Little butterflies. Big butterflies. Medium-sized butterflies. The butterfly theme continued on into the interior, where butterfly designs fluttered across the sofa's slipcovers, toss pillows, lampshades, towels, sheets, and bedspread. Four butterfly-decorated coffee mugs sat next to a Mr. Coffee embellished with a butterfly sticker.

When I chuckled, Debbie grinned. "Yeah, it's a bit much, and any woman driving a Jeep like yours might find Mustang, Cougar, or Fishin' Frenzy more suitable, but those trailers are already taken."

Debbie—she said addressing her as "Mrs. Margules" made her feel old—was a comfortable, denim-clad woman somewhere in her sixties, with deep laugh lines around her mouth and eyes. She smelled like turpentine, which made me like her immediately. Madeline always smelled like turpentine, too.

As I filled out the rental form in the office of her yellow house, I learned a little about my host. After retiring from teaching art at a Phoenix high school seven years earlier, she decided to fulfill her lifelong dream of running a B&B. Upon being shown this fifteen-acre property, which already had a run-down single-wide trailer in the back, she revised her dream. As soon as the sale went through, paid for by the sale of her Scottsdale condo, she bought several other trailers and used her artistic skills to renovate and decorate them. Recently she'd picked up a couple more at an auction, but hadn't yet finished the renovations.

"You'd be surprised how popular those little things are," she said. "In fact, the only reason I have a vacancy is because the woman who originally reserved it was in a car wreck a couple of days ago and is still recuperating. Nothing life-threatening, just a broken leg, but she's in traction for a while. Anyway, you can stay in Monarch until the eleven a.m. checkout time on Monday, if you wish. Just let me know as soon as you decide so I don't double-book. Oh, and I serve breakfast between seven and eight, here in the dining room."

I booked Monarch through Sunday night, explaining that I was taking a back-to-nature break from a heavy workload.

"Lot of that these days…people working two jobs just to get by."

While she ran Desert Investigations' Visa card through the system, I looked around. For such a conventional-looking woman, she had surprising taste in art. On the way to and from Monarch, I had already noticed a series of large, non-objective metal sculptures scattered around the property. The largest stood in a clearing, a seemingly jumbled-together construction of iron, bronze, pipe fittings, barbed wire, and rocks soaring more than six feet high. Despite its bulk, the piece was graceful, and after studying it for a moment, I thought it resembled a weeping angel. The bronze plaque at its base said MEMORY.

Here in the yellow house, the hallway showcased several Sonoran Desert landscapes, their loosely rendered style and vivid colors edging more toward edgy Expressionism than the tamer blurs of Impressionism. They were signed "D. Margules." But the office—although standard, with its rows of file cabinets, bookcases, and utilitarian desk—was decorated with a portrait of a dark-haired girl of about ten. Unlike the desert paintings, the portrait, also signed "D. Margules," was near-photographic in its realism.

"My daughter, Lindsey," she explained, when she caught me studying the painting.

Given Debbie's age, the girl could be in her forties by now. "She live nearby?"

"Nope. Here's your Visa back and your receipt."

In my line of work you learn what's your business and what's not, so instead of nosing into a possible strained relationship with her adult daughter, I asked, "What's a good place to eat in town? Something not as busy as Rock Springs."

"You like Mexican food?"

"You're not allowed to live in Arizona if you don't."

"Then I recommend Coyote Corral. The cook's the real deal, came up from Hermosillo last year to join her son. He runs the thrift store in town—stop by there if you get a chance. Great bargains on books, knickknacks, tools, whatever. Anyway, the Coyote's food is terrific and you get plenty of it. Margaritas are stellar. Oh, and you didn't ask, but Black Canyon Creek is just over the hill, and the fishing is particularly good when the level's up. If you take the right fork down in the valley, you'll come to the public access area. Trout and bass, mainly. Some perch. "

Mainly to sound friendly, I said, "Shoot, if I'd known, I would have brought my gear."

"No problem. Each trailer is equipped with basic fishing tackle. Just return it when you're through."

We discussed fish for a while, then I thanked her and left.

Finding my way back to Monarch wasn't as easy as I'd thought it would be. There were so many trees and brush—not to mention more metal sculptures with lofty names—between each trailer that I lost my way several times. First I ended up at the aptly named Gone Fishin' (pale blue with paintings of trout, bass, etc., swimming all over it), where a beautiful redhead with a dazzling complexion sat gutting a brook trout on the stoop. She looked up, gave me a wave, then returned to her bloody business. Then I stumbled across Mustang, where the brunette inhabitant wasn't as friendly. I liked the paintings of horses on the desert-tan trailer, though. After taking two more wrong turns and passing by several more cutely decorated trailers—Arizona wildlife was a recurring theme—I finally arrived at Monarch.

After showering and drying myself off with a butterfly-patterned towel, I slipped into fresh clothes: black tee shirt and black jeans, my usual wear. Then I headed into town.

Coyote Corral was everything Debbie promised. A surprisingly large combination restaurant and bar, the two rooms were only slightly separated by a half-wall of wood latticework. In the cozy dining area, red leather-ish booths lined the walls, leaving a space in the middle for a few tables, all filled. From my booth near the latticework, I could easily hear several conversations in the bar, most of it about horses or trucks.

The woman who cooked the delicious *chiles rellenos* I wolfed down might have been from Hermosillo, but the Coyote's owner certainly wasn't. Mario Genovese tended the standing-room-only bar while an attractive ash blonde who strongly resembled him waited tables. Shana Genovese Ferris. That meant Grace Genovese was home with the children. Not good.

As I mopped up the last grain of rice on my plate, I considered my wisest course of action. I could talk to Mario and Shana here, then drive back to their house and issue a warning to Grace. I hadn't liked what I'd seen earlier in the day, and suspected Grace was an enabler, albeit an unconscious one. It might be a good idea to pay a late-night visit to Wycoff, too. Yank his chain again. Get a few more food pellets.

In the best of all possible worlds, I wouldn't have to do anything. The GPS system on Wycoff's ankle bracelet would alert the computer at the Pinal County sheriff's office that he was on the lam and the authorities would take immediate action. But this wasn't the best of all possible worlds. Court-ordered ankle bracelets are notoriously easy to ditch. Chances were that Wycoff's remained at the Apache Junction house, making it appear he was obeying protocol. Then again, Wycoff might still be wearing the bracelet, but so were hundreds—perhaps thousands—of other felons across the greater Phoenix area. With so many to track, it could take days for some glassy-eyed computer geek at the sheriff's office to notice that this particular felon had flown the coop.

And by then…

I called for my check, and when Shana dropped it off, slipped her my business card along with a twenty. "Please tell your father to call me as soon as the crowd clears out."

Worry lines appeared at the corner of her hazel eyes. "This is about my uncle, isn't it?"

I nodded. "Your daughter isn't safe around him."

The warmth left her eyes. "Tell me about it."

"If your dad would prefer to talk in person, I'm staying at Debbie's Desert…"

"Oasis," she finished. "I doubt he'll have time for that, because he's pretty busy. *We're* busy, but I'll give him your card and have him call you." As she turned to take my Visa to the bar, I heard her mutter, "Not that it'll do any good."

When I returned to the hilltop overlooking the Genovese house, my worst fears were confirmed. Grace was speaking to Wycoff across the pasture fence and she had Bethany with her. Grace's eyes were only for her brother—they'd obviously been close, I suspected too close—but Wycoff never took his eyes off the little girl. How could Grace not notice? Perhaps she was so wrapped up in her own sisterly agenda she'd become blind to the obvious signs? *They're all wrong about him, Honey, he wouldn't hurt a fly*…the theme song of enablers and co-dependents everywhere.

Someone had to stop this.

Chapter Six

Because my trailer is not visible from Debbie's yellow house, I was able to park the Jeep on the far side of her turquoise truck and make my way on foot through the trees without anyone seeing me. While I had been scarfing down *chiles rellenos* at Coyote Corral, fat black clouds had gathered to the southeast, edging the humidity into the near-unbearable. One of Arizona's infamous monsoon storms was in the offing, but you can't order up weather to suit your needs. Fortunately, I had a clear plastic rain slicker in my backpack along with other necessities, so whatever Ma Nature threw at me, I felt prepared.

The zigzag hike up the hill to a sheltered spot overlooking the narrow valley took longer than planned, and by the time I scrambled into a thicket of brittlebush and scrub pine, the wind had risen. After donning my rain slicker, I hunkered down at the base of a tree, set my cell on vibrate, and settled in for a long wait.

Wycoff's beige Honda Civic had been moved off to the side to let Genovese and his daughter take the pickup to the restaurant. Bethany's Pink Princess bicycle now lay on the long veranda, sheltered from the coming rain. A towheaded boy, probably Luke, the little girl's brother, was busy replacing the bike's chain. As I watched through my binoculars, Grace Genovese came out the front door carrying a large covered platter, trailed by Bethany. The two started toward the pasture gate before a shout from the boy stopped them both. With the wind so high I couldn't hear any of the ensuing conversation, but it was clear the boy didn't want the girl to follow her grandmother to the RV. It was just as clear that their grandmother took issue with his disapproval, and a long argument followed that left Bethany visibly distressed. The drama ended with the girl joining her brother on the veranda, and Grace walking alone toward the RV. My binocs were strong enough that I could read the look on the boy's face. He knew exactly what kind of man his uncle was.

Several times I checked my phone to see if Genovese had called, but came up nada. Just three calls from Jimmy, one from wife-beating Hank Gunnerston, but none from the grandfather of an endangered nine-year-old. Too busy to protect her?

At ten, the lights in the house turned off. A few minutes later, the monsoon began. As monsoons go, the storm wasn't too bad, but the lightning was near-blinding and the rain was heavy enough that despite my raingear, I got soaked. At one point the combined noise of thunderclaps and screaming winds grew so loud it sounded like a fleet of Boeing 787s overhead. Although semi-sheltered from the worst of the downpour, I could still feel the wind pushing at me, trying to blow me off the hill and into the narrow valley below.

Around midnight the storm moved on, leaving the clean smell of ozone behind. It must have been raining just as hard in the mountains up by Flagstaff because the runoff turned the formerly gentle Black Canyon Creek into a raging torrent. Unfortunately, the torrent didn't rise high enough to jump the banks and sweep Wycoff's RV downstream. By the end of nature's spectacular display, the RV remained hunkered down on the bank, a flickering blue light from a television set lending it a spectral appearance.

Fleetingly I wondered what Wycoff could be watching. Reruns of *Leave It to Beaver*? *The Mickey Mouse Club*? A Shirley Temple movie?

At twelve-thirty the blue light flicked off.

Shortly after three, the Genoveses' pickup passed within ten feet of me as it topped the ridge and headed down to the house. Mario and Shana, their work at Coyote Corral finished.

Bethany was safe.

For the rest of the night, anyway.

Making a garrote is easy. You only need a strong cord or fishing line and duct tape, all in good supply at Monarch. A search through the kitchen cabinets procured each, along with a nice selection of fishing lures to go with the rod and reel I found in one of the closets. In less than ten minutes I had created a lethal and silent weapon.

Not that I needed silence. After last night's monsoon, Black Canyon Creek still raged, and the humidity in the air all but promised another whopper tonight. If Wycoff managed to get out a scream before the garrote tightened around his neck, the sound would be masked by the roar of the creek. Perfect. Now all I had to do was wait.

Ordinarily I dress in black jeans, but on special occasions I switch to cargo pants. In anticipation of this day, I had purchased a pair of nighttime camo cargo pants and matching jacket. Topping off that day's purchase had been the faux-leopard skin concealed-carry pocket holster for my .38 Colt revolver.

Between the two articles of clothing, I counted twelve pockets. I wouldn't need all of them, but it's better to be over-equipped than under. On the off-chance Genovese decided he needed to take care of business in town, leaving the coast clear for his foolish wife to allow Wycoff to "get to know" his niece, I set my phone on vibrate. After a quick breakfast of oat cakes and fruit compote at Debbie's cottage—the other tenants were nowhere in sight—I returned to my outpost on top of the ridge, an arsenal stashed in my new cargo pants.

I had never killed in cold blood before, which is not to say I have never killed anyone. When you're a cop and an armed suspect points a gun at you, you shoot first and ask questions later. But that's a different scenario. This killing would be flat-out murder.

At eight, Grace Wycoff Genovese took a covered plate out to the RV. A half hour later, she returned. At ten, Luke emerged from the garage with a motorbike. It roared to life, and when he passed my hiding spot, he came so close I could see he had his mother's hazel eyes. At noon, Grace took another covered plate to the RV, this time staying for a full hour. When she returned to the house, she carried several dirty dishes. Through my binocs I recognized the Spode china pattern one of my foster mothers—the eighth, I think, or maybe she was my eleventh—had inherited from her grandmother. Faience Chinoiserie, or a good imitation. Nothing but the Sunday best for her precious brother.

A little after eleven, Mario Genovese came out with Bethany. They loaded her Pink Princess bicycle into the bed of the pickup and drove off. This left Grace and Shana alone in the house.

Nothing much happened for the next few hours, so I killed time checking my phone messages. Still no calls from Genovese, two more from Jimmy. Feeling guilty, I texted him back that something had come up necessitating my stay in Black Canyon City, and to hold down the fort. While I was still typing, he called again, the phone vibrating nearly out of my hand. I didn't take that call, either. A string of text messages rolled in from Frank Gunnerston, who seemed to be having trouble accepting the fact that Desert Investigations would not help him find the wife he'd abused for so many years. Another text message came in from client Yolanda Blanco, who informed me she had followed up the lead we'd given her re her runaway daughter, and driven up to Flagstaff. Once there, she discovered that an hour earlier, Inez had bailed on the druggie boyfriend she'd been living with and split for parts unknown. Would Desert Investigations help locate her again?

After texting Gunnerston back and telling him what he could do with himself, I composed a more careful message to Yolanda, assuring her that yes, we would track her daughter down. Again. Then I texted Jimmy and told him to give Yolanda a fifty-percent discount on her next bill, and not to let her know we were doing it. Like most single mothers, she had more love than money.

So much grief in the world. So many people hooking up with the wrong partners. So many folks screwing up their lives for the most trivial of reasons.

So much purposeful blindness.

Ignoring another incoming call from Jimmy—he was about to set a new record for number of calls placed to me in a single day—I leaned back against an acacia and made myself comfortable, which was relatively easy in my loose cargo pants. Thanks to the padding in my new concealed-carry holster, my .38 didn't poke me too much, either.

About an hour later, when I was in danger of dropping off to sleep from sheer boredom, Genovese and his granddaughter returned. The truck's windows were closed and they drove so quickly I couldn't see their expressions, but when the truck started down the hill, I saw a purple-and-tan bicycle in the bed, its sales tag flapping in the wind. *Requiescat in pace*, Pink Princess. Soon afterwards, Luke came roaring over the hill on his motorbike. He looked upset.

Just before five the wind shifted. Earlier it had been little more than the usual light breeze sent over from California, but now it pushed a sky full of dark clouds up from Mexico. Phoenix was probably getting another haboob, the most severe type of dust storm, but at this elevation, Black Canyon City would only receive rain. From the denseness of those clouds, though, it appeared it would be a lot.

A little after six, Grace, clad in a rain slicker and carrying another plate full of food, headed for the RV while Genovese stood on the porch and watched her, Shana and Luke at his side. Bethany remained in the house. This time Grace exited the RV almost as soon as she went in. Once Grace rejoined the others, they all went back into the house together.

Maybe I wouldn't have to…

Wrong. At six-thirty Mario Genovese and Shana got into the pickup and drove up the hill on their way to work the night shift at Coyote Corral. As soon as they were out of sight, Grace came back out of the house holding Bethany's hand. I stood up, ready to run down the hill to stop them, but that turned out not to be necessary. When they reached the pasture gate, Luke slammed out of the house, ran across the yard, and snatched the girl away from his grandmother. Words were exchanged, but I couldn't hear them over the screaming wind. Their altercation continued for several minutes, finally ending with all three returning to the house.

The rain began at dusk, right around the time I heard the first notes of Native American flute music drifting up from Debbie's yellow house. CD or a musician playing for her own enjoyment? Then I heard chanting. Women's voices, not a CD. I pulled out more granola bars from my pocket and ate dinner, enjoying this odd serenade before the rain began to drown out the music.

The Genoveses' lights went out at ten; the RV's blue TV glow vanished almost immediately afterwards. By then, the downpour had become so heavy I could barely see past the surrounding brush. The worsening storm obliterated my view of the house, the pasture, and the Winnebago. Normal people would deplore such weather. Not me; I celebrated the fact that if someone in the house woke up, or if Genovese and Shana returned home early, they could not see past their noses.

Around eleven-thirty, the Winnebago became visible again. Wycoff, awakened by the storm, had turned on a light, and the glow pierced even the curtain of rain. Insomnia? I hoped all his dreams were nightmares. His light stayed on for nearly an hour, then blinked out.

After transferring several items from my backpack to those roomy cargo pants pockets, I slipped on a pair of latex surgical gloves—who knew what kind of nasty disease Wycoff had picked up in prison—then waited another half hour before making my move. The combined roar of rain, wind, and the near-deafening runoff down Black Canyon Creek covered my footsteps as I sloshed down the hill. My first stop was at Wycoff's Honda Civic, where I squatted down by the passenger-side wheel well, fished out the GPS module, and stashed it in one of my pockets. The transponder was no longer necessary, so no point in letting the authorities trace it to me. Not that I hoped to commit the perfect crime. Within hours of Wycoff's body being discovered, the police would come calling at Desert Investigations, and when they didn't find me there, I'd be the APB Star of the Day.

Maybe, after confessing to the Wycoff revenge killing—which I would do immediately—I would even confess to killing Norma. Whoever had done that deed deserved a medal, not a prison sentence. Perhaps it had been another now-grown foster child the Wycoffs had victimized. As for myself, I had only one regret— that I had decided not to use my Vindicator to take Wycoff out. Knives are messy. Although I had never met Mario Genovese in the flesh, over the past two days I had grown to like him, and I didn't want to splash blood all over his nice Winnebago.

GPS module secured in one pocket, Mag light in another, and my .38 nestled in the largest, I entered the pasture. Before leaving Scottsdale I hadn't thought to bring along rain boots, and by the time I made it ten feet inside the gate, mud and manure saturated my Reeboks, but that was the least of my worries. Since I couldn't actually see the Winnebago in the blinding storm, I could only guesstimate its location, which if I remembered correctly, was roughly a half mile south by southwest from the gate. If the wind and rain hadn't been so loud, I could have simply followed the roar of the swollen creek, but all I could do now was lower my face and head straight into the wind.

Despite everything, it was the longest walk of my life, even worse than...

I have a memory...

I was four years old. At least that's how old I think I was when my mother shot me in the head and left me for dead on that Phoenix street. After several months in a coma, I woke up. Unable to talk. Unable to walk.

I remembered learning how to walk again. The blue-dressed nurse in the room with all the bad machines had started off being kind, but today I heard an edge in her voice as she urged me on toward that hated padded walkway. "You're a big girl. You can do it."

To my young eyes, the walkway looked miles and miles long. I clung to the railings, afraid to move. My legs were matchsticks, and matchsticks couldn't hold up a little girl.

I shook my head. "Nhnnn!"

"Come on now, Missy. Left leg, then right leg."

What was left? What was right? I couldn't remember.

Mean Nurse put her big hands on one of my legs, pulling it forward. Unable to shift my balance quickly enough, I fell.

She hauled me up and none too gently placed my hands on the rails again. "We're going to do this until you get tired of not trying, Missy."

Missy. Was that my name?

"Nhnnn!"

"Complaining will get you nowhere."

"Nhnnn!" I hated Mean Nurse.

She knew it, too, but just said, "Watch the birdie."

Birdie? There were no birdies in this awful room.

"Look at the birdie, Missy!"

When I looked up, I saw something new. On the gate at the end of the narrow walkway someone had hung a cartoon of a big brown bird. Above Big Brown Bird were marks I recognized as words. I didn't know what they said, but I remembered the bird from the early morning cartoons one of the nurses, a nicer nurse than this one, always let me watch. Big Brown Bird was smart and fast and always outran the hungry coyote. Big Brown Bird made a noise like "Beep, beep!" so maybe that was what those words said.

I liked Big Brown Bird. He reminded me of me.

"Eeep, eeep!" I mimicked.

And took my first step and…

Now, as I staggered across the Genoveses' pasture, the rain hit me in the face so hard it felt like sleet. Maybe it was. The thermometer does strange things during a monsoon. It plays first with your skin, then your mind. Every now and then the wind—heightened by its sweep along the narrow valley—gusted even higher, making my rain slicker billow out around me. After traveling a few yards, I was soaked. But still I trudged forward, not knowing for certain if I was headed in the right direction.

As it turned out, I wasn't. The wind had tricked me, pushing me closer to the creek than was safe, but a lucky bolt of lightning lit up its rampaging surface. The only thing between me and that dangerous runoff was a cottonwood tree, mere feet from my face. Huddled beneath the tree was a lone horse, its eyes wide with fright. In the peal of thunder that followed the lightning flash, I could hardly hear his hooves as he bolted away. An even brighter flash revealed Mario Genovese's cattle, bunched tightly together under another tree, their backs to the wind. Standing apart from them were the three other horses and the Shetland pony.

I still couldn't see the Winnebago.

Using my flashlight was out—light can sometimes be seen through the densest rainstorm, and I didn't want the people back at the house to suddenly awaken and see a light bobbing across their pasture. But alert now to the dangers of walking blind, I halted beneath the cottonwoods, turned in the what I thought was the direction of the camper, and waited.

It didn't take long.

The next lightning bolt struck frighteningly near, reminding me how dangerous it was to stand under trees during a storm. Lightning loves tall objects, and the cottonwoods were the tallest object in the valley, so I moved out of the grove, leaving the animals to whatever mercy the storm might show them. But the lightning had done me a favor.

It had illuminated the Winnebago, less than fifty feet away.

I was about to become a murderer.

Taking a deep breath, I staggered forward again, ignoring the screams of the storm. My focus was on that creature in the Winnebago, that destroyer of innocence, that killer of dreams.

One step. Two. My mouth shut tight against the driving rain.

Mud and manure creeping past my ankles from the boggy ground.

Three steps.

Four.

Other steps followed, and soon the Winnebago loomed in front of me. My heart beat so loudly the world fell silent.

Could I really do this? Remembering Bethany's innocent face, I nodded.

Yes, I could.

And would.

I reached into a rear pocket for the kit of burglar's tools I'd fished out of my backpack, but when I tested the door handle, I discovered it unlocked. Wycoff must have felt secure, camped out here within shouting distance of his adoring sister.

Big mistake, perv.

I transferred my flashlight to my left hand and fished out the Taser with my right. I'd stun him first, and when he went down my garrote would end it.

I opened the door. Closed it softly behind me. Clicked on my flashlight.

Only to discover that someone else had done the job for me.

Chapter Seven

An hour later, with my wet clothes hung up to dry, I lay warm and snug in my bed at Debbie Margules' butterfly trailer, pondering my next move.

I had seen worse murder scenes, but not many. The killer, whoever he or she was, had not shown as much concern for the Winnebago as I'd planned to, and blood had spattered and dripped all over the floor from Wycoff's severed penis. Then there were the burns, eight of them evenly spaced an inch apart in an orderly row along his bare thigh. Approximately three inches long, their black-edges and blisters suggested they were administered while he was still alive.

Whoever had done this held more hate in his heart than even I did.

Outside, the storm raged on. Lightning flashed, thunder rolled, and the rain hitting the trailer's thin metal shell sounded like bullets. How long did I have before the sheriff banged on my door, too? I had signed my own name in the Desert Oasis guestbook and paid for my stay with Desert Investigations' Visa. At Coyote Corral, I had even handed my business card to Shana Genovese Ferris. Yet the idea of being hauled off to jail on suspicion of murder didn't alarm me. Something else did. I didn't believe in miracles but I hoped for one—that the swollen creek would jump its banks and sweep the Winnebago away, tearing it and its hideous cargo to pieces. Then there would be a chance that the cause of death would never be determined, and the killer would walk free. As far as I was concerned, hip-hip-hooray for him.

Or her. Women could be vengeful, too. Just ask any cop.

Maybe miracles did exist. For the first time in three decades I fell into a nightmare-less sleep.

The sun was shining when screams woke me up.

I tumbled out of bed, threw on clean clothes, and rushed out the door. The racket had awakened the other denizens of Debbie's Desert Oasis, and several of us, along with Debbie herself, followed the noise to see what was going on. When we reached the crest of the hill and peered through the early morning light into the valley below, we saw Grace Wycoff Genovese gesticulating wildly, running through the pasture toward her house. Mario Genovese had already made it through the gate and was running to meet her, clad only in his tightie whities, while Shana and her two children huddled together on the porch. Alarmed by the racket, the cattle and horses had retreated to the far end of the pasture, as far away from the Winnebago as the barbed-wire fence would allow them.

While I watched Grace make her way across the field, I marveled at her ability to scream so loudly and run at the same time. Her lung capacity must rival an opera singer's.

"What in the world's going on?" asked the redhead I'd seen the day before cleaning a fish on the steps of Fishin' Frenzy. Despite the activity below, I couldn't stop staring at her translucent complexion.

"Damned if I know, but from the screeching, you'd think somebody got murdered or something," replied the heavily tattooed brunette in Mustang. The grip of a Glock peeked out of the leather holster strapped to her hip. Earlier, as I'd zig-zagged my way through the mesquite grove to Monarch, I'd noticed a blacked-out Harley-Davidson Iron 833 parked in front of it. Biker chick? Or lone wolf?

The other denizens of the B&B hung back, a couple of them nervously eyeing the brunette's Glock. I didn't blame them.

"I've already called the sheriff," Debbie announced. Considering the caterwauling below, she sounded oddly nonchalant, which made me wonder if trouble was a common occurrence at the Genovese homestead.

The two Genoveses finally met up at the center of the pasture, and Mario wrapped his burly arms around his still-screaming wife. In movies, men slap women when they carry on like that, but Mario didn't. He just kept holding her. Eventually Grace's screams ceased, and with one arm still tightly wrapped around her, Mario led her toward the house.

"Show's over, folks," Debbie said. "Whatever's happened, Mario's taking care of her. The authorities will handle the rest." With a shooing motion, she ushered us back down the hill to her Desert Oasis.

Just before we reached our trailers, two sheriff's cruisers passed by, sirens wailing. The other B&B-ers stopped for a few seconds to watch their progress, but I kept walking, aware that I had already learned something interesting. Debbie was on a first-name basis with the Genoveses. Understandable, I guess. Despite its name, Black Canyon City was a small hamlet, and everyone here knew everyone else. Still...

Less than an hour after I returned to my butterfly trailer to rinse out the clothes I'd muddied the night before, the Yavapai County Sheriff's Department came knocking at my door. I had drawn a plainclothes female detective and two grim-faced male deputies, so it came as no surprise when the first words out of the detective's mouth were, "Ms. Jones, we'd like you to accompany us to the sheriff's office."

"All the way to Prescott?" I asked.

The detective—the shield she flashed said EASTMAN—smiled. "Oh, but it's such a pretty drive."

Prescott is famous for its gingerbready Victorian houses, so before the big SUV pulled into the sheriff's office parking lot, I took time to enjoy the view. Victoriana may seem odd in the desert, but in 1864 the town had been designated the capitol of the Arizona Territory, and building then began in earnest. Those beautiful old homes, proof that the city's prosperity had become its bane, attracting Californians fleeing that state's outrageous real estate prices. Now Gen X-ers clad in overpriced pseudo-Western wear bellied up to the same Whiskey Row bars as did the area's real life cowboys.

"Sure is a nice day," Detective Sergeant Linda Eastman said, after directing me to a metal chair in an interview room. The stiff chair, and the fact that the cop at the front desk had relieved me of my .38, made me uncomfortable, although I was determined not to show it.

"Love the sunshine," I responded. "Especially after all that rain."

If you've seen one interview room, you've seen them all. They're bare and ugly for a reason. Get trapped in one of those things and you'll say just about anything to get the hell out. Cognizant of the video camera trained on me, I decided to watch my mouth.

Looking very much at ease, Eastman leaned back in her chair. "As you're no doubt aware, there was an incident on the Genovese property sometime during the night."

"Horse get loose? Cow?"

"Now, now, Ms. Jones. You know better than that."

"I do?"

The door to the interview room opened and a uniformed deputy handed her a manila folder. She opened it and scanned through some papers, all the while humming something that sounded like "Maria," from *West Side Story.* An odd musical choice for an Arizona law officer, but maybe Eastman was originally from New York. Prescott didn't only attract Californians.

When Detective Eastman looked up, the smile and "Maria" were gone. "Says here the decedent's name is Brian H, as in Howard, Brian Howard Wycoff, once known to several children, including yourself, as 'Papa Brian.' That was before his trial for child rape, of course. He hasn't been known as 'Papa Brian' for, hmm, almost thirty years. Released from Florence Correctional Facility this past Monday."

"'*Decedent*,' did you say? He's dead? What was it? Heart attack? Snakebite?"

She ignored me. "Says here Mr. Wycoff's wife, Norma Wycoff nee Wilson, predeceased him by four days. Shot to death. Isn't that fascinating?"

"Recent statistics show there's been a rise in violent crime."

"Hmm. From what I read about that earlier case, when Mr. Wycoff was charged in multiple child rapes, there was talk of bringing Mrs. Wycoff to trial, too. You know, re several foster children, aiding and abetting, et cetera, et cetera. Due to her denials and a lack of evidence, that never happened." She put the folder down with a look of distaste. "Hardly the Beautiful People."

"Nice understatement."

"See, Mrs. Wycoff died pretty much in your own backyard, and now her husband turns up dead less than a mile from where you were spending the night. Cops don't like coincidences, Ms. Jones."

"Yet life is full of them."

Eastman flipped through the folder again, humming another bar of "Maria," this one slightly off-key. Was she trying to irritate me into a confession?

"It also says here Mr. Wycoff's sexual activities with children became known to the Scottsdale Police Department—that's where the Wycoffs were living at the time—after you tried to kill him with a kitchen knife."

"It was ruled self-defense."

She ignored me again. "You were on the witness list at his trial, but after two children testified against him, his attorney, no idiot, talked him into taking a plea deal." With that, she dropped the folder down on the table with an expression of distaste. "Besides you, four more children were about to testify, making seven kids total. Seven rape victims. *Seven, for shit's sake!* All of them ten years old or younger."

"I seem to remember something like that, yes."

Eastman leaned forward, as if about to share a secret just between us girls. When I was a cop, I had pulled that same trick.

"There were eight burn marks on Mr. Wycoff's body, Ms. Jones."

"Strange."

"One for each victim, perhaps?"

Shaking my head, I corrected her. "You just said there were only seven kids on the witness list."

I had wondered about that eighth burn mark, too. It was generally accepted that Wycoff had victimized more than the seven children on the witness list, but given the fact that children were so hesitant to make accusations against adults—especially molestation-type accusations—no one would ever know how many. Maybe even Wycoff had lost count.

Eastman was a good interviewer, and although she'd been open about the number of burns on Wycoff's thigh, she kept mum about the emasculation. Good cops always held something back, a detail about the crime only the killer would know.

"Where were you last night, Ms. Jones?"

There it was. She was through playing games and the interview would now proceed in earnest.

"I was asleep in a trailer covered with butterflies."

"Anybody with you?"

"I'm celibate these days."

"Lucky you. We've obtained a search warrant for your trailer. The techs are out there now, going over every inch of it, butterflies and all. Your Jeep, too."

"Try not to make a mess." Before returning to the trailer from the Winnebago, I had dismantled the garrote and with its pieces, thrown my gloves, muddy Reeboks, wet socks, and even the Taser into the raging creek, keeping only my beloved Vindicator as a reminder of what could have been. They were all halfway to Mexico by now, but the soles of my feet were still sore from my barefoot slog back to Monarch. Good thing my emergency backpack had held an extra pair of Reeboks.

Ignorant of my mental inventory, Eastman eased back in her chair again. "Did you kill Brian Howard Wycoff?"

"No."

"Did you kill Norma Wilson Wycoff?"

"No."

"Did you aid and/or abet the person who killed either of them?"

"No."

"Do you know who killed either of them?"

"No."

Detective Eastman closed her eyes for a moment, hummed a few more bars of "Maria," then stood up. "I'll have a deputy drive you back to Black Canyon City. Have a nice day."

My .38 had been handed back to me as I left, but considering everything, I couldn't figure out why I hadn't been arrested. Hell, if I'd still been a cop, I would have arrested myself. But here I sat, free as the proverbial bird, in the yellow house at Debbie's Desert Oasis, drinking herbal tea with Debbie and two other women while crime techs crawled all over Monarch and my Jeep. Some of the folks in the trailers toward the rear of the property had decamped after being cleared by the police, leaving our landlady grumbling about lost rent.

Since I had backed out of the Winnebago after taking only one step inside, I was not too worried about the authorities' interest in me. The night before, my camo pants' legs had been rolled up to my knees, so there would be no blood on them, and thanks to my latex gloves, I had left no prints on the Winnebago's door handle, either.

"I don't mean to be nosey, Lena, but why did they take you in for questioning?" asked Nicole Beltran, the beautiful redheaded resident of Fishin' Frenzy. With that amazing skin, I couldn't get a fix on her age, but she could be anywhere between twenty and forty.

"I was just, as they say in the movies, 'helping the police with their enquiries.'" The tea was delicious, a combination of berry, peppermint, and something else. Mango?

"Well, I don't like this," said Jacklyn Archerd, the pistol-packing biker in Mustang. Like me, she was dressed all in black, but her jeans were tighter than my cargo pants and her low-cut tank top revealed a lot more than my tee shirt did. Too thin-lipped and wiry to be conventionally attractive, she wasn't much older than thirty, but road-weathering had taken a toll on her face. Her copious tattoos didn't help. Both arms were sleeved-out with flowers and birds, and the name STEVIE was written in black and red Old English letters just below her collarbone. Note to self: Never tattoo a boyfriend's name anywhere on your person.

"The cops, I mean, not you, Lena," Jacklyn continued. "They decide they don't like you, they make stuff up. Some guy's dead down there. Murdered, you said they told you, so they're gonna be making up some pretty big stuff." Here she shot a look at Nicole. "And we, uh, you know..." She trailed off.

Debbie came over with another batch of blueberry scones. "I'm sure everything's going to be fine. The police know what they're doing."

"News to me." When Jacklyn raised her teacup to her lips, I noticed she wore no wedding ring, either. No jewelry at all, not that she needed it with all those tattoos.

"Jacklyn," Debbie soothed, "let's keep calm. Whatever's going on at the Genovese place has nothing to do with us."

My second scone was as delicious as the first, and for the next few moments I gave myself over to pleasure. The morning's brush with the law had left me unsettled, and I'd read somewhere that herbal tea and scones calmed your nerves. It seemed to be working.

"Either of you ladies stay here before?" I asked, merely to make conversation.

"Oh, yeah, we..." Jacklyn began, only to be cut off by Debbie.

"I do have my regulars." Debbie beamed around the table like a proud grandma. "Theme trailers are very popular these days. Bed comfy in Monarch, Lena?"

"Best night's sleep I've had in years." No lie there. Usually I woke up screaming in the middle of the night.

"What with all the runoff, fishing should be good today. You ought to try your luck down at the creek. The fishing tackle is in that tall closet in Monarch's kitchen."

"I noticed."

"Or if fishing's not your thing, there's a dude ranch in the valley about a mile further along. You could rent a horse and see the sights."

I told her I might do just that. We chitchatted for a few more minutes until the tea and scones were gone, then took separate paths back to our individual trailers. As I stopped to examine another of Debbie's large sculptures—*SEEING THE LIGHT* was constructed of copper, wood, and brick, with a few flashings of chrome—it struck me that the two trailers closest to the yellow house were occupied by single women. Unlike the people toward the rear of the property, Jacklyn and Nicole had checked in with no partners, no children. Mere coincidence, or something more?

Once I arrived at my trailer, I made an annoying discovery. While the Yavapai County techs hadn't made too big a mess during their search, they had confiscated my Vindicator, including my emergency backpack with its remaining stash of clean underwear.

So I was still under suspicion.

When I checked the tiny bathroom, I found that the damp clothes I had hung out to dry were gone, too. If worse came to worse, I could pick up a pair of jeans and a new tee shirt at the general store in town. Or since Detective Eastman hadn't ordered me to hang around, I could simply return to Scottsdale, but I hated to waste money. The rent on Monarch was good up to eleven Monday morning, and although I didn't care who had killed either of the Wycoffs, I had become curious about Debbie's Desert Oasis. Something was off here.

With a sigh, I climbed into my Jeep and headed for town.

The Black Canyon City General Store had everything the well-dressed PI could want, just not in the colors I preferred. Instead of black jeans or black cargo pants, I had to settle for beige-and-green camos. And instead of a solid black tee shirt, I wound up with a camo print there, too. As for underwear, white was the color of the day, but at least panties weren't thongs and the bras weren't underwired. The white socks were okay, too, since I didn't plan on hitting any fashion runways.

With two changes of clothing in my cart, along with a new backpack, I made my way to the checkout line and took my place behind a Stetson-wearing cowboy. He smelled like Horse, but in a manly sort of way. His cart was piled high with Ralston Purina. Come to think of it…I stopped looking at the dog food and lowered my eyes.

I'd know that ass anywhere.

Dusty.

I would have moved back in line but an elderly woman was already nudging my own ass with her cart, urging me to move forward to where Dusty was in the midst of breaking another woman's heart.

"Salome, you're lookin' finer than fine today," he told the checker, an overweight thirty-something with an acne-scarred face.

She blushed as red as her cheap lipstick. "You don't mean it."

"I never say anything I don't mean, darlin'."

Liar!

The poor woman blushed even deeper. "I'm, uh, I've lost a few pounds. This new diet…"

He didn't let her finish. "Now don't you go losin' too much, darlin', 'cause what you got, it's all in the right places."

It was all I could do not to gag. How in the world had I ever been naive enough to fall for that old line?

I was saved from announcing in a loud voice that the cowboy was a two-timing, forked-tongue piece of shit who almost got me killed, when the elderly woman behind me decided she'd forgotten something, backed her cart out of the line, and headed for the produce department. Seizing my chance, I ducked down my head and backed away, too. I spent the next few minutes lurking in the motor oil aisle until the cheating son of a bitch left the store.

By the time Dusty tore out of the parking lot in a tan Silverado with RED ROCK RANCH painted on its side, I had recovered enough to return to the checkout counter. When I reached the unfortunate Salome, I said, "Couldn't help noticing that good-looking cowboy you were talking to. Your boyfriend?"

"Don't I wish." Still flushed, she gave me a wobbly smile. "He looks just like Clint Eastwood, doesn't he? I mean, like back when Eastwood was lots younger and better lookin' than he is now."

"Cowboy live around here?" Please, God, let her say he was just passing through.

She nodded. "Rented hisself a little house down near the dude ranch. He's the head wrangler, knows everything there is to know 'bout horses."

And women.

The love-struck Salome continued singing the cheating son of a bitch's praises as she rang up my new wardrobe. "I went to a party down there once and he's got it fixed up real cute."

I bet his bedroom was real cute, too. Blondes, brunettes, and redheads draped over every picture hook and curtain rod, lolling across the bed, rolling around on the rug…

Forcing myself not to sneer, I said, "He sure looks like a man of taste."

Somehow I made it to my Jeep without bawling.

Chapter Eight

Ordinarily, a PI's life doesn't extend itself to fishing, but as I walked down the gravel road to Black Canyon Creek, I carried a rod and reel and a squirmy plastic bag filled with night crawlers dug up behind Monarch. The near run-in with Dusty had shaken me enough that I needed to settle down before making a final decision about the Wycoff investigation. Fishing was supposed to be relaxing, right?

As I topped the rise and looked down into the narrow valley below, I stopped for a moment. Laid out before me was a crime scene similar to the one I had seen in Apache Junction, only spread along several acres. The heaviest police presence swarmed around the Genoveses' taped-off Winnebago, where a sheriff's cruiser sat parked next to two tech vans and a coroner's wagon. A uniformed deputy stood outside the gate to wave curiosity-seekers away. At the house, I saw a white Chevy SUV emblazoned with the Yavapai County Sheriff's Department logo, plus what appeared to be an unmarked Chevy cruiser. They were parked diagonally behind the family's vehicles, blocking their way out.

I could only imagine what the Genoveses were going through. Getting grilled by the police is never fun.

At the bottom of the hill the gravel road forked left toward the Genovese house, and right toward a narrow trail leading straight down to the creek. The storm's runoff had lessened, but the current remained strong enough that the going could have been treacherous. After picking my way carefully down to the bank, I settled myself on a large boulder so deeply embedded in the ground it would have taken an industrial-sized bulldozer to move it. Best of all, my perch was less than a hundred yards downwind of the Genovese house. I baited my hook, and cast my line into the creek, forcing myself not to think of my ex-lover. Instead, I thought about the case.

Unlike Detective Eastman, I didn't hum, just listened to the birds and the water. They were all the music I needed. In counterpoint to the peaceful afternoon, the gentle breeze sometimes rose enough that it carried snippets of conversation between the deputies still stationed at the Genovese house, most of which I ignored now that the Big Bad Wolf was dead. Only once did one of the deputies mention the fact that the murdered man's wife had also been killed a few days earlier. Strange, wasn't it? A discussion of pedophiles followed, most of which I tuned out, but I tuned back in again when another one said, "Served her right, staying with a perv like that."

I thought so, too.

Two hours later, I had caught two rainbow trout and one largemouth bass, all of which I released. The high point of the afternoon came when I saw Grace Wycoff Genovese shoved into the unmarked cruiser and driven away. Another eyebrow-raiser arrived when I returned to the B&B and found Detective Eastman helping Debbie into the back of another cruiser. Neither woman looked happy.

"Are they arresting Debbie?" I asked Jacklyn, who was watching just outside the front door of yellow house.

The biker sneered at me. "Mind your own business."

I left her alone with her hostility and her Glock, and wended my way through the brush toward Monarch. Before reaching the trailer, I saw Nicole crying on the stoop of Fishin' Frenzy. Some women "cry pretty." She wasn't one of them. Black mascara streaked her cheeks, marring that flawless complexion, and her running nose was almost as red as her hair.

"Can I help?" I didn't have any tissues, but sometimes an arm around your shoulders can be steadying.

She waved me away. "Just leave me alone."

Before I could say anything else, my cell vibrated in my pocket. Expecting yet another call from Jimmy or wife-beating Frank Gunnerston, I fished it out and looked at the screen.

The call was from Mario Genovese.

An hour later I was sitting in a booth in the crowded dining area of Coyote Corral, enjoying a late lunch of *huevos rancheros* and listening to Mario Genovese give his version of the previous night's events. The place was packed but at first Genovese kept his voice so low I had trouble hearing him.

"Grace had his blood all over her and, uh, she'd tried to put his di—, uh, his penis back on…" he whispered. A handsome man with a dimpled chin and an outdoorsman's tan, his brown eyes were creased with worry. "I told you it'd been…"

"Severed. Yeah, you did." The memory wasn't pretty, but it didn't keep me from enjoying the *huevos rancheros*, some of the best I'd ever had. They were served with refried beans, garlicky Spanish rice, and hot rolled tortillas. Not knowing how he would react to my next question, I ate fast.

"Tell me, Mr. Genovese, putting aside Grace's display of histrionics, do you think there's a chance she did it?"

Instead of exploding, he answered, "She loved him."

"People kill people they love all the time."

"Grace wouldn't hurt a fly."

I managed to restrain my laughter by sopping up salsa with a tortilla.

Oblivious to my feelings about his wife, he continued. "Once the cops get through talking to her, they'll have to know she had nothing to do with it. Look, when my daughter gave me your card, I almost tossed it, but now I'm glad I didn't, because I want you to…" He stopped, took a deep breath, then continued. "Let me be honest here. I despised my brother-in-law, and yes, I made a big mistake in letting him stay in my RV for even one night, but Grace begged and begged and promised not to let him get anywhere near the grandkids and…"

I took a big bite of tortilla, swallowed it down, then licked salsa off my fingers. "She let Bethany meet him twice."

"She couldn't have!" The denial was so loud several customers looked our way.

"Twice, Mr. Genovese. I've had Wycoff under surveillance since he arrived at your place, and during that time I saw her encourage conversation between them two times. She even tried to take Bethany out to the RV, but your grandson stopped her." I lowered my voice to a whisper. "Has it occurred to you that maybe Grace loved her brother too much?" *Such as the incest kind of too much?* Incest was a common occurrence in pedophiles' families. That's one of the ways they get started. Our booth was now the center of attention. Funny how discussing a murder can make even un-nosy folks turn nosy.

"Maybe we'd better finish this conversation someplace else," I suggested. He hadn't yet told me what he wanted.

Genovese looked around, saw the fascinated faces, then stood up. "Outside. In back. There's something I need to ask you, something you could…"

Before finishing, he spun on his heel and headed for the hallway that separated the bar from the restaurant.

Intrigued, I followed him down the hall toward the rear exit, past an office, past the restrooms—Cowgirls and Cowboys—and out into the afternoon sunshine. He kept walking across the pickup-centric parking lot until he reached the Dumpster. The garbage must have been picked up recently because it didn't smell at all bad. In fact, the spot he'd chosen was quite nice. The Dumpster enjoyed a scenic view of acacia-covered hills rising behind it, and fluffy white clouds scuttling across a bright blue sky. Between pauses in our conversation I could hear semis roaring along I-17. Still, it was pleasant being outside after the crowded restaurant.

Picking up the conversation where we had left off, I said, "I'm talking about incest, Mr. Genovese. It might explain Grace's behavior." *And your obviously unhappy marriage.*

He looked miserable. "After that last breakdown I thought she was past her problems with him, but then Luke said…he said…"

"Your grandson told you she was dangling Brittany in front of him?"

He sighed. "I didn't want to believe it, but just in case, I was going to tell that son of a bitch to leave today and never come back. I was ready to give him the damned Winnebago if necessary, anything to get rid of him. Before he…" He ran his fingers through his thick hair. "Before he went to prison, before I put a stop to it, she'd sometimes drive down to Scottsdale to spend the weekend with him and Norma. Every time she came back she was…"

"Disturbed?" I finished for him.

"That might be putting it a bit strongly, but something like that, yeah. The last time I saw her, her eyes were bloodshot."

"Maybe she'd been drinking."

"Grace never drinks."

A terrible thought occurred to me. "Was this before Shana was born?"

After waiting long enough that I thought the interview might be finished, he answered, "Before. And after."

It took me a while to speak, too. "How did Shana act when she got back?"

"I…I don't know. I was more worried about how Grace was acting. Kids, they're down one day and up the next. Most of the time it doesn't mean anything."

But sometimes it does. "What finally happened? You said you put a stop to it. How'd that come about?"

"One time when they went down there, Grace and Shana, I mean, they stayed for a whole week, and when they got back Shana barely spoke for a week. Grace acted weird, too. Stupid me, I thought Norma was the problem, or maybe one of the other kids, you know, the foster children they took in, might have done something to her. It bothered me enough that I called Brian up and asked him what the hell was going on down there that had my daughter so upset. Was Norma being mean to her?

One of those foster kids? From what I heard, some of them were little hellions. Anyway, Brian swore nothing had happened, that when Grace was a kid she'd been moody, too, so it was probably a genetic thing. There was something about the way he said it that bothered me—it just didn't sound right—so the next time Grace told me she was going down there visiting, I forbid it."

"And?"

"And nothing. She didn't go."

From what I had observed about Grace, admittedly at a distance, she didn't appear to be the meek kind of woman who would accept her husband's every command as gospel. Had she also begun to suspect something was wrong?

"Did Shana ever say if anything happened, if her uncle…?"

He didn't let me finish. "If she had, I'd have killed him."

"How about Bethany? Did you ask her if her great-uncle had said anything out of the way?"

He thrust out his chin. "No need to. I'd warned her to stay away from him."

And little girls always do what they're told. "Mr. Genovese, you must be aware Norma Wycoff was murdered Tuesday, probably by the same person who killed your brother-in-law."

"All the news reports said that Norma was shot, at least that's what was reported on the news. And let me tell you, Brian sure as hell wasn't shot." The gloating expression on his face made me realize it was a good thing he'd been at the restaurant while Wycoff was being tortured, otherwise he might also have received an invitation to visit that ugly interview room at the Yavapai County Sheriff's Office.

Breaking up his moment of cheer, I said, "Well, Wycoff must have believed Norma's murder had something to do with his own crimes, or else why would he come running up here?"

"He told us someone was stalking him, some private investigator. I wonder who that could be."

I ignored the dig. "You didn't put two and two together when you found his body?"

"Grace found his body, not me," he corrected. "I just went in the Winnebago to make certain he was dead." He looked up at the crisp sky and sighed. "My wife's always been the excitable type, and what she was yelling didn't make any sense. For all I knew, the shithead—Brian, I mean—just got drunk and fell down and injured himself. He could've even still been breathing. So I went in and found…and found what I found. Rough way to go, but if anybody ever deserved it, he did. Still, I want you to…"

At that moment several customers exited the Corral, heading for the pickups parked near the rear of the gravel lot. They walked slowly, their attention riveted toward us.

"Sure sorry to hear about your brother-in-law, Mario," said a thin man wearing a John Deere gimme cap.

"Thanks, Jim," Genovese said.

"What I hear, it was no big loss." This from his buddy who was as obese as Jim was thin.

Jim nudged his pudgy pal. "Show some respect for the dead, can't ya?"

The two began to squabble. Genovese and I waited until they agreed that everyone should be spoken of with a certain amount of decorum when they died, at least in front of their families. Then they climbed into a lime-green pickup and drove away, only to be replaced by three cowboy types who felt it necessary to offer their own half-hearted condolences.

As soon as they left, I said to Genovese, "Maybe you should just go ahead and tell me what it is you want. Before somebody else comes over here to pay their half-hearted respects."

He rocked back on his heels. "Okay. I want to hire you."

"For what? To find out who killed your brother-in-law? Frankly, Mr. Genovese, I don't give a rat's ass who did."

Then Genovese said something that changed everything. "I don't care who killed that baby-raping bastard, either, Ms. Jones, but I'm afraid that once the cops get through talking to my wife, they'll come back for my grandson."

Here's the problem: I'm a sucker for kids. Not that I'm maternal, mind you, but having lost so much of my own childhood to violence, I'm more interested than the average person in ensuring that children be protected.

"Mr. Genovese, what makes you think the authorities might, to use your own words, 'come back' for your grandson?"

He looked down at the gravel, saw a Kit Kat wrapper near a cigarette butt, then bent down and picked up both. Then he walked over to the Dumpster and dropped them in the bin. Instead of answering me, he continued scouting the gravel for more debris. Typical avoidance behavior.

I waited.

After three more trips to the Dumpster he ran out of candy wrappers and cigarette butts and I ran out of patience. "Mr. Genovese?"

Out on I-17 a semi blasted its air horn. Here, a half-mile of hill between Coyote Corral and I-17, Genovese winced as if the truck drove right next to him. But he never took his eyes off the gravel.

"Mr. Genovese, answer my question or I'm driving back to Scottsdale right now. My Jeep's already packed."

He swallowed again. "He…he likes video games."

"So does every other thirteen-year-old boy in America."

"Violent ones."

I sighed. "Like every other thirteen-year-old boy in America."

"You don't understand. That's not the only thing."

"What else, then?" Getting this man to make sense was heavy going.

"It's…it's his girlfriend."

"A thirteen-year-old has a girlfriend? And even if he does, what does she have to do with any of this?"

"It's just puppy love," he muttered, still staring at the gravel, looking for more debris.

"Mr. Genovese, I'm tired of looking at the top of your head. We're either going to have this conversation or I'm splitting. Your choice."

He finally met my eyes. "The girl, ah, her name's Carolee, she attempted suicide last month. Cut her wrists, but thank God she cut the wrong way. She…She…Oh, hell. Supposedly it had something to do with her mother's live-in boyfriend. Cops went out and arrested him, but he made bond and is still in town, says everything Carolee told the police was a lie and he's going to sue for false arrest."

You didn't have to be a brain surgeon to figure that one out. "This Carolee, she accused her mother's boyfriend of sexual abuse, correct?"

He shot me a look of surprise. "Her mom told the cops it was nothing, that the girl was just looking for attention, that she's always making stuff up."

"This was before or after the suicide attempt?"

"Before."

"I take it your grandson believed her."

A nod. "Carolee's back home now from the hospital. I suspect Luke's been visiting her and that she's been talking to him about it, but I told him to ease up on the relationship, because who knows? Her mother might be right. I'd…I'd decided to talk him into seeing less of the girl even before this all happened because the mother, well, she's a heavy drinker and by the look of her skin and teeth, she's no stranger to meth, either. When the boyfriend mess blew up, I told Luke flat-out to stay away, and so did Shana, but of course he didn't listen. In a way it was a good thing he didn't, because he's the one who found the girl right after her attempt and called 9-1-1. They live in a trailer over there." He gestured in the general direction of the highway.

"They? Are you telling me that the mother's boyfriend is still living with them?"

"God, no, he's renting some old shack over by Rock Springs. Myra Jo, that's the girl's mother, she still sees him, though. They came into the bar together the other night. When I told him he wasn't welcome here, he slithered out like the piece of shit he is, but Myra Jo mouthed off, said she was going to sue. Doubtless got the lawsuit idea from her scumball boyfriend."

"Sue for what?"

He spread his hands wide. "Denial of her civil rights to get drunk on her ass every night? Whatever, it's a bad situation and I don't want either in my establishment, or Luke around any of them. I told Luke last night to stop going over there or I'd take away his video games."

Poor Carolee. An accused molester for a father figure, an addict for a mother, and now, thanks to Mario Genovese, in danger of losing her life-saving boyfriend. Yet this was no time to judge the man. In his place, I might have made the same judgment call.

"We're getting pretty far afield here. Tell me how much Luke knows about his grand-uncle?"

He bit his lip hard enough to make me wince. "That's the problem, Ms. Jones. Luke knows everything."

Chapter Nine

As we stood in the light of the beautiful day, Genovese told me that when Grace talked him into letting Wycoff stay in the Winnebago, he sat his grandson down and explained the nature of his grand-uncle's crimes.

"When I finished, I told Luke that under no circumstances were he nor Bethany to go anywhere near him. After that, I told Grace to make sure they didn't."

"And?"

"She promised." A spot of blood appeared on his bitten lip. He didn't bother wiping it off.

"Mr. Genovese, you realize I have to talk to Luke."

I could tell by his face he was about to say no, but before the denial was out of his mouth, he changed his mind. "Only if I'm present. Kid's thirteen, for Christ's sake!"

I shook my head. "Won't work, because the kid wouldn't tell me anything he didn't want you to hear." And thirteen-year-olds are good at keeping secrets from their parents and grand-parents.

"An attorney, then."

"Luke needs to talk openly to me, which he won't do with either you or some rent-a-shark hovering in the background. Given his age, I doubt he was involved in your brother-in-law's death, but I do need to ask him some questions. If I hear what I think I'm going to hear, then you have nothing to worry about."

Telling a grandfather not to worry about a grandchild was like telling the sun not to rise, but he understood my logic and reluctantly agreed.

"I need to talk to Grace, too."

"Uh, as to that…"

I didn't let him finish. "Yes, I know she's at the sheriff's office right now giving a formal statement, but I'm betting they'll cut her loose soon. And, yes, I understand that she's grieving, but if you want to hire Desert Investigations I have to interview her whether she likes it or not. Remember, if it hadn't been for her talking you into taking in Wycoff, none of you would be in this situation. Maybe not even your brother-in-law. Now, can I follow you back to the house? The sooner I talk to Luke, the better."

Luke was taller than the average thirteen-year-old boy, and more emotionally mature, which I put down to working on his grandfather's ranch. Working with livestock had given him a sense of responsibility, a trait that had fortunately kept Bethany away from Wycoff. Not to mention giving him a backbone. But it was that very backbone I was having trouble with now.

While his sister rode her new bicycle outside and his grandfather paced back and forth in the living room, Luke stood before me, arms crossed against his thin chest, defiance in his eyes. "I don't have to talk to you." He was a handsome boy, with his sandy hair, his mother's hazel eyes, and his grandfather's dimpled chin.

We were in Mario Genovese's den, a none-too-neat space furnished in Late Nineties Awful. Fake mahogany paneling, fake oak desk holding up an ancient iMac, brown indoor-outdoor carpet, two brown-and-gold plaid chairs. The only real wood in the room was a small and obviously locked gun cabinet in the corner. It held a Mossberg 500, a Vanguard rifle, and a small Rossi .22 caliber rifle—Luke's, no doubt. A family of hunters, from pesky squirrels to deer to big whatevers. Unless I was wrong, Genovese kept a handgun under the Corral's bar, too.

I sat in one of the chairs, while Luke remained standing. The den's small window overlooked the pasture, where a palomino and a pinto grazed near the fence. Luke seemed to prefer looking at them rather than at me.

"Luke, your grandfather hired me to keep you and the rest of the family out of trouble."

"We're not in trouble."

"Your grand-uncle was murdered on your property. That's a whole lot of trouble."

Bony shoulders shrugged. When Luke filled out, they would be he-man broad. His girlfriend, if she managed to survive her criminally negligent mother, would appreciate that.

He made a face to match the shrug. "What happened to him has nothing to do with us."

God bless kids. They confuse hope with truth. "The cops think it does, and your family has to live with the fallout whether you like it or not." I let that sink in for a moment then said, as if changing the subject, "Say, I hear you like video games."

"Me and everybody else I know."

"What kind?"

He warmed a little. "Oh, like *Call of Duty 4*, *Assassin's Creed*, *Jerico*, stuff like that."

The usual suspects. "Those games are pretty violent, aren't they?"

He flicked his eyes toward the pasture still preferring the horses to me. "Games're no worse than movies, and I don't see anybody getting all spastic over them."

We could discuss the pros and cons of violent video games all day, but I needed to step things up. "Where were you between ten and two last night?"

When he turned away from the horses, there was an expression of scorn on his face. "Where do you think I was?"

"My thoughts aren't important here."

"Hmph."

Most kids don't "hmph" well and Luke was no exception. I tried not to smile, to leave the kid his dignity. "If you weren't here, you can't provide an alibi for anyone in this house, which includes your sister, your mother, and your grandparents."

Horrified, he responded, "Mom and Gramps were at the Coyote and a million customers would have seen them!"

"There was a storm, remember? I'm betting a lot of the usual crowd stayed home. But your mom and gramps aside, how about your grandmother?" For good measure, I added, "And Bethany."

He looked at me like I was crazy. "I know what you're getting at, and nobody went out to the 'Bago. I would have seen them."

"Not if you were asleep. Or gone."

"I, uh, I…" He darted a look at the iMac.

Again, I had to force myself not to smile at this artless kid. In a way he reminded me of my goddaughter. "You snuck onto the computer last night, didn't you, Luke?"

He hung his head. "Gramps'll kill me if he finds out."

"Oh, I doubt that."

"Yes he will. I'm not supposed to use it if he's not in the room with me."

Lena, don't you dare smile. "Were you e-mailing Carolee? You girlfriend?"

"Yeah," he told the brown carpet.

Good. The e-mails would be dated and timed, providing an alibi for at least one member of the Genovese family. "While you were in here messaging away, did you happen to hear or see anything?"

Thin shoulders hunched over, he finally collapsed into the chair across from mine. "Just Grandma snoring. She's awful loud. Gramps is always after her to get her nose operated on and she says she will, but she wants to make sure she's all better first. She was kinda sick there for a while."

Luke didn't realize it, but he had just alibied his grandmother.

"Snoring can be a problem when it wakes everyone up. Besides your grandma, did you hear anything else? A car, voices outside, whatever?"

He shook his head. "Just the storm. Loud? Geez! That storm was something, wasn't it? Took down one of our cottonwoods."

And loud enough to cover a tortured man's screams. Then something Luke said struck me. "What do you mean, your grandmother was 'kinda sick'?"

He blushed. "I shouldn't have said anything. She's okay now, so she promised Gramps she'd call the EMT, or ENT, the nose doctor, whatever they're called, and get something scheduled next month. But this was, uh, before my uncle…you know, got killed." He looked out at the pasture again, where the palomino and the pinto were having some sort of disagreement. Ears back, they faced each other, yellow teeth snapping. Threats duly delivered, they trotted off to opposite ends of the pasture. Too bad humans couldn't settle their disagreements in the same sensible way.

"It's okay to tell me what was wrong with your grandmother, Luke. I hope it was nothing serious." Whatever the illness, maybe it had affected her judgment.

"Breast cancer," he told the carpet. "But they got it in time."

"Mastectomy? Chemo?" Sylvie, my Scottsdale PD frenemy, had once undergone a long bout of chemo, and she'd been pretty loopy during that time, ascribing her loopiness to "chemo brain." She'd even started dating a fellow cop, something she swore she would never do. It had taken her another three months for her to return to her usual, razor-sharp self and dump him.

"Yeah, both. Radiation, too, Mom said."

"How long ago?"

"Couple years. Before Mom and Bethany and me moved in here."

"Glad to hear she's better. But you know, Luke, with that motorbike of yours, you must be pretty familiar with the area around here, all the trails."

Aggrieved, he raised his voice again. "It's legal! Just as long as I don't take it out on the highway!"

"What I meant was, you must know if there's another way to get to the Winnebago without going past your house."

Light dawning, he relaxed. "Yeah, there's a dirt trail that comes down the hill behind the pasture. It's too narrow for cars, but it's great for bikes and horses."

And murderers on foot.

When my next few questions elicited no more useful information, I escorted Luke back into the living room, where his grandfather gave him an anxious look. Luke made a beeline to the front door. Before it closed behind him, I caught a glimpse of Bethany outside, hovering over her new bike, a small wrench in her hand.

"I bought her a new basket, too," Genovese explained. "Told her she had to put it on by herself but forgot to tell Luke."

"Speaking of Luke, Mr. Genovese…"

It was interesting to watch his face when he learned that his grandson had been e-mailing the forbidden girlfriend in the middle of the night. He didn't know whether to cheer or be furious. I kept reminding him that the timing gave Luke a perfect alibi, and that his recollection of Grace's snores alibied her, too.

"Never thought either would be a good thing," he grumbled, mollified.

The Genovese living room was more up-to-date than the den, and considerably more feminine, with a soft green Berber carpet, matching floral love seats, chairs heaped with color-coordinated pillows, and a bronze-and-glass étagère showcasing miniature teapots. A collection of Wedgewood plates lined the walls. Every flat surface was taken up with family photographs, mostly of Luke and Bethany, from cradle to now. Over the upright piano hung a formal studio portrait of the children's mother. Before work and worry had prematurely lined her face, Shana had been stunning.

Reminded, I asked, "Where's your daughter?"

"Working. Daytime bartender called in sick again, so she's covering."

"Pulling a double shift?"

He shrugged. "Run a bar, that's the way it works."

"She's not too upset over her uncle?"

"You're kidding, right? She liked him even less than I did, almost stroked out when she heard he was staying in the 'Bago."

I made a mental note to track down Shana, but first things first.

"How many customers did you get at the Coyote last night? What with the monsoon and all, I'll bet you closed up early."

Since I'd been sleeping the sleep of the innocent, I hadn't heard his truck pass the Oasis.

"You don't know the folks around here. A whole pack of them stayed 'til closing, like they were afraid to get their feet wet or something. Hell, one old boy went and got his dog out of his truck and brought it in. Fed the ugly thing tacos all night."

"When did your last customer leave?"

"Closing time, two o'clock. What with the cleanup and all, Shana and I didn't get out of there until after three. Damned dog made an awful mess, but even worse was the guy who puked all over the bathroom. Told him next time, he's eighty-sixed for life."

I raised my eyebrows. "You allowed a customer in that condition to drive?"

"You think I'm crazy? He gets in a wreck, kills himself or someone else, my name's all over the lawsuit, so hell, no, I didn't let him drive, just called his wife and told her to come and pick him up."

"When was this?"

"Just before closing. It took her, me, and Shana, all three of us, to get him to her car."

"None of your other customers offered to help?"

"Did I mention he'd puked all over himself, too? Anyway, by the time she showed up, everybody else had split, leaving us to do the honors."

As unlikely as it seemed, it sounded like Genovese and his entire family were alibied to the hilt. "Did you…?"

The sound of a car door closing outside, then footsteps on the porch, cut my question short. I heard a child's questioning voice—Bethany's—mingled with a woman's. Then the front door opened and Grace walked in, fresh from her grilling at the sheriff's office. Red-eyed and frowsy-haired, she looked like hell but wore a fake smile for the girl's sake. It disappeared when she saw me.

"Who are you?"

Before I could answer, Genovese explained my presence.

Grace wasn't pleased. "We don't need a private detective snooping into our business. There's already been enough of that."

But Bethany, who had followed her in, was thrilled. "A detective? Just like on TV?"

"Exactly," I answered, only half-truthfully. "I'm here to help your family."

Grace was having none of that. "Listen, you…"

Before she could continue what sounded like a get-out-of-here-and-don't-come-back order, Genovese interrupted. "Let's do this in the den."

At first it didn't seem like Grace would comply, but then changed her mind. Turning back to the girl, she said, "Go help Luke with that basket, okay? Remember, your grandfather told you to work on it yourself, not have him do everything for you."

As soon as the girl left, Grace threw me an ugly look and walked toward the den, her gait as stiff-legged as a robot's. She didn't bother to check if we followed.

Earlier, I had only thought of her in relation to her sicko brother, but now I saw another side. Although a pushover where he was concerned, she had no trouble being confrontational with others.

Contrary to popular opinion, enablers aren't necessarily weak. It's tempting to believe they are when they have no income of their own and need to rely on their mates for financial support, but in actuality, that's seldom the case. Before the Wycoffs had been outed for the monsters they were, Norma Wycoff ran a busy print shop, ordering supplies, balancing the books, hiring and firing the help without a qualm. She had also been a cake-baking deacon at her church and the Mace-toting commander of the local Neighborhood Watch. People who knew her, when later questioned by the police, described her as a no-nonsense woman. Yet I knew that if her child-raping husband said the sun rose in the west, Norma would nod her head and agree—while the sun rose in the east right in front of her.

No, you didn't have to be weak to be in denial. You just had to be obsessed, and if there's one quality present in all enablers, it's that they are as obsessed with their pedophiles as their pedophiles are with children. Knowing this, I dreaded the upcoming interview.

This time I didn't chase her husband out of the den. On several occasions Norma Wycoff had been violent, and considering the stress Grace was under, I wouldn't put it past her, either. If nothing else, the man might serve as a calming agent.

"I'm sorry for your loss, Grace," I said, once we'd seated ourselves in the den's ugly chairs, Genovese taking the one behind his desk.

No answer from the woman other than a red-eyed stare.

"If I'm going to help you and your family, I do have a few questions."

Still that stare. Goosebumps rose on my arms, but I kept my voice steady. "Were you aware that under the terms of Mr. Wycoff's release he had to remain within Pinal County jurisdiction unless approved beforehand to move elsewhere?"

More nothing.

Genovese leaned forward. "Grace, please."

She flicked her eyes toward him, but her head didn't move. "A brother has a right to be near his sister."

"Even when the brother has confessed to multiple counts of child rape and there are two children on the premises?"

"People give false confessions all the time. The cops make them do it."

Although I already knew the answer, as a matter of form I asked, "Where were you between ten and two last night?"

"Sleeping." She tugged on the necklace at her throat, a silver dove winging its way across a gold cross.

"You didn't go out at all?"

"It was storming."

As if people never took long walks in rainstorms. "So you don't know if Luke was here all night."

A brief flash of alarm across her face. "I heard him! Luke… Luke was in the living room. All night!"

"How do you know that if you were sleeping?"

"The TV woke me up. He was watching it."

A practiced liar, but not a good one. Now for the real question. "When was the last time you saw your brother? Alive, I mean."

"When I took him his dinner."

"Did you talk?"

"Of course."

"What did you talk about?"

"The weather."

Jesus, talking to her was like pulling teeth. "Anything else?"

"We prayed together."

"Your brother was a religious man?"

"He was a *godly* man."

I thought about that for a moment, then said, "A false confession is a lie. Correct me if I'm wrong here, but I always thought godly men don't lie."

Her rebuttal was classic. "He was scared back then, you know, back when it all happened, so he told the police what they wanted to hear."

"You're saying he was a weak man?"

"We are all weak compared to the glory of God."

Seeing a possible chink in the armor of denial, I zeroed in. "But Grace, weakness can manifest itself in various ways, and in your brother's case, pedophilia was one of them."

Her voice rose. "My brother's no pedophile! He was railroaded! Railroaded by the police and by...by..." She searched for the word. "...by those little *brats*. They're the ones who killed him!"

Seven little brats, all of us supposedly in cahoots with each other? With difficulty, I resisted the urge to slap her. "Then you're convinced he was innocent of those crimes."

"My brother would never do anything like that."

"You weren't worried about him being around your granddaughter?"

"It's a sin to separate people who love each other." She turned her red-eyed stare away from me and onto her husband, bile seeping out of her voice like pus from a festering sore.

The urge to slap her intensified. Grace's interpretation of "sin" was highly creative—turn your back on child rape while loving thy brother waaaay too much. "Okay, let's say—just theoretically, you understand—that those, ah, brats didn't kill him. Who do you think did?"

The red stare returned to me. "The whore on the hill."

"Huh?"

"You heard me."

"Yes, I did, but not being from around here, I don't know who you're referring to."

The red eyes narrowed into slits. "You should, since you've been staying with her."

Her husband cleared his throat. "Grace. Don't."

"Don't tell me what I can say and what I can't," she snapped.

I turned to Genovese in bewilderment. "Who is she talking about?"

He raised his hands in a helpless gesture.

Further enraged by his lack of cooperation, Grace clenched her fingers into claws and screamed, "It was your darling Debbie! The whore on the hill!"

I couldn't take any more so I stood up. "Thank you for your time, Grace. You've been very helpful."

As I walked out of the den, I snuck a look back at Mario Genovese, who was staring at his wife like he'd never seen her before.

Chapter Ten

Ten minutes later I was back in the butterfly trailer, figuring what to do next. Now that the Genovese family appeared to be alibied out, I no longer cared who had killed Brian Wycoff, so sticking around was a waste of my time. As for wasting my Monarch rent money, I no longer cared about that, either. And then there was Dusty. Added to the uncomfortably close presence of an ex-lover and the possibility of running into him, a return to Scottsdale looked pretty good despite the Valley's more intense heat. I was just about to start packing my new clothes when someone knocked on the trailer door. When I opened it, I saw Nicole, the redhead in Fishin' Frenzy. She had changed into a neatly tailored suit and designer pumps, and was carrying a briefcase. Behind her stood Jacklyn, the gun-toting brunette in Mustang, in her usual black leather pants and black halter top. Seeing the women up close like this stirred my memory. I'd seen both of them before, but where and when eluded me.

"Can we come in?" Nicole asked.

I nodded. Their eyes weren't quite as red as Grace Genovese's but getting there, and the hostility they'd shown me earlier had vanished.

"The cops still have Debbie," Jacklyn said. With her Glock, tattoos, and black leather she should have looked tough. Instead, she looked vulnerable.

"They're taking her formal statement, that's all," I said. "I had to give one, myself. So did the victim's sister."

It was like I hadn't even spoken. "You have to do something," Nicole said, her voice firm in contrast to her porcelain-complexion looks.

The women's abrupt departure from their earlier mind-your-own-business attitudes confused me. "*Do* something? Like what? I'm finished here."

"Debbie looked you up, said you might be just what we need."

I had paid for Monarch's rental with Desert Investigations' credit card, so it would have been easy to find our website, but that begged the question. Surely Debbie Margules wasn't in the habit of doing background searches on her tenants. More to the point, why would an inoffensive artist who ran a cutesy B&B need the services of a private detective?

"If Mrs. Margules—Debbie—needs anyone at this point, it's an attorney. I'll be happy to recommend one." In my line of work you bump up against dozens.

Jacklyn started to say something, but Nicole brushed her aside. "She already has one, more or less, and that's me. The problem is, it's been a long time since I handled criminal defense cases. These days I specialize in real estate law, mainly commercial, so I can't do much more than counsel her to keep her mouth shut during the interrogation. Which she will, if I know her as well as I think I do, but I'm leaving for the sheriff's office to see what I can do. She's been gone too long. If worse comes to worse, I know an excellent defense attorney in Phoenix, but when I called his office I found out he's on vacation in Bermuda and won't be back until late next week. So for now, I'm it. You, too, if you'll agree to come aboard."

A former defense attorney who now specialized in real estate law? She had to be older than she looked. Much older, and possibly the regular client of a superstar cosmetic surgeon.

Since I hadn't yet told Genovese I would work for him I remained free to indulge my curiosity. Gesturing toward the butterfly-print sofa, I said, "Maybe you'd better sit down and tell me what's going on."

They sat, and Nicole took a deep breath. "The other day Debbie threatened to kill that Wycoff guy, and everybody at Coyote Corral heard her."

That's another thing about my line of work; the surprises just keep coming.

Hiding my shock, I said. "Two questions. One, why did Debbie make the threat, and two, how did she know who he was? Mr. Wycoff didn't exactly announce his arrival via bullhorn."

The two women looked at each other in silent communication. Then Jacklyn, brushing back a stray lock of black hair, replied, "We all knew him. Knew about him, anyway. What he had done."

"Forgive me if I don't quite understand, but the Wycoff trial took place almost thirty years ago. Sure, it was all over the newspapers, but why would you still remember something like that?" The minute the words were out of my mouth, I realized that both women were somewhere in their late thirties or early forties—the right ages to have been his victims.

My suspicion must have shown on my face, because Nicole vented a bitter laugh. "Not us. But Debbie's daughter, Lindsey, was nine when she disappeared, and at the time, Debbie and her husband—Ed's dead now—lived only a couple of blocks from the Wycoffs."

While checking into the B&B, I'd seen a painting of a little girl around that age, but when I mentioned it, Debbie had brushed me off.

"When exactly was this?" I asked Nicole.

"A year before Wycoff was arrested."

Before I could respond, Nicole added, "And why do I remember 'something like that'? Because every single time another child disappears, the media shows up on the doorstep of every family who's suffered through the same heartbreak. Like mine. Yes, that's right, Lena. My daughter, Candice, was ten when she was taken." Her gorgeous skin had paled, but her voice remained firm.

Unlike Jacklyn's, whose voice wobbled when she said, "My son was seven. And Sophia's daughter was eight."

Shaken to the core by this recital of misery, I asked, "Who's Sophia?"

"She was supposed to be here with us this weekend, but she's in the hospital," Nicole explained. "In traction from a car accident. That's the only reason you were able to rent Monarch. She'd planned to stay in it. Butterflies are her thing."

The plot of one of my favorite mystery novels described how the victims of a heinous crime had gotten together to deliver the rough justice a murderer deserved. Had I, bent upon my own desire for revenge, stumbled into a similar situation? From past experience I knew that revenge killings aren't only the stuff of fiction. They happen in real life, too. I also knew that women, either through anger or grief, were every bit as capable as men of being the perpetrators. Take the women at Debbie's Desert Oasis. If what they told me was true, all three had lost children—four, counting the bed-ridden Sophia. Maybe none of them, including the hospitable Debbie, looked like killers, but at the time, Brian Wycoff hadn't looked like a pedophile, either.

In the kitchen area was a small stool that had doubled as a stepladder during my search through the cabinets. Without saying anything, I fetched it.

Taking a deep breath, I sat across from the women whose faces I now recognized. "Maybe you'd better start at the beginning."

Chapter Eleven

Years earlier Debbie, Jacklyn, Nicole, and Sophia had come to know each other through their attendance at the meetings of Parents of Missing Children, a Phoenix offshoot of Parents of Murdered Children.

"At first we all belonged to PMC," Jacklyn explained, "but our situations were different. Unlike the others, our children could still be alive, like Elizabeth Smart or Jaycee Dugard. At least that's what we hoped."

I couldn't begin to imagine the pain these women must have endured for them to actually hope their children were kept imprisoned as someone's sex slaves. Yet I said nothing, because there was nothing to say.

"We do everything we can to keep their cases alive," Nicole said. "When another child goes missing, we allow ourselves to be interviewed holding up the age-progressed pictures of our children the police artist made for us, hoping that someone will recognize them."

That was why Nicole and Jacklyn looked familiar. At one time or another, I had seen them on television. The two had remained in their original homes—as did Sophia, they said—in case their children ever found their way back. Debbie, however, had lost all hope.

My suspicious mind made me ask two terrible questions. "When exactly did your children go missing?"

"Candice disappeared on her way home from school over eight years ago," Nicole answered. "The school was only three blocks away. I'd originally planned to pick her up as usual, but that day she asked if she could walk home with some other girl, so I let her. As it turned out, the girl—her name was Robin—woke up sick and didn't go to school, so…" When she shrugged, it was like she was trying to dislodge a hundred-pound weight off her back.

Self-loathing tainted Jacklyn's voice. "Stevie was taken from the park playground nine years ago when I had my back turned, flirting with some stupid guy."

"And Sophia? What about her?"

They looked at each other, and a message of some sort passed between them. "Go ahead and tell her," Jacklyn said to Nicole. "It can't hurt Sophia since the poor thing's been, uh, in traction for almost a week, remember."

Nicole sighed. "Sophia's daughter, Trish, vanished thirty-two years ago. She was eight."

In other words, Sophia's daughter had disappeared while Brian Wycoff was still free as the proverbial bird, free to terrorize and rape small children. Maybe even kill them.

Until one of them grabbed a kitchen knife and…

If the story about Sophia's car accident checked out, it left one viable suspect: Debbie Margules, whose daughter also went missing before my nine-year-old self ended Wycoff's predatory career. Debbie's kitchen had plenty of knives, and from the various metal sculptures on display around the property, she owned an acetylene torch, too. No wonder she was still at the sheriff's office.

"Is that attorney in Bermuda really good?" I hoped Nicole would tell me he was Johnnie Cochran, risen from the dead.

"The best," she assured me.

"It's not a coincidence you two are up here in Black Canyon City at the same time, is it?"

Nicole shook her head. "We've come up here at the same time every year since Debbie opened this place. August is when her daughter and my son both disappeared, different years, of course. She had the idea that all of us should be together around the anniversary date. Get away from it all, maybe fish a little, and in the evening, participate in healing ceremonies instead of sitting home and crying by ourselves. Strength in numbers and all that. It was working, too." She paused. "Up until now."

After swallowing the lump in my throat, I asked, "So what do you want me to do?" But I already knew the answer.

"Find out who actually did it."

It's not often in my job that I come up against a moral quandary. In fact, it had happened only twice in my years in law enforcement. Frankly, I didn't care who killed Brian Wycoff, but I liked Debbie Margules and respected what she had done to help these grieving women. But, here's where it got complicated. I used to be a police officer, and police officers are sworn to uphold the law, however unfair that law might seem. We are never, under any circumstances, supposed to act as judge, jury, and executioner.

Then again, the other night I had been prepared to execute Wycoff myself. Only the fact that someone else had already done it kept his blood off my hands.

Cops do kill. They kill in self-defense and they kill to defend others, which is where things start getting gray around the edges. I had been ready to kill Wycoff in order to protect Bethany and any other child who might cross his path, but I wouldn't have tortured him. And I wouldn't have allowed suspicion to fall on anyone else. If necessary, I would have confessed.

Did I see Debbie Margules as a murderer? I've always believed anyone is capable of murder, depending on the provocation, but did I see her as a torturer? Again, that depends. Would a grieving mother torture a man into telling her the location of her child's grave?

Possibly.

But the number of those burn marks could suggest something else. Eight burns, seven known victims. There had been seven children on the witness list at Brian Wycoff's trial; I was only one of them.

Who else was out there I didn't know about?

"You always bring your work clothes when you go fishing?" I asked Nicole, as we zipped up I-17 on the way to Prescott, where Debbie was being interviewed. If actually arrested, she would be kept in a holding cell until transferred to the jail in Cordes Junction.

Nicole smiled. "I spent five years in the Girl Scouts, where they taught me to always be prepared." Catching my expression out of the corner of her eye, she added, "Some clients of mine are attempting to buy a stretch of land near Cottonwood, and before I left Phoenix we set up a Sunday meeting with the parties involved. Since I knew I'd be up here for several days, I packed my 'work clothes,' as you call them, to save me the drive back and forth. You have a problem with suits?"

"Not on others. Myself, I find them confining."

"You and Jacklyn, two of a kind."

"I don't own a Harley." But maybe someday…

Outside Nicole's silver Lexus, scrub turned into pine and saguaros became few and far between as we climbed in elevation. Cattle grazed on the lush vegetation. It was, as Detective Yvonne Eastman had said, a pretty drive. When we took the State Route 69 turnoff, the cattle disappeared, replaced by new housing developments, then, as we passed through Prescott Valley, apartment blocks and trailer courts. Finally Prescott's beautiful Victorians came into view.

Nicole waved at one small, gingerbready house. "You wouldn't believe what that thing cost. Nine hundred thou for an eleven-hundred-square-footer, two bedroom, one bath, no garage, built 1886 and in need of repair."

"I couldn't even afford the heating bill." Because of the elevation, the Snow God visited Prescott every winter. "It is pretty, though."

"You looking? I work with several realtors in the Scottsdale area and I can…"

"I'm all set."

"A girl can't live above her office for the rest of her life."

She *had* done her homework. I wasn't sure whether I liked that or not.

The weekend traffic, comprised mainly of Phoenicians escaping the worst of the August heat, slowed to a crawl as we made our way through the downtown area to the sheriff's office, and it was only with difficulty that I warded off more offers of realtor referrals. To be frank, I don't like houses, no matter how nice they are. Houses remind me too much of the places I had stayed back in the day when home ownership appeared to be the only requirement to becoming a foster parent. Yes, I know the system has changed, and yes, I'm aware that applicants now had to endure background checks that would freak out an NSA agent, but I'll take an apartment any day, thank you very much. In apartments, your neighbors can hear you scream.

"Here we are," Nicole said, pulling into the sheriff's parking lot. "Sure do love the weather up here."

She had me there. I wasn't looking forward to returning to the Valley's heat, and if the interview with Debbie went the way I thought it would, I'd be back in the city while they were still frying eggs on car hoods.

There are three ways you get immediate help in police stations. The first is when you're a suspect, the second is when you're bleeding, and the third is when you arrive with a briefcase-carrying attorney. Within minutes we were cloistered in an un-bugged room with Debbie Margules, who appeared strangely relaxed.

"Took you long enough," she said to Nicole.

"I had to talk Ms. Jones here into coming in with me. You haven't given a statement, have you?"

"All they got from me was my name, telephone number, address, social security number, and date of birth. All of which they already had."

Nicole turned to me. "Told you so."

Debbie wasn't finished. "You'll be gratified to know that nice Detective Eastman ran out and got me a veggie burger, iced tea, and carob-dipped strawberries."

Nicole and I smiled. When we'd come into the room, Eastman had been stationed by the door, humming "Maria." She didn't have much of a repertoire but at least she was on pitch.

"Eastman gone now?" Debbie asked.

At our nods, Debbie continued, "Like I said, I didn't tell them anything, although she did her best, and in a way it was quite entertaining, but I want to go home now." The corner of her left eye twitched, proving her earlier calm a mere act.

Nicole nodded. "I'm pretty certain that can be arranged. Wait here." She stood up and went in search of Eastman.

While we waited, we talked fish. They were biting.

"It's always like that after a storm," Debbie said.

"I've never done much fishing before."

"You should. It's very relaxing."

"I thought you were a vegetarian."

"I eat fish. But even if I were a pure vegetarian, I wouldn't force my dietary beliefs on anyone. Besides, fishing is rather Zen, which is why most fishermen—and fisherwomen—are such upright citizens. Things get them all bent out of shape, they don't grab their guns and shoot up the local Elks Lodge, they just arm themselves with rods and reels and head for the nearest body of water."

We discussed the virtues of trout and bass until Nicole came back, Detective Eastman in tow. They were both smiling.

"You can go now, Ms. Margules," Eastman said. "But we'd appreciate it if…"

"If I didn't leave town." Debbie smiled, too, although the twitch didn't leave her eye.

"Exactly. Now, do you need me to show you out?"

"We can find it, thanks."

"Then have a nice day." Eastman sauntered away to the strains of "Maria."

Once we were back on the road, fish disappeared from the conversation.

"Nicole and Jacklyn have already told me about Parents of Missing Children and what happened to you all, so I'm up to speed there," I informed Debbie. For ease of conversation, we were both sitting in the Lexus' backseat as it purred down the highway. "What I need now is for you to tell me about the death threat you leveled at Brian Wycoff at the restaurant. And I want to know how you found out he was staying at the Genoveses' in the first place."

Her calm demeanor had disappeared once we left the parking lot, and incipient tears welled in her eyes, whether from fear or relief, I couldn't tell.

"The gals had been up here since last Saturday, and by Thursday they were getting a little restless, so I suggested we go down to the Coyote Corral and have dinner and a few drinks, maybe pick up some tamales for Friday. Mario's cook is terrific and the green tamales are vegetarian and…"

Interrupting what sounded like the beginnings of a soliloquy about the excellence of Mexican-veg cuisine, I said, "I'm sure they're delicious, but I need to know how you found out about Wycoff's presence in Black Canyon City."

I could see Nicole frowning in the rearview mirror over my snappish tone, but I didn't care. The minute we reached the B&B, I was packing up and driving back to Scottsdale. I wanted to get there before dark, heat be damned.

Debbie swallowed. "Sorry. My nerves…" She swallowed again, then said, "It was just…just…kind of a coincidence, I guess. Midway through the meal I excused myself to go to the ladies' room—too much Dos Equis, probably—and to get there, you have to pass by Mario's office. Anyway, the door was ajar and I saw Grace in there with him, and even though they were trying to keep their voices down, I could tell they were having a fight. Um, I don't mean a physical fight, although both sounded pretty heated. It was over Wycoff. He'd shown up at the house and Grace was all for letting him stay in that RV of theirs as long as he wanted, but Mario said he didn't want him anywhere near his grandkids, that if he wasn't gone by Monday he was calling the sheriff. He was furious, and Grace was crying...."

She took a deep breath. "I was in shock, hearing that...that awful name again, but somehow I made it into the ladies'. I stayed in there so long Nicole came to check on me."

"Did you know he was Grace's brother?"

"Not when I first moved up here, that's for sure, or I'd have found a different property to buy. In a different town. Maybe even a different state." A note of sadness crept into her voice. "You know, Grace and I used to be friends."

"Until Grace told you who her brother was."

Debbie shook her head. "Mario told me."

Now we were entering "whore on the hill" territory. "This was when?"

At first I didn't think she was going to answer, but then she said, "Two years ago, Mario and I got, ah, close. He and Grace were separated at the time so I didn't see anything wrong with it. And he was so lonely! Those two have always had their troubles. Even though their place is down in that valley, sometimes when the wind was right I could hear them arguing. But he didn't want to break up the marriage. Catholics are like that where family's concerned. Anyway, while they were separated and she was living with her sister down in Phoenix, that's when we had our affair. And when he told me about his brother-in-law."

"Pillow talk?" It wasn't hard to imagine. Your guard gets dropped when you're lying in bed next to someone who's just made you happy.

Her face flushed. "He said she was all messed-up sexually, and he blamed her brother for it, said that he'd...he'd messed with her when she was a kid."

What a surprise. "When she was around nine, maybe?"

She stared at me. "How'd you know?"

I tried to keep the bitterness out of my voice. "A lucky guess." For the first time I felt pity for Grace. With Wycoff for an older brother, she'd really had no chance. When he started molesting her, where were their parents? Didn't they notice something was wrong? But maybe they did. Maybe like so many parents of budding pedophiles, they decided to look the other way, to pretend nothing was happening. Or maybe they blamed Wycoff's behavior on Grace. Just like Norma blamed his behavior on me and all those other children. God, I could only imagine what Grace had gone through as a child.

On second thought, I didn't have to imagine. I knew.

As the exit ramp for Black Canyon City came into view, I asked Nicole, "When Genovese and Grace were arguing at the Coyote Corral, you were there. Did you hear it?"

She kept her eyes on the road, but I could read her bitter expression in the rearview mirror. "Everybody heard."

"Jacklyn, too?"

"What did I just say?"

Oh, hell. A whole damn bar full of suspects.

Chapter Twelve

The more I thought about the Wycoff killings the less I believed they were perpetrated by some Johnny-Come-Lately vigilante who hung out at the local bar. Instinct told me the crimes were rooted in the past. If I decided to help Debbie, the past was where I needed to go.

And I was not looking forward to it.

During the drive, two names had occurred to me—both of them from my own past—so when Nicole dropped me off at the Oasis, I hurried up to the butterfly trailer and called Jimmy. "I hate to bother you," I told him, "it being the weekend and all, but I need a favor."

Remembering that my partner had volunteered to work the Inter-Tribal Pow Wow up on the Navajo Rez, I was surprised when he answered the phone on the second ring.

"Thanks for finally calling me back," he said, speaking loudly enough that I could hear him over the drums and yips in the background. "I've been trying to reach you for days."

"Sorry about that, but I've…"

"We've been getting threatening phone calls at the office."

Threats aren't unusual in our business. Someone is always getting pissed off by our investigations, so Jimmy and I have learned to ignore them. So why was he so worried all of a sudden?

Trying to lighten him up, I forced a chuckle. ""Maybe we'll break our record for the week."

More drumbeats. More yips. "Lena, they didn't sound like the usual…"

"Then we'll have to batten down the hatches, won't we? Look, I called you for a reason."

"Not for the pleasure of hearing my voice?" More than a drop of sarcasm there.

I let it slide. "I need a favor."

A sigh. "What kind of favor?"

"I need the address and phone number for Guy DeLucca. He was a social worker with Child Protective Services back in the bad old days." DeLucca had placed me and the other victims with the Wycoffs, although I didn't tell Jimmy that.

"Can't it wait until Monday? I've agreed to act as a judge for the Men's Fancy Dance competition."

"You're kidding me."

Traditionally, Fancy Dance—an energetic dance performed with rattles, bells—and lots and lots of beadwork, feathers, and sheep "fluff"—was usually performed by Plains tribes, such as Comanche, Kiowa, or Arapaho. Jimmy was Pima, and although he was a whiz at Chicken Scratch, Fancy Dance was outside his circle of knowledge.

Another sigh. "I'm judging the judges. Last year there were complaints because one of the judges turned out to be related to the winner, and…"

I interrupted. "To keep nepotism from rearing its ugly head, you were picked to do the dirty work. I get it. Look, I hate to be so pushy, but it's important. I've already tried to get in touch with DeLucca and found out his number and address are unlisted."

"Social workers' numbers usually are. Besides, my computer's back at the office." I heard cheering in the background, a horse's whinny, someone—not Jimmy, I hoped—muttering what sounded like curses in Pima. Or was it Navajo? "That's why God created laptops, and I happen to know you never go anywhere without yours. Isn't that pow-wow taking place next to the trading post? I'm pretty sure they have Wi-Fi up there."

More muttering. "The Men's Fancy Dance competition takes place in half an hour."

"Then you've got time."

Belatedly realizing how rude that sounded, I hastily added, "Something else. I need the same info on Sergeant Linda McCracken, formerly of the Scottsdale Police Force, long before my time there. Say, you still have a cousin in the Medical Examiner's office, don't you?"

"Yeeesss." Slow. Suspicious.

"Ask him what caliber bullets were dug out of Norma Wycoff's brain."

"You're kidding, right?"

"I'm stone cold serious, Almost Brother."

"Don't you think you're asking a lot of favors for someone whose calls you never answer?" He waited for my answer. When he didn't get one, he said, "Oh, all right. I'll call my cousin. And as soon as the Fancy Dance competition is over, I'll fetch my laptop and find DeLucca and McCracken for you."

Before I could thank this paragon of patience, he hung up.

To kill time, I looked around Monarch and began to count butterflies. I made it up to a hundred and fifteen before I realized the hopelessness of the task. With my mind engaged in such trivia, Dusty kept sneaking in. Dusty telling me he loved me. Dusty telling me I was the only woman for him. Dusty's wife—the wife I didn't know he had—aiming that big-ass .50-caliber Desert Eagle at me.

Maintaining close relationships is difficult at best for former foster children, but the violence of my own background made it even harder. Shuttled from one home after another, only a crazy person would dare to love. So even as a child, I knew better than to set myself up for heartbreak. And yet I had loved. I had loved Reverend Giblin and his wife. I had loved Madeline, I had loved the Prestons.

And God help me, I had loved Dusty.

Disgusted by the memory of my own foolishness I grabbed

the rod and reel out of the kitchen cabinet and walked down to Black Canyon Creek.

The creek still raged, but I didn't mind. The chuckling of the water, the whit-whit-whit song of cactus wrens, and the whispering breeze through the cottonwoods calmed me. Not expecting any luck, I cast and recast my line into the creek, taking care not to snag it on the branches floating by. As I sat there on a dry boulder, it occurred to me that there were worse ways to spend one's time. Like mourning over the past. What was that saying? Yesterday is gone, tomorrow is but a dream, the only thing we truly have is today, this moment.

So I gave myself up to it.

An hour later, just as my casting arm had begun to tire, my phone rang.

I took the call, only to find that people were still singing and dancing out there in Navajo Land.

"How'd the Men's Fancy Dance judging go?"

"Won by an Arapaho out of Oklahoma, not related to any of the judges as far as I could tell."

"And you could tell."

"That's why they picked me. Anyway, you're in luck. I was able to reach my cousin, the one who works for the ME, and here's the scoop. Two .22LR bullets, of all things, killed Norma Wycoff. Not exactly heavy artillery."

"It means the perp definitely came through the back, because people would have noticed somebody walking down the street with a rifle."

"My thoughts exactly." A pause.

"And?" I asked, waiting for the other information I'd requested.

The pause lengthened uncomfortably until he finally said, "I'm still waiting for a thank you, Lena."

I duly complied. "What about those addresses and phone numbers I need?"

A sigh. "First addy, Guy DeLucca, 5840 North Bonadventure, Phoenix, early retirement twenty years ago, medical, lives alone. Yeah, unlisted phone number but I managed to get it anyway.

555-760-4237. Second addy, Linda McCracken, formerly Scott-sdale PD sergeant, also early-retired, in her case due to getting shot up in the line of duty. Partial paralysis. She's at 47298 West Esmeralda Way, Peoria, 555-174-2973, lives with her daughter Delores, a Phoenix PD cop, never been shot. Not yet, anyway."

After I thanked him again, he became less testy, so we chatted for another few minutes about office stuff, then said our friendly goodbyes.

Thus ended my fishing for the day. As I trudged back up the hill to my butterfly trailer, I placed a call to DeLucca, but wound up with voicemail. Maybe he was out fishing, too. Still feeling anxious about Debbie's situation, I decided to head back down to the Valley of the Sun anyway, so after notifying Nicole of my plans, I grabbed my new backpack and hit the road.

The problem with driving is that it gives you a chance to think. Even though I was blasting a Phoenix heavy metal station at top volume, that son of a bitch Dusty kept sneaking his two-timing way into my brain.

Dusty.

Dusty's soft drawl. Dusty's gentle hands. Dusty's muscular back. Dusty's…

"Shit!" I yelled, shocking the man cruising next to me in a red Jaguar XKE convertible.

"Sorry!" I yelled, allowing the Jag to pull ahead.

Giving up, I turned off the heavy-metal station and let the memories roll in.

In Hollywood parlance, Dusty and I had "met cute." I was a cop, he was speeding, I pulled him over. Long story short, his slow-talking cowboy charm swept me off my black-booted feet.

Our relationship was great for a while, although I did notice that from time to time he would pull a disappearing act for a week or two. But I've never been the clinging type, and by then I had opened Desert Investigations and was so busy that I hardly noticed. Yes, I know. The folks in Al-Anon have a word for it: denial. If I had been more astute, I would have paid more attention to the frequent smell of liquor on Dusty's breath, to his often blank look when I referred to an event we'd attended together a month, or even a day, ago.

The truth was, Dusty was a drunk.

Like many drunks, he was good at hiding it. At least he was until the time he returned from Las Vegas, stalked by the redhead he had married during a six-day bender. As if that weren't bad enough, the redhead tracked him all the way to my apartment above Desert Investigations, where she proceeded to shoot up the place. I only managed to escape serious injury because the redhead—Joanne, I believe her name was—was a New York native who had never owned a gun before. That was the end of Dusty's and my relationship. I didn't care that he had entered rehab, I didn't care that he annulled his "marriage," I didn't care that he swore how much he still loved me.

I didn't care, I didn't care, I didn't care. Given my childhood, I already had all the bad memories I needed. There was no point in accumulating more.

But sometimes the nights were so lonely....

Halfway back to Scottsdale my phone rang. Retrofitted hands-free system or not, I don't like talking while navigating the whacked-out Valley freeways and was about to let it roll over to voicemail, when I heard a man's baritone. I remembered that voice even though it had been almost thirty years since I'd last heard it.

"Ms. Jones, this is Guy DeLucca. You left a message for me earlier. Call me back at the same number. I'm home now." He hung up before I could reply.

Instead of a call-back, I took the Bethany Home exit off Interstate17 and headed east toward the Biltmore area, a sorta-upper middle class enclave built around one of Phoenix's premier resorts. Some of the new McMansions nudged the one million mark, but DeLucca's wasn't one of them. His tiny cottage, one of the original homes in the area, appeared ramshackle compared to its upstart neighbors, and the land was worth more than the house. The roof needed repair, the front gutter had snapped in two, and the wood siding looked like it hadn't been painted since Nixon was president.

DeLucca's doorbell was broken, so I knocked. He opened the door immediately, displaying no wariness. But he looked hard at the scar on my forehead.

"Lena Jones," he said. "Formerly known as Little Girl Doe."

The social worker I remembered had been a fit, good-looking man somewhere in his twenties, with thick dark hair brushed back in a semi-pompadour. Now his hair had vanished and his once-trim waistline bulged. Creases furrowed his face, the deepest of them dug around his watery eyes.

"Mr. DeLucca, I presume."

His sad smile revealed yellowed teeth. One of the canines was missing. "Come in, come in. Don't stand out there in the heat."

Inside, it was much cooler, partially because of the blinds shut against the blazing sun. The house's interior wasn't quite as bad as its exterior, although the furniture showed considerable wear. Scratched oak plank flooring, ho-hum brown sofa and chairs, oak coffee table, end tables, and bookshelves displaying divergent tastes—from history to botany to the culinary arts, with an emphasis on desserts. Other than the books, the décor was so monotonous the whole room could have been ordered en masse from a catalog directed at people who were more interested in longevity than appearance. The only other items displaying personal taste were the weapons artfully arranged on the wall: a U.S. Cavalry sword circa 1865; a vintage-WWI Browning Auto-5 self-loading semi-automatic shotgun; and a Walther PPK/S pistol, the German honey of World War II.

In keeping with the military motif, framed photographs on the bookcase behind DeLucca displayed various wars, yet similar faces. From the men's uniforms, I surmised that DeLucca, his father, his grandfather, and even his great-grandfather had all served in the U.S. Army. One photo showed a man—probably his father—receiving a Silver Star. Another showed DeLucca himself as an honor guard at the Tomb of the Unknown Soldier.

"Family tradition," DeLucca said, aware the photos had caught my attention. He pointed out something I hadn't noticed: his father's Silver Star sitting in a frame on one of the oak end tables. "A reminder of the sacrifices he and others made. Some say it's only a symbol, but I happen to believe symbols are important."

I felt compelled to ask, "And your father sacrificed…?"

"Two legs."

As he led me to a brown chair, I wondered if there were similar traditions in my family. But I did remember one sacrifice—my father gunned down in an attempt to save the children. I could still hear their screams in my dreams.

To push the memory back into the shadows, I sipped at the glass of instant iced tea he'd fetched me. It still had undissolved crystals floating on top. "If I remember correctly, you're the person who named me."

A faint smile. "When you first started talking, I thought you were saying 'Lena.' Was I wrong?"

"I'm fine with Lena, but what about the Jones bit? You couldn't think of anything more original?" I hoped my smile tempered what might be interpreted as criticism, because over time, I began to realize he had done the best he could with the limited information he'd possessed.

DeLucca gestured toward one of the photographs. It showed him at a much younger age, with another man. The two stood in a jungle clearing, dressed in ragged battle gear.

"The 'Jones' was for Corporal Jason Elroy Jones," DeLucca explained. "A childhood friend. Jason and I served together in 'Nam. His hair was the same color as yours."

"Oh."

"Jason never made it home."

"I'm sorry."

"He was brave. As are you, so the name fits. But I sincerely apologize if you don't like it."

I peered carefully at the photograph. The younger DeLucca, smiling despite the threat of dense jungle behind him. The blond man next to him was smiling, too. The man prior to the ghost.

"I like it more now, Mr. DeLucca. But I'm not sure I agree with you about symbols. Sure, they help us remember, but sometimes we have to forget in order to survive. At least that's what I've found."

"Point taken. No apology will ever be enough for what I did to you, to those other children, I…"

"You didn't do anything to me or anyone else. Brian Wycoff did. And his wife knew all about it."

"If I hadn't…"

"They had a beautiful house, came across as nice people, and there were no red flags. Their neighbors, the people at their church, they all swore up and down the Wycoffs were the salt of the earth."

"I should have known…"

"None of us can read minds. Now I don't want to hear anything else about it, all right?" Smiling, smiling.

He sighed. "Okay."

But we both knew it would never be okay.

"Look, Mr. DeLucca, I contacted you in hopes that you can help me with something."

"Anything."

Judging from the look in those haunted eyes I had the feeling that if I'd asked him to take a dive off the twenty-fourth floor of the Hyatt Regency he would, but my request wasn't as extreme. On second thought, maybe it was.

"You've heard Norma and Brian Wycoff were murdered, right?"

"It's been all over the news." From the edge in his voice, I knew he hadn't shed any tears.

"Someone I know, a very nice lady, is being looked at as a suspect."

He frowned. "Why?"

"She and her attorney want me to look into it, just in case charges are brought against her."

"You didn't answer my question. Why is this woman a suspect? Women usually don't go around murdering people."

I didn't bother countering that I'd known several women who had done exactly that. In order to keep the conversation on track, I explained about Parents of Missing Children and Debbie's Desert Oasis. "To make matters worse, the B&B is a short walk from the ranch where Wycoff was murdered."

As I talked, his frown deepened. "So you're saying the police suspect her simply because she has a missing daughter? That she believed Wycoff might have been involved in her child's disappearance?" His outrage matched my own.

More to calm him than anything else, I said, "It's not such a big leap, considering how close the Wycoffs' house was to hers when her daughter disappeared. Just a couple of blocks, from what I hear."

"Still, suspecting her based on mere coincidence is ridiculous."

"I think so, too, but the police are the police, and they have to follow up. I can assure you that none of them personally give a damn about what happened to the Wycoffs, but they can't let killers off the hook regardless of who the victim—or victims— are. As far as the state of Arizona and the various jurisdictions are concerned, Wycoff had paid in full for his crimes."

A snort of disgust. "Twenty-five years for ruining the lives of at least seven children? Not nearly enough."

Oddly, that statement made me realize something for the very first time.

"I'm not ruined," I assured him. *Banged up around the edges, maybe, but not ruined.*

He bowed his head in agreement.

"Maybe the others aren't, either. People…" I had to clear my throat before continuing. "People can overcome amazing hardships."

When he raised his head again, a shadow had crossed his eyes which had nothing to do with the closed blinds. "Two of those children went on to commit suicide later. Did you know that?"

It took me a moment before I could tell him I was all too aware of that tragic fact.

"The others…" His voice trailed off. "Let's just say you've done the best of them. At life, I mean."

"You've been following me?"

"I've kept tabs on you all. But don't worry, I've never crossed over into stalking territory, just the odd computer check or two to see how you were getting along. Plus, you make it onto the evening news from time to time. Do you enjoy the fame?"

"Not especially." I pointed at my scarred forehead. "I used to think my appearance would jog someone's memory and I'd finally find out what really happened to me, and who my parents are. Or were. But that never happened. Look, I didn't stop by just to chat; I'm here for a reason. Because of the case I'm working, I want to get in touch with the others, and you can…"

He lifted his right hand, palm up. "Stop right there, Lena. Their names are confidential and I won't reveal them to anyone, not even you."

I frowned. "But they're no longer minors."

"Doesn't matter. And before you go getting any bright ideas— you are an investigator, after all—those court records are sealed and will remain so."

"Mr. DeLucca, one of them might know…"

"They don't know anything."

"How can you be sure of that?"

"Leave them alone!" he ordered. "They've been through enough." He straightened his back and crossed his arms in front of his chest, the universal sign for *Back the hell off.*

I thanked him for his time and left.

The only drawback I see about apartment living is that we renters never have enough room for storage. No attics, no basements. Because of that, we seldom turn into packrats, and shy away from anything we don't really need, keepsakes of the past among them. As a foster kid, I'd never had much baggage anyway—at least not the material kind—and during my early adult years I'd lived in tiny studio apartments until I leased the two floors for Desert Investigations. Being habitually short of space, I'd fallen back on that old remedy of renters everywhere: the commercial storage unit. South Scottsdale abounds with them, both air-conditioned and non.

Stor-More, located off Hayden Road just north of the Tempe border, was non, which was one of the reasons I seldom visited the unit in the summer. The other reason is that I'm not a fan of the scenery along Memory Lane.

Still, sundown found me in that sweltering, dusty place, rummaging among cardboard boxes until I found the banker's box I was looking for. For a while I just stared at the thing, hesitant as always to even touch it. In fact, there had been times in the past twenty-five years that I'd been tempted to take the box out in the desert and burn it. Now I was glad I hadn't. Why I'd held onto it, I don't know. It was a box of nightmares, and burning would have been the wisest course.

But today I needed the information in that box. Shivering with disgust, I lifted it, pulled down the accordion door on the unit, secured the lock, and drove away.

Once at my apartment above Desert Investigations, I stashed the box in the furthest corner of the living room, out of my sightline as I nuked a container of ramen for dinner. Instead of eating I sat there for a while, staring at my bowl. I finally gave up and left the table.

Steeling myself, I grabbed a pen and notebook and approached the box again. Opened it. Lifted out the scrapbooks and the folder of newspaper clippings. Set them aside. Pulled out the envelope of eight-by-ten color glossies. The first shot showed a child's size four dress, which was about my age when I last wore it. The blue had faded to a muddy gray, the bright bloodstains darkened to brown. After holding the photograph longer than necessary, I set it aside.

Second photo: formerly white shoes and socks, more blood spatter.

Third photo, a little girl's panties, not as bloody as the dress.

I didn't bother looking at the photographs of myself lying comatose in a hospital bed. Too disturbing.

I put the photos back into the envelope and picked up a folder of newspaper clippings. They were brittle and yellow with age, but still readable.

First clipping: the header on page three of the *Arizona Republic* read CHILD FOUND SHOT. The following story detailed how an unidentified Hispanic woman had carried the child into the Emergency Ward at St. Joseph's Hospital in Phoenix, then disappeared, leaving no information other than saying she'd found the little girl lying in the street on Thomas Road. She thought the child might have fallen from the white bus she'd seen disappearing around the corner. Upon examination, the girl was discovered to have a bullet lodged in her right temple. Her condition was listed as critical.

Second clipping: same newspaper, same page, dated four days later. SHOT CHILD STILL UNIDENTIFIED. The story, in which the comatose child was referred to as Little Girl Doe, described her as pale-complexioned, with long blond hair, green eyes, and—other than the bullet wound on her temple— seemingly well cared-for. After surgery, her condition had been upgraded to serious. The authorities encouraged anyone who might know of a missing child fitting that description to step forward. The dress she'd been wearing was blue.

Third clipping: same newspaper, page seven, dated two months later. SHOT CHILD AWAKENS FROM COMA. An unnamed hospital source was quoted as saying, "The poor kid doesn't seem to have any awareness of who she is or who her parents are. She can't walk or even talk." The article went on to say that the police were actively pursuing leads in hopes of learning Little Girl Doe's identity.

Fourth clipping: different newspaper, dated five years later. The forty-eight-point Gothic headline on the front page of the *Scottsdale Journal,* shouted: CHILD STABS MAN WITH KITCHEN KNIFE. The story, which described the assailant as the nine-year-old foster daughter of the victim, said, "Because the assailant is a minor, her identity is being withheld."

Brian Wycoff, a Scottsdale resident, was named as the child's victim. Further down, the Wycoffs' neighbor, Mrs. Imelda Bassel, was quoted as saying, "I heard this horrible screaming, at first a child's, and then a man's, and the next thing you know I saw a little girl run out the door covered in blood. I thought maybe she was hurt and I tried to get her to come to me, but she ran away, so I called the police. It was only when I saw the paramedics carrying Brian out that I realized he'd been hurt, too. This is so awful, he was such a sweet man. I'm praying for him and Norma, his lovely wife. They both belong to my church, and you've never met two nicer people."

The only statement the police would give was that the investigation was ongoing. Meanwhile, the article assured its concerned Scottsdale readers, the unnamed assailant had been apprehended and turned over to juvenile authorities.

Fifth clipping: a week later, front page of the *Scottsdale Journal*. The coverage had taken a dramatic turn, and for the next dozen or so clippings, reporters stopped using the word "assailant" when referring to the unnamed child, substituting the word "victim." Wycoff had become the "accused assailant." One of the reporters managed to get a quote from Linda McCracken, identified as the first Scottsdale PD officer on the scene, who found the unidentified child hiding behind a Dumpster two miles from the house where the stabbing had taken place.

"Considering everything that had happened to her," McCracken said, "she appeared calm, but maybe she was in shock. She sat in the back of my patrol car with her hands folded like a little lady. Never at any point did she pose a threat to me nor to anyone else."

The photographers had caught up with McCracken as she left the courthouse. She'd kept her head down, but you could still see the classically clean lines of her features, her long dark eyelashes, her shining hair.

Moved, I reached out a hand and caressed her face.

Chapter Thirteen

That night I dreamed about the white bus and my mother screaming, "I'll kill her! I'll kill her myself!" then the noise of a gunshot almost simultaneous with the kick that propelled me though the door. Then nothing but black until I woke up to the glare of hospital lights.

Dreams aren't linear. Instead of seeing a white wall…

I looked out on a dark forest, where children were running through the woods. Then the trees disappeared, replaced by a bright sun shining over collection of rough cabins and teepees strung out across a meadow. Nearby, a group of men and women weeded a garden, while in the distance, children—the forest children?—played tag around a tall man dressed in white as he looked on. Night fell again, revealing a fire pit encircled by the garden people. The man in white sat off to the side with a golden-haired boy who looked just like him. The circle people were listening to a young red-haired man as he played the guitar and sang "Michael Row the Boat Ashore." After a while, my father changed chords, segued into "Rock My Soul in the Bosom of Abraham" while everyone sang and clapped along with him. One of the finest singers was my mother.

Then we were back in the forest, but this time, the children were screaming…

Just like I was screaming when I woke up.

Chapter Fourteen

Still shaken from my dream, I showered, donned my running gear and my concealed-carry fanny pack—unlike my pocket holster, the fanny pack provided a more balanced run—and headed for Eldorado Park.

In summer, when the temps routinely shoot past the hundred-fifteen-degree mark, we runners hit the trail early, thus the park was busy when I arrived. As I huffed along with the others, drops of sweat sprinkled the concrete path. One of the reasons I chose that location during summers was because olive trees shaded much of the park's trails, cutting down on the collective misery. By six-thirty I'd reached Tempe Town Lake, and took a short break on the pedestrian bridge overlooking the water. As I gulped down Gatorade, I spotted several egrets fishing in the shallows, every now and then spreading their snowy wings to cool off. One of the smaller egrets speared a fish and gobbled it down before his larger buddies could take it away from him. Or her. When it came to egrets, I couldn't tell the difference.

Rested and rehydrated, I turned around and jogged more slowly back to where I'd parked my Jeep in the Eldorado lot, and returned to Old Town Scottsdale. When I pulled up, the thermometer on the side of my building read 105. At seven-thirty a.m.

Oh, what fun.

By eight, I was showered and dressed in fresh clothes, my .38 back in its pocket holster. Deciding to take a chance by not phoning ahead—cops can be funny about phone calls from people they don't know—I drove straight to 47298 East Esmeralda Way, Peoria. There was always a chance the bullet scar on my face would do for me what a disembodied voice couldn't.

As luck would have it, both retired Police Sergeant Linda McCracken and her daughter, Officer Delores McCracken, were home.

They lived in a small Mediterranean-style townhouse on Phoenix's northwest side, tucked into a planned community of single-family houses, garden townhomes, and a boutique-ish shopping center. It was easy to spot the McCrackens' unit because of the wheelchair ramp leading to the front door.

A tall woman in her thirties, muscular and narrow-eyed, answered the doorbell, her entire body on alert. The daughter. When I introduced myself, she immediately looked at the scar on my temple. Finding it, her expression changed from cop caution into delight.

"You're the little girl my mom told me about! Only you're not so little anymore, are you?"

Before I could answer, she ushered me in and yelled, "Mom, get out here! Guess who just dropped by? It's that PI we saw on the six o'clock news last month, the one you said was called Little Girl Doe!"

A hum, a whispery sound, then a gray-haired woman in a powered wheelchair emerged from the hallway. Sergeant Linda McCracken. The years hadn't been merciful. The left side of her craggy face drooped, and her left arm had contorted into a claw. But her eyes were as kind as I remembered.

"I recognized you the minute that reporter started talking to you." Her voice hadn't changed, either, still gruff but with an underlying note of warmth.

After I'd given her the demanded hug, she gestured me over to the sofa. "Sit, sit."

I sat.

Their house wasn't what you'd expect of two women living together. The overstuffed furniture was designed for comfort, not appearance, and I saw no frou-frou, no flouncy toss pillows, no pictures of family or cats. Only the *de rigueur* gun cabinet that played host to a plethora of firearms, from a small .22 rifle to an AK-47. The wall next to it displayed commendations and photographs of both women in dress uniform. Bookshelves lined the other walls, the books organized in categories: history, science, economics, and row upon row of mystery novels, many written by L.D. Hutchinson. I'd read several of them, and had been struck by how well-versed the author was in police procedure.

"You like mysteries?" Sergeant McCracken's smile lifted the corner of her face that wasn't paralyzed. Her daughter had hurried into the kitchen to get us iced tea, the usual hostess offering during Valley of the Sun summers.

"Especially Hutchinson's. He always gets it right."

That crooked smile again. "*She* gets it right."

I got it, too. "Your daughter?"

Sergeant McCracken nodded. "Partly. We collaborate. Hutchinson was my mother's maiden name. Delores comes up with the characters and plot, I write the dialogue and descriptions, and do the fact-checking." She raised her good hand and pressed her forefinger to her ruined mouth. "But it's a secret so don't tell anyone."

I laughed. "That explains why L.D. never shows up for book signings. But why the secrecy?"

"We'll let the cat out of the bag when Dolores retires from the force, but not until then. You used to be a cop. Can you imagine working next to someone you're afraid might put you into a book?"

"That would creep me out," I admitted.

She winked. "There you go."

Just then Delores returned with the iced tea. She took one look at her mother and said, "You gave away our secret, didn't you?"

"Little Girl Doe knows how to keep her mouth shut."

"I'm Lena Jones now," I reminded her.

"Of course. That social worker gave you the name."

"No imagination," her daughter snapped, taking a sip of her iced tea. "Jones, for Pete's sake."

"And why not Smith?" Sergeant McCracken proposed. "Or White? Or Gray?"

"Oh, Mom, you never could come up with decent character names. Remember that time when most of your characters' names began with the letter 'C'? And a lot of the others' names ended in 'Y'?"

The two bantered good-naturedly for the next couple of minutes, each trying on different names for me, which ranged from Delores' choices of Tova Svenson because, she said, with my blond hair and green eyes I looked Swedish, to the Eastern European, like Ilsa Milovic, for similar reasons. She proved correct about her mother's lack of naming expertise when her mother held out for the relatively bland "Carol Green." As entertaining as it all was, I wasn't a character in a mystery novel. I was real, and today I had a very real problem.

"Not that I'm not enjoying the process of finding a more suitable name for myself, ladies, but I'm here to see if you can help me out with a case I'm working on."

They alerted like hunting dogs catching a scent.

"You're talking about the Wycoff case, right?" Sergeant McCracken said, her good hand clutching at her wheelchair's armrest. "But why would you care? Considering what they did to you and the others, I thought you'd be tripping the Light Fantastic all over Scottsdale."

I told them about Debbie Margules and the women in Parents of Missing Children, and how Debbie had come under suspicion.

The two looked at each other. They didn't say anything right away, but Sergeant McCracken finally broke the silence. "If that woman killed the Wycoffs, I wouldn't blame her one bit. Of course, if you tell anyone I said that, I'll say you're lying." She softened her statement with a lopsided smile.

"I don't know much about the Margules case other than what I read, but I worked the Archerd case," Delores said, her expression grim. "Jacklyn Archerd's son, Stevie, was taken from El Camino Park several years ago. Never found. The mother being affiliated with one of those biker gangs—I think it was the Moguls—that didn't help the public's perception any, and people blamed her. Some even thought she'd killed the kid herself or had one of her biker buddies do it for the insurance money."

"Stevie Archerd was insured?"

"For five thousand dollars. That might not sound like much, but there were rumors of a drug problem, so it could have meant a lot. We couldn't prove anything and after a while, the trail went cold." The harsh look on her face told me where her own suspicions lay.

I remembered the tattoo across Jacklyn's chest, and the pain in her eyes when she talked about her son. There being nothing I could say that would change Delores' mind, I switched cases. "How about the disappearance of Candice Beltran? Either of you know anything about that?"

They both shook their heads. "Just what I read in the papers," the old sergeant said. "That poor mother. Nicole, her name was. When it happened—Delores and I both followed the case—she was in such terrible shape we thought for sure she'd wind up in a psychiatric hospital or a suicide, but she didn't. Got a law degree instead. We see her every now and then on TV, talking about missing children. She's become quite the advocate."

Now that their memories were primed, it was time to bring up the real reason for my visit. Directing my next question to Sergeant McCracken, I said, "I've gone through some old newspaper clippings trying to find the names of the kids on the witness list at Brian Wycoff's trial, but since they were all under age, the two who testified before he struck a deal were just referred to as Minor A and Minor B. Did you ever get wind of their names? Or the names of the other four minors on the list? They'd all be around my age now, so…"

She shook her head as much as she was able to. "That courthouse was locked down tighter than a crab's ass. They kept the kids secluded in separate rooms so they wouldn't catch sight of each other. So, sorry. Can't help you there."

"Me, neither," Delores said. "I've heard nothing about any of them, and most of the people involved in the trial are retired by now."

I wasn't too disappointed because that was pretty much what I'd expected, although it never hurt to try. "What can you tell me about that social worker, Guy DeLucca? I know he testified."

Sergeant McCracken' face became more lopsided when she frowned. "Poor shit was so distraught over placing you and those other kids with the Wycoffs that he shot himself a week after the trial ended. Didn't die, from what I hear. Civilians with guns. They don't know how to do it right."

At that, her daughter gave her a sharp look.

McCracken caught it and laughed. There was no irony in her voice when she said, "Don't you go worrying about me, Delores. If I'd wanted to off myself, I'd have done it years ago, and with considerable more expertise than poor old DeLucca. As it is, I'm too busy worrying about how Rhyne O'Malley's going to react when he finds out his wife's been cheating on him."

It took me a second to remember that Detective Rhyne O'Malley was the protagonist in the duo's books. "He'll go on a bender," I pointed out. Their sleuth had been carrying on a long love affair of his own, but with Wild Turkey.

"Oh, no, he won't!" she cackled. "Rhyne joined AA in *Death Over the Rainbow,* which gets released in September, and neither Delores nor I want him falling off the wagon just yet. Three books from now, maybe, but we need him sober for a while. Our readers were beginning to worry about him."

For the next half hour we talked crime, both fictional and real, until Sergeant McCracken's head began to droop. As she slid off into Dreamland, I had a memory…

My nine-year-old self thought I'd killed him.

Children's minds are strange things. Not being able to stand the abuse anymore, I'd begun planning Papa Brian's murder more than a month earlier, working myself up to it a little at a time, stifling my fear, letting my hatred grow until I was ready. Then, on that terrible Thursday morning, the morning Norma volunteered at her church, I gave my dog Sandy away. Papa Brian had warned me that if I ever told anyone, he'd blind Sandy first, then kill him slowly.

So I kept quiet.

Sandy was the only thing I cared about anymore.

That day, that terrible and wonderful day, before Papa Brian came home early, as he always did on Thursdays, I went down to the kitchen and found the knife. It was the one I'd seen Mama Norma use when she cut up chickens for frying. How was I to know the blade was neither long enough or strong enough to gut a full-grown man?

But at least, an hour later, it got him away from me for good.

As Papa Brian lay screaming on the floor, I ran.

I ran, and I ran, and I ran. I ran down the block, across the park, and into the neighborhood beyond, where the houses were bigger and the alleys were wider. I was headed for the Pima Rez, having got it into my mind that I would build a teepee and live there for the rest of my life. Or at least until my parents came back for me.

I never made it.

Around 84th Street I developed a crick in my side and couldn't run anymore. All I could do was hide myself between a large Dumpster and a cement block wall.

That's where Officer Linda McCracken found me. She was younger then, and pretty. The bullet that came for her was still fifteen years in the future, so when she spotted me, she left her squad car idling and walked toward me slowly, using the same tone of voice I'd used with Sandy that day I found him shivering by the side of the road.

"I won't hurt you, Honey." McCracken's soft voice sounded like safety, but I knew better. Papa Brian had a soft voice, too.

Giving up, not knowing what else to do anymore, I let her approach, even though I recognized the lie, even though I knew she was going to shoot me with that big gun she carried in her holster.

Officer McCracken kept her word. She didn't shoot me. Instead, she knelt down—and not minding my bloody clothes—wrapped her strong arms around me and kissed me on the forehead.

"There, there, Honey. It'll be all right. I promise."

Before I left her house, the old sergeant's head had sunk almost to her chest, but not so low that I couldn't return that long-ago kiss.

Chapter Fifteen

Life isn't fair. Everyone knows that, but every time a tragedy happens, we are stunned by the unfairness of it all. Parents disappear. Children are abused. Good cops get shot.

Juries free the guilty and convict the innocent.

I was still inwardly railing about the unfairness of life when I made it back to my apartment above Desert Investigations. Increasingly concerned about Debbie Margules and her precarious situation, I called Jimmy again and told him what I needed. Once the sputtering ended, he said, "That's near-impossible."

"You've done it before."

"That was a wholly different situation. Give it a rest, Lena."

"I wouldn't ask you to if it wasn't necessary. I'm really worried about that woman."

"Chances are they'll never charge her. You know as well as I do the cops won't knock themselves out over this case, regardless of what they say in the press conferences."

"On the off-chance you're right, how about it?"

His silence told me it was time to soothe some ruffled feathers. "Pow wow still going fine?" I could hear drumming in the background, people clapping.

His tone was lighter when he answered. "Yeah, and now that the Men's Fancy Dance judging is over, I can relax. There's Indians from all over, even a group of Mohawks from New York and some Seminoles from Florida. Talk about a great turnout!

Listen, Lena, it's been nice talking to you and all, even when you're wanting the impossible…"

"*Near* impossible, you said. Remember?"

"I have to get back to my cousin's fry bread wagon. Couple hours ago her daughter went into early labor, so she's shorthanded."

And that was that.

Frustrated, I paced back and forth around my apartment for a while, not knowing what to do next. After a half hour of that, I decided to burn off my excess energy at the gym. Today being a Scottsdale Fight Pro kind of day, I was soon flipping Sean Finnegan, my usual workout buddy, over my head. As soon as he picked himself up, he responded in kind.

"We have to stop meeting like this," he said, helping me to my feet.

I flipped him again.

He took the second fall with good grace, and after we finished roughing each other up, we shared a raspberry power smoothie at the drinks bar. Sean was a firefighter, male-model handsome, and if he hadn't been gay, I'd have been all over him. But such is life. As the Rolling Stones song goes, you can't always get what you want.

Most of my restlessness burned away, I returned to my apartment and watched the late afternoon news. A bullet-riddled body had just been dug up near the White Tank Mountains west of Phoenix. Yesterday hikers had found two bodies in the desert less than a mile away, both having died from natural causes; one felled by a heart attack, the other from heatstroke. Same day on the other side of the Valley, at the base of Weaver's Needle in the Superstitions, a hiker from Minneapolis had also collapsed and died from heatstroke. His golden retriever survived, but just barely. An Apache couple found the dog collapsed in the shade by its master's body, and shared their water bottles with it, the man being beyond help.

I decided there should be signs posted at the airport saying, NEVER HIKE ALONE. IF YOU HIKE, TAKE ONE GALLON OF WATER PER PERSON WITH YOU, MORE IN JUNE, JULY & AUGUST. REPEAT: NEVER HIKE ALONE.

Good ideas are nothing if not acted on, so I picked up my landline and punched in the number of my U.S. Representative. Instead of the Honorable Juliana Thorsson, whom I'd come to know during my last case, my fourteen-year-old goddaughter, Alison, picked up.

"Hi, Lena."

"Hi, Ali. Your mom home?"

"Yeah, but she's working."

"She's always working. Let me talk to her anyway."

"She told me to screen her calls."

"Remember that Banned Books backpack you wanted?"

"The one she said I couldn't have because I'd copy down the titles and read my way through them?"

"Yeah, that one. I'll get it for you if you let me talk to her."

"MOOOOOMMMM! It's IMPOOOORTANT!"

Juliana picked up the extension. "Stop bribing the kid, Lena."

"What, you were eavesdropping?"

"Mothers always eavesdrop. What do you want this time?"

I told her about my idea for the Sky Harbor Airport sign, but she didn't greet it with enthusiasm.

"You need to stop watching the news. I heard about those poor tourists, too. But we could paper the entire city with those signs and people would still go hiking out there unprepared."

"But we should do something!"

An irritable sigh. "Do you think we haven't tried? Signs similar to the one you're requesting are already up at the airports and bus terminals. They're just not being paid attention to. Now, Lena, I'm happy to know you're concerned about the public welfare, but I'm busy putting together a piece of legislation that will tighten last year's rewrite of the eminent domain statute, and I have to get back to work on it before I lose my train of thought. You want to talk to Ali again?"

"Put her back on."

"I never left," Alison said, once her mother hung up the extension. "When do I get the backpack?"

"I'll order it tomorrow."

"Today."

"It's Sunday."

"Nothing's closed on Sunday anymore. But it's on sale at Amazon for $79.95, shipping free, guaranteed overnight. Oh, and I think you should get it stuffed with some of the books, like, *Lady Chatterley's Lover* or something."

"Don't be greedy."

We talked books for a while, then about her boyfriend, Kyle, then school. Before I ended the call, she'd cadged me out of *Catcher in the Rye, The Color Purple,* and *Their Eyes Were Watching God.* I'd been able, thank the Lord I wasn't sure I believed in, to talk her out of *Lady Chatterley's Lover.*

Talking to Ali always cheered me up, so after a quick ramen dinner, followed by a pint of Ben & Jerry's Save Our Swirled ice cream, I felt strong enough to continue the job I'd started the evening before. Only this time I bypassed the photos and newspaper clippings and picked up the scrapbook I had begun working on during Brian Wycoff's trial.

Fortified by the ministry of Ben & Jerry, I opened the scrapbook. The cover said: THIS IS LENA JONES' BOOK.

The first few pages were scribbles about Brian Wycoff, what he had done to me, and how sorry I was that I failed at killing him. I had drawn a picture of him bleeding from the stomach. There was a lot of red on that page.

Toward the back of the scrapbook I saw a shaky drawing of a smiling man dressed in Jesus robes. Abraham. Vampire teeth sprouted from Abraham's still-smiling mouth.

Near the end, I had drawn a picture of children running through trees. The children were covered by red dots.

The final page showed a red-haired man with Xs for eyes. My

father. He lay on his back, surrounded by trees and red-dotted children. The children had Xs for eyes, too.

That page was the reddest of them all.

I closed the scrapbook.

Then I went into the kitchen and ate my way through another pint of Ben & Jerry's Save Our Swirled.

The night was another bad one. Over and over my mother screamed, "They killed them and it's my fault, it's all my fault!"

So much red.

Chapter Sixteen

"Good grief, Lena, what happened to you?" Jimmy asked as he came through the office door.

I had arrived at the office earlier than usual on a Monday because at some point I'd become afraid to go back to sleep. I was on my fourth cup of high-test Graffeo Dark and even my teeth were vibrating.

"Hard workout at Scottsdale Fight Pro," I said.

"Workouts don't cause red eyes."

"Insomnia."

"That does." The pow wow had been good for him. His bronze skin had picked up even more color from the sun and his mahogany eyes shone. Even his long black hair, now falling several inches past his shoulders, appeared glossier. I made myself look away and think about Dusty instead.

I am such a fool.

Jimmy wasn't through with me. "This case isn't good for you," he said.

"It's no different than any of the others." Outside, a couple of tourists stopped to look at the array of turquoise jewelry in the window of Ken Littlefeather's store. He wouldn't open for another two hours. Name withstanding, Ken wasn't Indian; he was Italian, from New Jersey, and his...

"The Wycoff case isn't like any other case, Lena. It's bringing up some bad stuff for you."

"I can handle it."

"Just look at yourself, woman. You've aged ten years in one week."

"That's something a woman loves to hear."

He took two steps toward me. I took three steps back.

Dusty. Think of Dusty. Think of that cheating son of a bitch and his pistol-packing wife, the bullets that had almost struck me, think of anything, anything, but don't ever think about letting Jimmy get any closer.

I could feel Jimmy staring at me.

"Lena, you…"

The turquoise-hunting tourists walked on to the next store, an art gallery with idealized paintings of the desert that pretended the desert was not a killing ground.

"Leave it alone, Jimmy," I said, backing up another step, keeping my face turned toward the action on Main Street.

Out of the corner of my eye I could see Jimmy shrug. Then he turned and walked over to his computer station. Sat down. Turned on his computer. "Okay. Police any closer to arresting someone in the Wycoff case?"

"Last I heard they're still looking at Debbie."

Even a frown couldn't mar the perfection of his earth-colored face. "I don't like the sound of that. From what you've told me, she's had a rough enough time without winding up in a jail cell."

"Tell me about it." I fetched my partner a cup of coffee, which surprised him, then gave him time to settle in. A half hour later I glanced at his computer screen and saw that he was running background checks for a grocery store chain we had under contract. Background checks are our bread-and-butter, but something more immediate was on my mind.

"Jimmy?"

"What?"

"Remember what I asked you to do yesterday?"

He stopped typing. Without turning around, he said, "You wanted me to find the names of the kids on the witness list at Wycoff's trial."

"Right."

"Which I told you was impossible, that the court records were sealed."

"As much as I hate to repeat myself, you said *near*-impossible."

"Same thing."

"No it's not."

He finally turned around, his dark eyes serious. "Please give it a rest. There's nothing to gain by dredging up old history. The man's dead. He's no longer a danger to anyone."

"Didn't I just tell you that Debbie Margules remains under suspicion?"

"So do you, probably."

"But…"

"Tell you what. If Ms. Margules does wind up getting arrested, I'll see what I can do. But only then. The minute I start poking into sealed court documents, red flags will go up all over the Maricopa County system, and could eventually lead to my own arrest. Having once spent some time in a jail cell myself, I'm loathe to repeat that dubious pleasure, thank you very much. Deal?"

"Deal."

We worked in companionable silence for the next hour, me doing billing and answering phones, Jimmy continuing his background checks. Just before noon, I received a call that made my adrenalin level spike. One of my contacts had spotted Inez, client Yolanda Blanco's runaway daughter, panhandling in front of the Greyhound Bus Depot.

"Gotta go!" I yelled at Jimmy. "Someone's spotted Inez!"

Ten minutes later I was headed west on the I-10 toward Phoenix.

Most bus depots are not located in high-rent districts, but the Greyhound Depot broke the mold. Adjoining Sky Harbor Airport, it sat amidst sculpted parkland, looking more like an upscale business office. Still, bus stations don't always attract society's A-listers, and when I spotted the eighteen-year-old by a kiosk in front, she was surrounded by a crowd of low-lifes. It was easy to see why. A beauty by any standard, her light tan skin glowed with good health, more than making up for her scruffy Levis and torn Arcade Fire tee shirt. She had also gained a few pounds since going on the lam. They looked good on her.

But I could tell she was scared. One of the lowlifes, a big dude who towered over her by almost a foot, was tugging at her sleeve.

I slipped my .38 out of its pocket holster and exited the Jeep.

"Back off, buddy," I told Big Dude.

"Mind your own business, bitch," he replied. He smelled of Eau de Street, made even more pungent by the heat.

I flashed my ID and turned so he could see my .38. "This young woman *is* my business."

Big Dude backed off. So did his pals.

The fear in Inez' eyes diminished but didn't go away. "Who the hell are you?" she asked, jutting out her chin in a show of fierce. Living with a druggie teaches a girl that kind of skill.

"Someone your mom hired because she's worried about you."

"She needs to mind her own business. I'm of age now, and she can't tell me what I can or can't do. I'm living my own life."

"How's that working out for you?"

She turned away, but not before I could see her blush.

"Look, Inez, your mother's been around more than you realize, and because of that, she can spot trouble a mile away. Your boyfriend, Glen?"

"Ex-boyfriend," she muttered, still turned away.

"My office ran a check on him and he's been arrested four times on burglary charges."

"He was framed."

"Four times?" I slipped my handgun back into its pocket holster. "Let me make a suggestion. It's just a suggestion, mind you, because you're right, you're an adult and neither I nor your mom can make you do anything you don't want to do. If you don't like what I have to offer, I'll just drive away."

When she faced me, the fear had been replaced by a flash of hope. "What kind of offer you talking about?"

"That you get in my Jeep and let me drop you off at your mom's. Once you go inside, I'll wait for a half hour, and if you decide for any reason that you don't want to stay, I'll drive you anywhere you want to go. Even back here."

She snuck a glance at Big Dude, still lurking under the depot's overhang and eying her greedily. "You promise? Anywhere?"

"Promise. If you have another druggie boyfriend in mind, I'll take you to him, too."

She looked down at the ground and muttered something like, "...all a bunch of assholes." Then she looked up and said, "Okay."

On the way to Yolanda's house, Inez opened up. "I'm pregnant. That's why I left. She's such a prude she'd kill me if she ever found out."

I'd guessed about the pregnancy; so had Yolanda. "Pregnancy is a hard condition to hide, but nah, she's not going to kill you. That's against the law, and as you've noticed, your mom is very law-abiding these days."

After a few moments of silence, she said, "What do you mean, *these days?*"

I gave her a smile. "I think you and your mom need to talk. You know, woman-to-woman. All about guys and stuff, starting with your dad."

"He's dead." She looked forlorn.

"There's 'dead' and there's 'dead.' Talk to your mother, Inez. You'd be surprised how much you two have in common. And I happen to know she likes babies."

An hour later I entered the air-conditioned comfort of Desert Investigations.

"How'd it go?" Jimmy asked, his face tense.

"Mother and child reunion, just like the Simon and Garfunkel song. Everybody hugging, bawling, the whole bit. Girl's gonna stay and they're out shopping for baby clothes as we speak."

"That's good news." But the worried expression didn't go away.

"Why the long face, then, Almost Brother?"

"We got a call while you were gone. From Nicole Beltran. The attorney."

My happy face disappeared. "Debbie's been arrested."

He nodded. "Something about a problem with an alibi. According to Beltran, Ms. Margules might not have been where she said she was at the time of Norma Wycoff's murder. There's more, but you'd better call and get it directly from her. Beltran, I mean, since Ms. Margules can't exactly get to a phone now, having already used her one-call privilege."

I took a deep breath. "Jimmy, those names you said you'd…"

"Already on it. Getting them might take me a couple of days. Sealed records and all that."

Somehow I refrained from putting my head in my hands. "Two days is a long time when you're sitting in a jail cell."

"Been there, done that, didn't even get a lousy tee shirt."

When I returned Nicole's call, she told me why Debbie's alibi didn't hold water, she hadn't been where she'd said she'd been the night before or the morning of Norma Wycoff's murder. No one had seen her the night of Brian Wycoff's torture/murder, either. After voicing my disbelief, I told Nicole what I might be able to do.

In response, she said, "Since I'm an officer of the court, I'll pretend I didn't hear that."

"Pretend away. With Debbie locked up, what's going to happen to her B&B?"

"I'm on vacation, and I'd planned to check into at one of those nice Sedona resorts after we'd finished our get-together at the Oasis, but hell, I might as well stay on and take care of the place for her." She didn't sound happy. "I'm not much of a cook, though. Maybe you…?"

Despite the seriousness of the situation I had to chuckle. "I don't think Debbie's guests would enjoy instant ramen for breakfast. Can't Jacklyn help?" Not that the gun-slinging biker chick had seemed any more domestic than myself.

"She had to go back to Phoenix, remember? I called her with the update and she said she'll try to get someone to cover her shifts for her, but didn't sound optimistic. If I'm careful maybe I can keep from poisoning the guests."

On that note we ended the call.

Jimmy and I had been working quietly together for a couple of hours when the office door opened and a monsoon of rage blew in. Frank Gunnerston, he with the "runaway" wife.

"Where's my wife!?" he thundered.

"As far away from you as she can get," I answered, opening the desk drawer where I kept my .38.

Gunnerston was so worked up he didn't notice. "I paid you good money to find her!"

"Which we did."

"Then give me her address! I paid for it!"

"As I have told you on several occasions, Mr. Gunnerston, the fact that she has taken out an Order of Protection against you mitigates your situation. You should have told us about that. But tell you what I'll do. I'll accept half the amount due and we'll call it even."

"You're not getting a dime, bitch. In fact, I'm gonna sue you for withholding of services!"

Frank Gunnerston just missed being handsome. His height and big build made him resemble a linebacker, but there was a brutish cast to his deep-set eyes that his sloping forehead did nothing to relieve. From a distance, he still looked pretty good, though.

But right now he was in my face.

Jimmy stood, his hands clenched. "Back off, buddy."

Gunnerston sneered. "Fuck you, Indian."

Realizing what could happen next, in one swift move I plucked my .38 out of the drawer and cocked it. "Listen to the man."

A .38 revolver isn't a big gun, but when it's aimed at your balls, you pay attention. Not being totally stupid, Gunnerston raised his hands and stepped back.

"I only want what I paid for."

"You're not getting it, which is why I'm agreeing to settle for half the fee billed. Now go home and cool off."

"I meant it when I said I'll sue!"

"See you in court, Frank."

Jimmy didn't sit back down until Gunnerston left. While he's a gentle man, he can be a terror with his fists. Gunnerston didn't know how lucky he was I'd pulled the gun and diffused the situation before Jimmy broke his jaw.

I winked at Jimmy. "That was fun."

"For you, maybe." His fists were still clenched. "Please don't tell me you're actually going to settle for fifty percent."

"Not anymore. Now I'm holding out for the full amount, and if he doesn't cough it up, I'll sue *his* ass and get the entire amount plus court costs."

I hate bullies.

Of course, there were different types of bullies. Among them were the straight-out, hard-voiced kind, frequently paired with ever-ready fists; then there were the silken, whisper-soft people who got their way by use of manipulation. I don't know which was worse: the brutes or the sneaks. But I try not to think about bullies too much. They gave me bad dreams.

Such as the one I had that night…

It was Sunday, and Abraham had called everyone together. We gathered in the meadow, near the fire ring, eager to hear his next teaching. Pure in his white robe, smiling gently, his voice was soft as an angel's as he shared his latest Revelation.

"God spoke to me last night."

"Glory be!" our friends shouted. So did my mother and I. My father remained silent.

"God told me what we must do to remain in his favor."

"Glory be!" we shouted again.

"What did First Abraham do?" he asked.

Confused faces. When the Bibles had been taken away, only Abraham's was left. Our Abraham. The only man who knew the true nature of God, the only man who could be trusted to truthfully interpret that confusing holy book. Unlike the rest of us, Abraham understood its every passage.

Still the gentle smile. "First Abraham knew there could be no salvation without obeying God's word. Every word! First Abraham walked that difficult path, and he found salvation. Therefore we—as people of God—must walk that path, no matter how difficult."

"Glory be!"

My father frowned. He alone of all the other men had refused to obey Abraham's last Revelation. "We need to get out of here," he whispered to my mother.

"He didn't mean it," she whispered back. "He's just testing us."

As Abraham talked, my father continued, "You're wrong, Helen. Yesterday he ordered Jonas to turn his wife over to him. You know how he's been looking at Sylvia."

My mother laughed. "Sylvia's beautiful. No wonder Abraham's been looking."

"He did more than look last night."

"You need to stop listening to rumors." Her smile was almost the same as Our Abraham's.

But that night Abraham sent for my mother.

Chapter Seventeen

By noon the next day, Jimmy announced he had broken into the old Maricopa County criminal court system and found the names of the children on the Wycoff witness list. Not only that, but he'd run a follow-up check on them and knew where they were now. The printout he handed me was almost three inches high. I would have been happier about this break, but I was too shaken up by last night's dream—last night's memory, actually.

"You feeling okay, Lena? I thought you'd be thrilled." He was looking worried again. I wished he would stop that.

"I'm feeling hunky-dory." I couldn't get the memory of my mother's tears out of my head. *Abraham had sent for her.*

"If you want, I'll do the interviews."

Jimmy's offer gave me the first smile of the day. He hated what we called "street work," preferring the insularity of his keyboard. "I can handle it, Almost Brother."

"Hmm."

"Really. I'm fine."

He stared at me for what seemed forever, then said, "Tell you what. You look like you need a break, so before you start working your way through that printout—and it's an unhappy one, I assure you—why don't you come out to the Rez with me for lunch? I barbequed a big fat chicken last evening and made this huge garbanzo bean salad. It's more than I can eat, and it looks like you could use the protein. You've been living on nothing but ramen again, haven't you?"

"What's wrong with ramen?"

"Lack of nutrition, for one." He stood up. "C'mon. The drive there and back won't take much longer than getting served at one of the restaurants around here, and I can assure you the food's every bit as good. Better, even."

"Barbeque, did you say?" Unhappy as I was, I hadn't been able to eat breakfast, and my stomach was growling.

"Braised with my famous secret sauce."

Fifteen minutes later, I was sitting in Jimmy's trailer facing a plate of food that would have intimidated a professional wrestler. As a recording of R. Carlos Nakai's flute songs played in the background, he served me half a chicken, a cilantro-spiced garbanzo bean salad with avocado chunks and red onion, and a whopping glass of iced tea. Yes, Jimmy was right. The food overshadowed the offerings of any Scottsdale restaurant.

So did the ambiance. While others might love white linen and crystal chandeliers, I preferred Jimmy's taste in décor. The carpet in his trailer matched the color of the mesas surrounding the Rez, and Pima-patterned pillows livened up a butternut leather sofa. He had built the coffee table himself out of saguaro cactus spines, studding them with errant pieces of turquoise. It wasn't furniture, it was *art*.

But the cabinetry in the kitchen area remained his masterpiece. The cupboards were covered with his paintings of the old Pima gods: Earth Doctor, the father-god who created the world; Elder Brother, who after defeating Earth Doctor in battle, had sent him into hiding in a labyrinth beneath the desert; and Spider Woman, who had tried in vain to make peace between the two.

"You could make a small fortune selling stuff like this," I said, gobbling down another forkful of salad.

"Oh, I do okay."

No lie there. As a full partner in Desert Investigations, he could have bought himself a nice house in Scottsdale, but preferred living on the Rez near his large extended family. Although raised by a white adoptive family in Utah after the deaths of both his parents, he had found a deeper peace here among his tribal roots.

I swallowed, picked up what was left of a drumstick and began to gnaw.

Jimmy had been right about something else, too. Being out here on the Rez again diminished the horror of last night's dream. During the drive over in his pickup, we'd seen a small herd of javelina trotting through the underbrush, along with another rare sigh: a female coyote loping a dry wash with two adolescent pups trailing behind. The sound of traffic had been replaced with the songs of cactus wrens and the whistles of red-tailed hawks. Plus, it was cooler out here. Well, that's what happens when you don't cover Nature with cement and asphalt.

Drumstick finished, I asked, "What's for dessert?"

"Prickly pear ice cream. Made it myself."

I must have gained ten pounds on that meal, but I didn't care. The ice cream, which he served with a cinnamon stick plunged through the double scoop, hit new heights of flavor, and when I finished, I heaved a happy sigh.

"Feeling better now?" he asked, refusing my help in clearing up.

"Yes, yes, and another yes. By the way, what's with all that building material you have piled out in back?"

He gave me a cagey smile. "I'll show you when I'm done."

Jimmy was always building something, whether a small kiva to be used for communing with the gods, or a computer lab add-on to his Airstream. It would be interesting to see what was coming next.

A half hour later, back at Desert Investigations, where I—fortified by good food and even better companionship—read my way through Jimmy's printout. The thick pages detailed the tormented lives of the other foster children who, along with me, had been slated to testify against the Wycoffs. Out of the six other kids who had agreed to testify against Papa Brian, two were dead.

Five years earlier Errol Bidley shot himself in the abandoned south Phoenix warehouse where he'd been squatting, and just last year Molly Arness had hung herself off the Mill Avenue Bridge. That left Tamara Clemson, who was currently serving a five-year sentence in Perryville Prison for multiple DUIs, one that had ended with the vehicular homicide of a four-year-old boy; Gayle Mitter, who'd moved to Los Angeles, where she'd been arrested twice for prostitution and once for the possession of illegal substances; Casey Starr—original name Fairfield—who now owned a company named Cyber-Sec; and Magda Pierce, nee Wallace, a flight attendant for Canyon Airlines.

Out of the seven of us, only the last two had wound up with normal lives. Three, if I counted myself, but given my dreams, "normal" is not the best word to describe me.

Not liking what I was about to do, I jumped into my Jeep and set off for the nearest Wycoff victim: Magda Wallace Pierce, at 203561 Bluebird Circle, in the Arcadia District. With luck, she would be home. If not, I would try again tomorrow.

The Arcadia District is the least Phoenix of all Phoenix neighborhoods. With its older homes, lush green lawns and towering trees, it could have been any nice Midwestern suburb. Only every now and then did faux Territorial or Mediterranean architecture intrude upon the fantasy.

As I neared Magda's house, a coy Cape Cod knockoff, a woman wearing a flight attendant's uniform drove by me in a white Honda Accord. I pulled over to the curb and waited, allowing her time to park her car in the garage and enter the house. Women—especially women with a history of being sexually attacked—don't like strangers approaching them on the street, so I decided to give her ten minutes to do whatever she needed to do: put away groceries if she'd shopped on the way home; pee, if she'd been sipping bottled water all the way from Sky Harbor Airport.

Time up, I exited the Jeep and rang her doorbell.

After a long look through the door's peephole, the door opened revealing a still-attractive brunette in her forties, wearing a sharply tailored blue jacket and slacks. She gave me a smile that didn't reach her eyes.

"Hello, there! What may I do for you?"

Coffee? Tea? Peanuts?

I had rehearsed my speech, such as it was, on the drive over, so I was as ready as a person could be for having the temerity to bring up the worst time in someone's life. "Hello, back." I smiled, too, but hoped mine look more sincere. "I'm a private investigator…" here I pulled out my ID, "and I'd like to talk to you about someone you once knew. It's very important."

The smile went away and the suspicious eyes flickered. "If you mean my ex-husband, I have nothing to say. He can thank his girlfriend for what happened. I had nothing to do with it." She started to close the door.

"I want to talk to you about Brian Wycoff," I told her. "An innocent woman's life may depend on it."

In a way, that was true. If convicted of double murder, Debbie Margules would spend the rest of her life in prison. Or worse, since Arizona still had the death penalty. Maybe, given who the so-called "victims" were, a judge might go easy on her, but it could easily go the other way. Justice is supposed to be blind; sometimes it actually is.

The second I said "Brian Wycoff," competing emotions began fighting it out across Magda Wallace Pierce's face. Fear, disgust, curiosity.

Curiosity won. "Come on inside, Ms. Jones. It's hotter than blazes out there. Want some water? I'd offer you iced tea, but I've just returned from a flight."

Water would be great, I told her. While she bustled into the kitchen, I looked around. The house was considerably more upscale than it would have been on a flight attendant's salary alone, so I guessed at a healthy divorce settlement. Not a lot of warmth to the color scheme, though. Cement-gray carpet, two matching gray-on-gray sofas, a scattering of tables that were a mixture of expensive new and auction-house antiques. No family photos.

She was back in a minute with a filled ice bucket, two glasses that looked and chimed like Waterford crystal, and four bottles of Perrier. The perfect hostess, she tonged several cubes of ice into the glasses, then poured as if the liquid was fine wine.

Service accomplished, the flight attendant politesse disappeared and the true woman emerged. "This is about that fucker's murder, right?"

"And his wife's."

A sneer. "She deserved it. I told her what he was doing to me, and you know what she said?" Not waiting for an answer, she added, "She said it was my own fault, that I was a little whore."

"She said the same thing to me."

She looked confused for a moment, then after a quick glace and the scar on my forehead, it cleared. "Oh. Right. You're the one who stabbed him." The first genuine smile lit her face. "Good on you, girl." Then the confusion returned. "Since he did the same things to you he did to me, why do you care who killed him? Whoever did it, did the world a big favor. Same for Norma. In some ways, she was more evil."

I explained about Debbie Margules and how she was sitting in jail about to be indicted for a murder she didn't commit.

"God, the poor…" She swallowed. "First she loses her daughter, probably to Wycoff, and now…" Her voice trailed off again, then she cleared her throat and continued, "I get it. You're going to find out enough to spring her. Then what? Surely you're not going to keep looking so you can turn the real hero over to the police."

A smart woman, she'd put her finger on the very conundrum I was struggling with. To effectively clear Debbie of murder charges would mean I'd found the real killer, someone the Wycoffs had hurt as much as they'd hurt Magda Wallace Pierce and a host of other vulnerable children.

"Frankly, I haven't gotten that far," I told her. "But I'll think of something."

"Good luck with that."

"Where were you when Papa Brian was killed?"

She actually laughed. "I was wondering when you'd get around to asking me. If necessary, a handsome-but-married pilot can testify that I was in bed with him in his double-queen hotel suite in Birmingham, Alabama. I arrived home to the happy news."

"How about Norma's death?"

Another lilting laugh. "In the air over Texas on my way to Pensacola, Florida."

"I can check, you know."

"Check away, Lena. My hands are squeaky clean. Unfortunately."

We chatted comfortably for a while in unspoken agreement to avoid any more talk of the Wycoffs. While we made our way through the Perrier, I learned about her ex-husband Charles, who had developed a severe gambling problem while accompanying his girlfriend—the woman he'd left Magda for—to the local casinos, and then started embezzling from the insurance company where he worked. Charles' trial came up next week, and Magda was still undecided whether to attend. I also learned that that she'd met her husband in a group home, several years into her adventures through the CPS system.

"I thought he seemed normal, considering," she said, allowing a wistful tone into her voice. "He received a scholarship to U of A, and as soon as I aged out of the system, I moved down to Tucson to be with him. That's when I started taking classes myself. After what we'd both been through, our future looked bright. But you never know about people, do you, no matter how together they may seem?"

I agreed that you didn't, reminding myself to double-check her great-sounding alibi.

An hour later, I sloshed my Perrier-logged self out to the Jeep and drove through the increasing heat back to Desert Investigations. There was no point in trying to reach Casey Starr, nee Fairfield, yet. Cybe-Sec didn't close until five.

Seeing Jimmy still scrolling his way through background checks, I pitied him. How could a man as energetic and physically fit as he was spend most of his working hours hunched over a computer? I remembered something he had once told me about his love for puzzles. As a kid he had read the entire Sherlock Holmes canon several times, and the third time through decided to find work in a puzzle-oriented profession. Thus the white-hat hacking and subsequent partnership at Desert Investigations.

During one lull in the clicking and clacking, I called out, "Hey, Jimmy!"

"Huh?" He looked up at me with glazed eyes. He always had that expression when searches ran particularly deep.

"Have you ever been fooled by someone?" Then I remembered his disastrous love life, and added, "Other than women."

"All the time."

"Really? *All* the time?"

He sat back in his ergonomic mesh chair and sighed. "Lena, very few people turn out to be what you thought they were when you first met them. Take me, for instance."

I laughed. "You? You're exactly what I always thought you were."

Mahogany eyes burned into mine. "And what's that?"

"A nerd who neither looks nor acts like a nerd."

"Those are the 'what-I'm-nots.' Tell me the 'ams.'"

I tried again. "You're a great cook. You like Thai food and fry bread. You watch *National Geographic* specials. You turned your trailer into a work of art. And you're the best hacker in the business."

"Anything else?"

"You're loyal to your people."

"Go on."

"Go on to what? That's it, isn't it?"

After a pause long enough to make me feel uncomfortable, he said, "You don't know me at all."

Disturbed for some reason, I spent the next couple of hours checking out Magda Pierce's alibi through my contacts at

Canyon Airlines. After several phone calls, I concluded she was telling the truth. I don't know why that surprised me, but it did.

A little after five, Jimmy proclaimed himself finished for the day. "Want to come over to my place for dinner, too? I was thinking shrimp on the barbie, with ratatouille side."

Given the excellence of the lunch he'd served me, I seriously considered it, then decided not. "Sounds great, but I'm going to see if I can chase down Casey Starr. He's probably home by now. "

"He lives all the way out in Litchfield Park. Shouldn't you call first?"

"And give him the chance to refuse a meeting? I'll risk it."

Jimmy grunted a goodbye and left.

Phoenix was becoming more and more like Los Angeles, a collection of suburbs in search of a city. Our freeway system isn't as clogged as L.A.'s, but rush hour in the Valley of the Sun is still no picnic. Thanks to the jackknifed semi blocking two lanes on the I-10, it took me more than an hour to reach Litchfield, when it shouldn't have taken more than thirty minutes.

Sweaty and irritable, I finally reached the Litchfield turnoff. The rest of the drive was a snap. A former cotton-growing area turned planned community on Phoenix's far west side, the landscaping was almost as lush as Arcadia's. Chez Starr, a faux-stucco Territorial knock-off, even overlooked a man-made lake.

According to Jimmy's printout, Cyber-Sec, Casey's company, was doing well. So was Kay Starr, his wife, who headed up the Engineering Department at Maricopa College. No children, though, and given Starr's background, I wondered if that was by choice. Neither of them had an arrest record, and both were frequent volunteers at St. Mary's Food Bank. In short, the all-American family, minus the 2.3 kids.

PI's don't trust perfection, so I approached their front door with the same forethought I'd approached Magda's, hoping for the truth, prepared for lies.

Starr wasn't home.

Neither was his wife.

Frustrated, I hopped back in my Jeep and drove to a small strip mall I'd passed earlier, where I ordered a gyro at Nikko's Greek Cafe. I ate slowly, giving the Starrs time to meander home. The service was as fast as the décor was spare, so by the time I finished eating, only a half hour had passed. To kill more time, I walked next door to the Yoghurt Yurt and had a raspberry cheesecake sundae with chocolate chips and granola sprinkles.

Then I climbed back into my Jeep. The upholstery felt scorching by now, so I had to cover the driver's seat with the blanket I kept in the back. Reminding myself to buy heat-resistant seat covers, I tooled out of the lot and back to Chez Starr.

The Starrs were still gone. It occurred to me then, that they might have been on vacation—most sane and well-heeled Phoenicians leave the city during summer—so I gave in and phoned their number. Voice mail. A pleasant male voice told me to leave a message and he'd get back to me as soon as possible. Giving up, I made my way along the diesel-fumed interstate toward Scottsdale.

Driving in non-congested traffic gives you time to remember.

Remember Papa Brian telling me to keep our little secret or he'd kill my dog. Mama Norma telling me what a slut I was. Sandy, my dog Sandy, the only thing in the world it was safe to love, looking at me with absolute trust in his eyes.

My fault, all my fault.

I should have kept him with me instead of giving him to those other girls. Sandy and I could have run away together and found a home for the both of us, a home with loving people.

And before we ran, I should have used a bigger knife.

When I arrived at my apartment, I showered off the sweat and the fumes and the memories.

Needing something to drown out the noise in my head, I wrapped myself in a bath sheet and clicked on the TV with the remote. The local news wasn't helpful with its muggings and shootings and melting glaciers. Neither were the cable offerings. Supposedly real housewives, bearded duck-hunters, Kardashians.

Irritated, I turned off the TV, stepped around the bankers' box I had brought in from the storage locker, and wandered into my bedroom. I stood there for a while before realizing it was too early to go to bed.

Bed?

Roy Rogers and Trigger bedspread. A duplicate of one I'd had for one brief, happy time as a child.

To the side, a nightstand with a horsehead lamp, another duplicate of a bygone room.

Sue Grafton's *X* open on the nightstand.

A glass of water next to *X*.

Underneath the window, a chest of drawers. Pine.

Closet. No monsters in there now. Papa Brian was dead.

Still restless, I changed into clean clothes and went back into the living room. Sat down. Clicked on the TV again. More muggings, more shootings, more Kardashians. Clicked it off.

Tired of sitting there picking at my cuticles, I stood up.

Looked around again.

Sofa covered in Navajo rugs.

Satin toss pillow that said WELCOME TO THE PHILIPPINES.

Painting by an Apache artist over the sofa.

Chair covered by another Navajo rug.

What the hell?

I was taking inventory again.

Confused, I went into the kitchen and opened the refrigerator door. Mustard. Ketchup. Two-day-old leftovers from the Thai restaurant across the street. The contents of the freezer revealed a months-old, half-finished carton of Rocky Road ice cream crystallized to a fare-thee-well. I tossed it and the other leftovers into the garbage. Now the refrigerator was empty except for condiments.

Maybe I should organize my bedroom closet?

I was halfway down the hall again before I caught myself. What was there to organize? Just several pairs of black jeans and black cargo pants, black tee shirts, three pairs of black Reeboks.

And that damned box where I'd stashed the damned paisley-printed scrapbook.

I let out a breath.

Looked at my hands.

The cuticles were bleeding.

Why was I doing this to myself?

Because I couldn't help it.

Despising my own cowardice, I opened the box and took out the scrapbook. Looked through the articles, the photographs.

Let the memories come.

Let myself see the deep green forest, the hovering night. The cold blue light in Golden Boy's eyes. My father running with the children. Men running after them through the trees. Gunshots. The screams as the children were hit. My father, clutching a baby, as he fell.

What had happened next?

Abraham said something, gave an order. What was it? What had Abraham said as he handed the rifle to his golden-haired son?

"You're a man now. Old enough to do a man's work."

Shot through the gut, my father lay helpless. The baby, thrown out of his arms as he hit the ground, squalled.

"Finish them according to God's holy word," Abraham demanded as he handed the rifle to my twelve-year-old husband.

Let myself hear the gunshots as Golden Boy finished off my father and my baby brother.

Two more shots.

Let myself hear Abraham's words of praise. "God is pleased, son!"

Let myself hear my mother's shrieks as Abraham's men restrained her.

Let myself see my twelve-year-old husband beaming under his father's approval.

And for the first time in more than thirty years, I let myself cry.

Chapter Eighteen

Jimmy stood up when I entered the office next morning.

"What's wrong?"

Still feeling weak, I sat down at my desk. "Turns out I'm married. And I have...I *had*...a brother."

"Oh, Lena."

The next thing I knew, he was leaning over me, his hand on mine. How odd. We never touched. Over the scent of fresh-brewed coffee, I could smell toothpaste and some kind of herbal shampoo. And cologne. When had he switched from Polo and started wearing Paco Rabanne?

"Tell me," he said.

I took a deep breath, then told him.

At the end, he said, "That marriage isn't legal, Lena."

I swallowed. "It still happened. And my baby brother's still dead and I don't even remember his name and my father's dead and I don't remember what happened to my mother and what kind of world is it when you can't even remember your own brother's name?"

I couldn't stop babbling and I didn't like the tight feeling in my throat.

His hand squeezed mine. "We'll find whoever did this to you."

I stopped. Took a deep breath. "Did to *me*? I'm alive, aren't I? The others aren't." I had never felt so empty.

"Did you see your mother killed?"

"No. But she's..."

He put a cautionary finger against my lips. "Don't say it, because you don't know for sure."

I drew back. For some reason, his touch, although warm, made me feel even more benefit than before.

"Lena, do you...?"

I shook my head. "Enough. No more."

Without another word he returned to his computer and after one last long look at me, resumed typing.

From what I could see, he was scrolling through newspapers. Did he think he would find something new, such as an article we hadn't already read a hundred times before? What was the point, anyway? What was done was done, and this continual rooting around in the past, looking for that mythical state termed "closure" never solved anything. People needed to just...

Then it occurred to me that Debbie Margules, Jacklyn Archerd, Nicole Beltran, and all the other members of Parents of Missing Children wouldn't agree with that line of thinking. Although fearing the worst, their search for their children had never ended.

Inspired by their courage I forced myself to think about Golden Boy, about what he'd said to me in that grim forest.

"Don't be afraid, girl. I protect my property."

I was property then. That's all.

Property.

Abraham had called my mother property, too, when he'd sent for her. All the women in the group were his property, he constantly reminded us. I was the sole exception because he'd transferred my title and registration to Golden Boy.

Remembering, my grief slid away, replaced by a deep, burning rage.

"Lena, are you okay?" Jimmy's voice brought me back to the present.

"Never been better," I lied.

After a workday that never seemed to end, I hopped on the freeway again and headed to Litchfield Park. This time I had better luck and the door to Casey Starr's house opened just as I raised my hand to press the bell.

"Saw you coming up the walk," a handsome man said. White teeth gleamed.

With his extraordinarily sculpted face and body, Casey Starr could have wound up as a screen star, but instead he'd become intimate with computers and was thus set for life, even when his looks went south with age.

"Hello, Miss Whoever-You-Are, your face looks familiar. Didn't I see you on TV once? When you shot some guy?" He was still smiling.

"He lived."

"And you were raised in foster homes, right?"

"Right."

"And you're still looking for your parents?"

Casey Starr must have had one hell of a memory, because the interview in which I'd discussed that part of my life had taken place five years earlier. At the time I believed going public with my story would bring answers to so many questions, but I'd been wrong. It only added new ones.

Producing my ID, I said, "I wanted to talk to you in private, if possible."

The smile left his face—funny how that happens—but after a brief pause, it returned. "Now that you've intrigued me, you might as well come on in since I'm the only one here. For now, anyway."

He led me through a nicely appointed, if rumpled, living room. Toss pillows on the floor, family photographs knocked over, torn pieces of paper littering the Saltillo tile. Four flame-point Siamese kittens and their mama smirked up at me, then resumed tearing up more paper.

"Those are Kay's. My wife's." The hint of a scowl marred his perfect face. "I'm not wild about the little vermin, but happy wife, happy life, right? Me, I want them out of the house as soon as possible, so she's agreed to at least sell the kittens."

I looked at my watch. It was almost seven.

"She's working late?" I asked, as he took me into a mahogany-rich den and settled himself behind one of the facing twin desks. Unasked, I took the chair near the other one.

"A department meeting. She'll eventually come storming in here in a vile mood." He smiled again, as if he found his wife's bad temper amusing.

From the photographs in the living room, I had already noticed that Mrs. Starr was a beauty, although the glint of steel in her eyes hinted at something more. Casey Starr hadn't married for comfort, that was for sure.

"This is about the Wycoffs, I presume." He'd had no trouble putting two and two together.

"You presume correctly."

"They were unpleasant people."

My turn to smile. "That's one way of putting it."

Most child molesters have a gender preference. With Papa Brian, it was girls. However, he was capable of crossing gender lines when a girl wasn't available, which is what had happened when Casey Starr was placed in his care. Judging from the grown man, Starr must have been a beautiful little boy.

"Whoever offed the bastards deserves a medal," he said, but with an odd lack of rancor behind the statement.

"No argument there."

"So why do you care?"

He listened as I discussed Debbie and the other women from Parents of Missing Children. When I finished, he said, "How unfortunate."

Unfortunate? What an inadequate word for tragedy.

"Mr. Starr, may I ask you where you were last Tuesday morning and Saturday night?"

"You can ask, Ms. Jones, but I decline to answer." Now his smile looked a bit on the seductive side. This was a man who was used to dealing with people, especially females.

"Why not? And you can call me Lena."

"On advice of my attorney, that's why not. Would you like his number?"

He reeled it off as I wrote it down, not that I'd bother to call. Attorneys being attorneys, he'd take up ten minutes of my time to tell me nothing, then bill his client for an hour.

"That's it, then?" I asked. "You're going to say nothing?"

The smile broadened just enough I could see a crooked incisor. The imperfection somehow made him even more seductive. "Wrong, Miss Lena Jones, the oh-so-beautiful private investigator. I'm going to invite you to have some iced tea, and then I'm going to ask if you'd like something else."

Chapter Nineteen

"Why do you have little white hairs all over your black tee shirt?" Jimmy asked the next morning, while I stood in front of the coffee machine, waiting for my coffee mug to fill.

"Came from a cat."

"You don't have a cat."

"Yesterday I didn't have a cat," I grumped. "Today I do."

Jimmy tried hard not to snicker but couldn't quite pull it off. "A white cat, I see."

"Flame-point Siamese, actually. White with peach points."

Another snicker. "Your entire wardrobe is black, so that's going to work out well."

"No shit, Sherlock."

"What's its name?"

"Snowball."

This time he yelped out loud. When the yelps died down, he wheezed, "Oh, lord, Lena Jones has a cat named Snowball!"

Stung, I growled, "Easier to remember than Siam Hanghal, the thing's legal name."

He guffawed. "This is rich. Who pawned it off on you?"

"Casey Starr."

More laughter. "Gotta watch those dotcom guys."

Jimmy wouldn't shut up until I agreed to let him meet the cat. Well, kitten, since it was only twelve weeks old.

Upstairs, my apartment looked like it had been tossed by the cops. Good thing I had tucked my personal files back into the bankers' box. The kitchen garbage was overturned, used coffee filters and ramen bags were strewn around, and an entire roll of toilet paper had been dragged in from the bathroom and shredded into confetti.

After rampaging all through the apartment last night and depositing its hair everywhere, I had thought the tiny demon would be sacked out in the expensive KittyKondo I'd purchased at PetSmart on the way home from Litchfield. But no, after making that aforesaid mess and clawing out the stuffing from one of my Navajo print toss pillows, it was now climbing the drapes.

"That's some cat," Jimmy said.

"Yeah."

"I see you bought a cat condo."

"Yeah."

"And three bags of kitten food."

"Yeah."

"And twenty pounds of kitty litter."

"Necessary, I was told."

"Would you look at that fancy cat carrier! And all those cat toys! Lena, you must have spent a bundle."

Embarrassed for some reason, I explained, "Cat toys aren't cheap."

"I especially admire the fake fur catnip mouse, although he seems to prefer the toss pillows and drapes."

"Might be a she. On second thought, maybe not."

Having achieved the drapes' summit, Snowball ran across the curtain rod, took a dive toward the sofa, continued across the sofa back, sprang onto the chair, and from the chair, leapt onto my shoulder where he/she dug in with his/her claws.

"Athletic, too," Jimmy said, admiringly.

I removed his/her claws from my shoulder, hoping I wouldn't bleed too much.

"Bet that hurt." Jimmy started laughing again.

"Don't start with me, or I'll put him on *your* shoulder."

Snowball, who wasn't much bigger than my palm, lay in my

hand, purring. It was an oddly soothing sound, so soothing I could feel my usually high blood pressure dropping.

"Now that you two have met, what say we go back to work?"

"Gonna bring your cat?"

"Too destructive. Or haven't you noticed?"

Once back in the office, Jimmy eased up on me out of pity, and we worked together without squabbling for the rest of the morning. At noon, in celebration of my new role as a pet-owner, I walked across the street to the Thai restaurant and brought us back some Panang curry and chicken satay.

"My turn to treat," I said, refusing to take his money.

When we were through eating, Jimmy looked at me with a serious expression and said, "I didn't want to ruin your appetite, but while you were over there, we received another threatening phone call."

"So?" I gathered up the empty food cartons and put them in the trash.

"Whoever it was said that if you didn't watch your step, he was going to take you out, and I don't think he meant on a date. Not a consensual one, anyway. Like before, he was trying to disguise his voice but I'm pretty sure it was Frank Gunnerston."

I sighed. "Him again."

"Like a bad penny."

For wife-beaters, pride is always more important than love, thus they can't handle rejection, the ultimate blow to their pride. When I had discovered Gunnerston's violent history and dropped him from our client list, he had taken that as a rejection, and he'd been right. His feeling of outraged pride had grown after showing up at Desert Investigations and I scared him off with my .38. That had only made it worse because another man—Jimmy—witnessed it. The fact that Gunnerston was still trying to find his wife, long after she escaped his reign of terror didn't bode well for his ability to forgive and forget. If anything, it sounded like he'd transferred his hostility from her to me.

"We need to keep a good lookout," I told Jimmy. "He might show up here again, this time packing."

Jimmy nodded and I reminded myself to clean my revolver that night. How long had it been? Three weeks? Four? I hadn't been to the firing range for two months, but what with the Valley's dust and all...

I was typing in the last of my notes on the Wycoff case when I noticed something missing from the interviews. I had talked to the women at Debbie's Desert Oasis, to Mario and Grace Genovese, and to two of Wycoff's victims, as well as their former social worker, but for some reason I'd never gotten around to interviewing Shana Genovese Ferris, Mario and Grace's daughter. The mother of two children herself, she might have had a motive to kill her uncle if she had discovered his obsession with Bethany. But who would have told her? The second I asked myself that question, I remembered young Luke arguing with his grandmother when she'd attempted to take the little girl out to the RV. He might easily have shared his concerns with his mother.

I stood up and grabbed my new emergency backpack, now plump with fresh clothes. "Jimmy, I have to drive back to Black Canyon City and talk to someone." I looked at my watch. It was headed for late afternoon, and I hated driving back and forth in the heat. "Depending on how things go, I might be gone overnight."

Then I remembered the crowd at the Coyote Corral who had overheard Mario arguing with Grace about allowing her brother to stay on their property. "Maybe even a couple of nights." I headed for the door.

"Aren't you forgetting something?" Jimmy asked, before I could make it out.

I paused. "Forgetting about what?"

"Snowball."

Out of shock, I almost dropped my backpack. "What am I going to do? The little thing's just a baby. I can't leave it alone, but I've still got to do my job."

He looked at me pityingly. "Welcome to the wonderful world of pet ownership. Tell you what. Leave me the key to your apartment and I'll look in on him. Or her, whatever."

"*Look in on*? But it'll get lonely!" I knew all about loneliness.

Jimmy was, if nothing, a man of surprises. "If you want, I can do a little pet-sitting for you, spend the night with your, ahem, 'baby.' Pet it, play with it, let it tear my hands to ribbons, all that fun stuff."

"You'd do that for me?"

"I like cats. And I don't want you to worry."

I walked back to my desk and opened the center drawer where I kept my spare keys taped to its underside. After handing them over, I said, "I appreciate this, Jimmy."

Load lifted, I headed for my Jeep.

I hadn't planned my escape from the Valley wisely. Early rush hour had already begun, so the traffic was bumper-to-bumper until I made it to Anthem, where I stopped for gas. It occurred to me, not for the first time, that as much as I enjoyed driving my open-air Jeep, it might be wise to purchase a vehicle with better gas mileage and better protection from the elements. I could still keep the Jeep for weekend jaunts.

After filling up, it was smooth sailing all the way to the Black Canyon City turnoff, where the temperature felt ten degrees cooler. Feeling optimistic, I pulled into Coyote Corral's parking lot next to Shana's Volvo. If no complications arose, I should be able to take care of business and make it back to Scottsdale by sunset, thus relieving Jimmy from cat-sitting duties.

I should have realized from the number of cars in the parking lot, that the place would be packed. Some of the customers were enjoying an early dinner in the dining area but most stood three-deep at the bar, drinking their way through the Happy Hour special. Shana, looking exceptional in a tight blue tee shirt and matching shorts, ran back and forth from one end of the bar to the other, delivering slopping pitchers of beer and tequila shots.

Every now and then she bumped into her father, who looked as frazzled as she did. Trying for an interview now being pointless, I turned around and walked back to my Jeep.

Ten minutes later I was signing the guest register at Debbie's Desert Oasis. Here the parking area was only half full, so I guessed some of the fishing folk had either checked out or driven farther north for the day to wherever the fish happened to be biting. The door to the little yellow house was open, allowing a soft breeze to float through, carrying along the scent of scrub pine and creosote bushes.

Soon attorney Nicole Beltran and I were sitting in Debbie's office, discussing my progress—or lack thereof—on her case. As we had passed through the living room, I'd noted it was decorated in a style best described as Arizona Cute, with a Navajo rug hanging above the ranch-style sofa, an earth tone braided rug covering a scarred wood floor, and a collection of Kachina dolls on the bookshelf. But Debbie's office was strictly business, the only jarring note being the oil painting of Lindsey, her daughter. I'd once read that some parents of missing children erected shrines to them in their homes, but so far I had seen nothing like that in Debbie's house, just the portrait. Maybe that was the only reminder she needed.

I thought about the bankers' box sitting in my living room, and the memory-haunting contents inside. Sometimes it was better to forget.

"Any news on your investigation?" Nicole's question interrupted my trip down Memory Lane.

I pulled my mind away from that terrible box. "Ah, nothing concrete. What are the chances of Debbie being granted bail?"

She shook her head. "With a double murder charge hanging over her head? Doubtful, but I'm trying. You want to stay in Monarch again? A couple of fishermen were in there yesterday, but they checked out this morning and I've already cleaned it up. Fresh sheets."

"Might as well, since it was beginning to feel like home. Anything happening with Jacklyn since I left?"

"She's having no luck getting her shift covered at the Iron Cross, so she's stuck down there until next Monday. Maybe you'll come up with something by then."

I wanted to tell her that within days Wycoff's real killer would be caught and Debbie freed, but my earlier optimism was dead as ashes. There were just too many people with good reasons to kill the Wycoffs.

"These things take time," I told her.

She didn't look surprised. Movie star complexion notwithstanding, she was, after all, an attorney and knew from experience that investigations could crawl.

"By the way, Nicole, in the phone message you left with my partner, you said Debbie's alibi fell apart. What happened?"

She pressed her lips together as if trying to keep her anger inside. Failing, she snapped, "I told her not to say anything to the authorities, but she didn't listen. Remember that female detective, Eastman, I think her name is?"

"Yvonne Eastman, right. The one into *West Side Story.*"

"It's must be Debbie's favorite movie, too, because despite my previous warnings, she eventually cozied up to Eastman and the next thing you know, was telling the cop her life story, right down to the part where she drove down to Apache Junction the day that son of a bitch was released, just to check him out."

"She *what*?!" This was news, and not the good kind.

The expressions on Nicole's face ran the gamut of sorrow to exasperation. "Not only that, but she told Eastman she sat in front of his house for a couple of hours, hoping to see what he looked like now so if she ever saw him visit his sister, she'd recognize him. When he never came out, she gave up and drove back here. At least she said he never came out of the house."

"Did she mention seeing his car?" Since there's more than one way to ID someone.

"Beige Honda Civic. Older model. Yeah. Said she even wrote down the license plate number."

As a PI, I've long known that intelligent people can do dumb things, but this took the cake. "Debbie blurted out all that just because she and Eastman share the same taste in music?"

"That and the fact she figured she'd get found out anyway. Why, you might ask? Because when scoping out the Wycoff house in Apache Junction, she parked too close to a fire hydrant and got ticketed. She also figured the neighbors might have noticed the truck, too, since she was driving her bright turquoise 1956 Ford F100 pickup. You know, the one that has DEBBIE'S DESERT OASIS, BLACK CANYON CITY, WHERE THE FISH ARE ALWAYS BITING. on both front doors. With her phone number under it."

It was all I could do not to bury my head in my hands. "You and Jacklyn didn't notice she was gone, for what, four hours minimum?"

"We were fishing. And talking. So much so we probably scared away the fish, which would account for us coming back empty-handed while everyone else nearby was hauling out bass by the truckload."

I didn't like asking the next question, but it was necessary. "Were you and Jacklyn in each other's sight all the time?"

She gave me a hard look. "Every single second."

It sounded good, except that they alibied each other, and as such, I took her story for what it was worth: nothing. "Glad to hear that, but you know, I was just wondering—do you think Debbie really believes Wycoff had something to do with her daughter's disappearance?"

"She's always believed that, wouldn't you? Back then, he lived only a couple of blocks from Debbie's house, and Lindsey had to pass his place in order to get to school."

Nicole was right. I thought Wycoff had grabbed the kid, too. "I can understand her wanting to kill Wycoff, but why would she kill Norma?"

Nicole's flawless face twisted with contempt. "I would think that should be obvious. The woman had to know what her husband was like, right? To keep her own nest feathered, she covered

up anything connecting him to the crime and alibied the hell
out of him when the cops canvassed the neighborhood. Detective Eastman's not stupid, so she would have figured that much
out. As for the legalities, Norma's murder may not have taken
place on Eastman's turf, but since Brian died up here under the
auspices of the Yavapai County Sheriff's Office, they're claiming
jurisdiction. The authorities in Pinal County, where the Wycoffs
live now—ah, *lived*—are fighting with Yavapai County over
prosecutorial rights as we speak, which adds to the boondoggle.
Whichever side wins, Debbie's in a world of hurt. There could
even be two trials, one here, and another down there."

I looked at the Hopi Kachina dolls on the bookshelf. From
their placement so close together, two of them appeared to be
fighting, although one was armed with eagle feathers, the other a
gourd. Not for nothing were the Hopi called the People of Peace.

Nicole heaved a sigh. "Lena, I have less than a week left on
my vacation, and then I have to get back to work. Whatever
you can do, you'd better do it fast."

Considering everything, Debbie couldn't have dug a bigger
hole for herself with a backhoe. That's what PIs were for; helping the hole-diggers.

"Did the sheriff's people search her studio?" I was thinking
of the acetylene torch Debbie owned, which could easily have
made those eight burn marks on Wycoff's thigh.

Nicole nodded. "Yep, with a proper search warrant. Believe
you me, I checked every word. Professionally put together, professionally served. Sometimes I miss the days when these small
sheriff's offices didn't know their asses from a hole in the ground."

I tore my eyes away from the Kachinas. "Did they find anything useful?"

"Among other things, they took away her sculpting tools."
Seeing my expression, she added, "Yeah, her acetylene torch,
too. Along with a collection of chisels and knives."

Chapter Twenty

The Coyote Corral was even busier when I returned, but the bulk of the crowd had moved toward the dining area, and the night shift had arrived to help out. Shana remained a dervish behind the bar, while her father kept busy shuttling heaping trays of food from the kitchen. I added to his load with an order of cheese enchiladas and a Diet Coke. Hoping to catch her between drink orders, I took a seat at the bar. Shana was genial enough when she served my Coke, but after that confined her attentions to the other end of the bar and let a different bartender name-tagged LIZ refresh my drink. I didn't blame Shana for giving me the cold shoulder. If a relative, however unpleasant, had been murdered on my property, making me suffer through a full-on police investigation, I'd feel leery about talking to me, too.

As it turned out, eating at the bar had its advantages. While sipping slowly at my Coke, I overheard the conversation of the two men next to me. From the tenor of their voices they sounded fairly young but their faces were so weather-beaten they looked older. As I listened, I learned one of them had been at the Corral the night Wycoff had been killed.

"Never saw Cyril get so wasted," the skinny man with the red beard said. He had hit on me when I first sat down, but had taken my rejection with good nature. "Puked all over hisself and had to be carried home."

"Hell, I'd drink like that if I was married to Roseanne, too," the burly one replied.

Red Beard let that go. "Awful thing about Jeff's trailer gettin' swept away like that, isn't it? Not enough left to be salvaged, 'cept some scrap metal."

During the next half hour and another Diet Coke, I learned more about Jeff Somebody's trailer contents than I needed to know, but when Red Beard and Burley came back around to Cyril Somebody, I sharpened my ears.

"Didn't know Cyril was in here the night that guy was offed," Burley said.

"That's because you was outta town visitin' your daughter, or you'd a been in here drunk on your ass, too," Red Beard responded. "Good thing he was too wrecked to walk, what with him feelin' the way he does about them baby-rapers."

A silence stretched between them for a moment, counter-pointed by the noise around us. Then Burley added, "Too bad about his little girl, wasn't it? The one that got molested?"

Red Beard grunted. "She's livin' with her mama now, some town in Indiana, I hear."

Another silence, then as if they couldn't bear to talk about Cyril's little girl anymore, they switched back to the trials and tribulations of Jeff, and the upcoming fund-raiser.

Cyril.

I committed the name to memory.

The caffeine in the Coke was making me jittery, so I pushed my glass away and walked down to the other end of the bar where Shana was taking a breather. She didn't seem happy at being cornered, but when I suggested a meeting at Casa Genovese the next day, she said in a resigned tone, "Might as well get it over with now. What with everything that's happened, Mama's a mess and I don't want her bothered again." She jerked her head toward the hallway. "Let's go into the office. Liz can take care of the bar for a while, but you'll have to make it quick. The night crowd's gonna start rolling in soon."

The office was in back, halfway down the hall to the rear exit, and it looked like most bar offices everywhere. Banged-up oak desk littered with unfiled invoices and a ratty old computer, two cheap chairs, neon beer signs and a poster of the Budweiser Clydesdales decorating the unpainted cement block walls.

Once we sat down, Shana again denied leaving the Corral at any time during the night Wycoff was murdered.

"Look," she said, a frown line marring her perfect features. "I'll admit I detested my uncle, but I wouldn't kill him. Threaten him, maybe, which I confess I did, but when Mom told me what'd been done to him...My God! If you think either me or my dad is capable of doing something like that, you're flat-out nuts. The sheriff's people have been all over us for the past couple of days, asking this, asking that, finding out everything about us right down to our shopping habits and movie preferences, and I'm just damned sick of being questioned. Frankly, I hope they never catch who did it." She flashed me an angry look. "I don't have to talk to you, you know."

"I know, Shana, and I appreciate you taking the time."

Mollified, she calmed somewhat. To keep her from returning to her volcanic state, I asked, "What about this Cyril guy, the one who got so drunk that night your uncle was killed? What do you know about him?"

She started to answer, but just then the office phone rang. Muttering under her breath, Shana reached across the old oak desk and picked up the receiver. Listened. Shook her head.

"Nope."

Shook her head again. "Nope."

She listened some more, then snapped, "Look, you're going to have to quit calling me. Nope means nope, same as 'Hell no, ain't gonna happen.' Get it?" She made a face at the big Budweiser poster hanging on the wall. I doubted it was the Clydesdales that she found disgusting.

"Nope, no, nada, nein, nyet, and fuck off, okay? I'm hanging up now."

As she lowered the receiver, I could still hear a man on the other end of the line talking. He sounded unhappy.

"Sorry about that," Shana said, resettling into her chair. "Gary. My ex. He wants us to get back together and won't take no for an answer."

I wondered if she was enduring a Hank Gunnerston situation. "Bad divorce?"

She gave me a cynical smile. "The old story, caught him cheating with the art director—we ran a small ad agency down in Phoenix, and the art director was his third, for Christ's sake!—and I finally had enough even though I was only one semester from getting my bachelor's in marketing. Dumb timing, yeah, but there you are. Anyway, I grabbed the kids and left, never went back except to pick up their things. Shoulda took the Mercedes while I was at it, but that's me all over. Act first, think second. So yeah, I guess you could call it a bad divorce. I'm only working here until Gary finds a buyer for the agency and I get my share of the proceeds. Then I'll see what I can do about partnering with another ad shop back in the Valley and move out of my parents' house. Dad's okay, but Mom…" She frowned. "Enough about that. Where were we when my soliloquy about Mr. Pants-Down interrupted our conversation?"

I refrained from asking if the art directors had been male or female. "I was asking about Cyril."

"Oh, yeah. Cyril Sanders. He belongs in AA, not helping the Corral pay its light bill. If Dad thought it would do any good, he'd eighty-six the poor guy for life, but then he'd just drink some other place and they might not get him home alive like we always do."

"Something bad happened to his daughter, I hear."

She looked down at her lap, where her fingers were fussing with several turquoise and silver rings, all of Zuni design. "I don't know anything about it firsthand, because I was still married and living down in the Valley at the time, but from what Dad said…" Then she looked back up at me, her eyes, so hard when she talked to her ex, had gone soft. "Some guy snatched Cyril's kid on her way to school. Poor little thing was only five. He let her go afterwards, but being traumatized, she couldn't give the cops much of a description. And Cyril…" She took a deep breath. "He was always a heavy drinker, but after that he could set a record for the number of tequila shots downed in a half hour."

Her story jogged my memory. "Wasn't there a similar molestation incident up here, the one with Luke's girlfriend? Carolee, I think her name is. Your dad told me her mom's boyfriend molested her."

"Seth. A real creep, that's for sure. But 'similar'? Listen, whoever took Cyril's kid was a stranger, and besides, that happened something like ten years ago, so I don't see…" Light finally dawned. "Wait a minute. Do you believe Cyril could have…? No. If Cyril thought that Seth had anything to do with hurting his little girl, it would've been Seth who was killed and castrated, not my uncle."

I found it interesting that she didn't deny Cyril was capable of murder.

"Where does he live, this Cyril?"

The hardness returned to her eyes. "Why can't you leave him alone?"

"Because Debbie Margules is sitting in the Yavapai County Jail, that's why. And I want to get her out."

"Debbie? In jail? You can't be serious!" Her face turned as white as the blaze down one of the Clydesdale's face.

"Apparently Debbie didn't tell the authorities the truth about where she was when Norma Wycoff was killed. They got a warrant to look at her property and came away with certain, ah, items that could have been used in his death." *And emasculation.*

"But she would never…" Ashen now, Shana shook her head. "Debbie Margules is one of the kindest people I know. You're wrong about her."

I watched her carefully as she reached over and picked up an invoice from the desk, pretended to study it for a moment. When she looked back at me, some color had returned to her face although her hand trembled. "That's too bad. About Debbie getting arrested, I mean. No one in his right mind would believe she killed my uncle, let alone did the other things I hear were done to him. But some people will do anything to protect a child, won't they?"

She should know. Choosing my words carefully, I said, "I was surprised when I found out that your mother allowed your uncle to stay on the property, considering the fact that your children were there, too."

"Mother never did have any sense where he was concerned." She looked down at the paper in her hands. Judging from the Clydesdales trotting across the top, it was for beer.

I did some quick math in my head. Shana was in her late thirties and could possibly have come in contact with Wycoff before he went to prison.

"Did you ever have any problems with your uncle?"

"He lived in Scottsdale, we lived up here."

"Your mom never took you with her when she visited?"

"No." She wouldn't look at me.

"You were never alone with him?"

"No, I said!"

I found her denials interesting since Mario had told me the opposite—that Grace had taken the young Shana to visit Brian and Norma at least once. But it was time to back away. "Okay. When you were growing up, what did your mother tell you about him?"

"Only that he went to prison for something he didn't do."

"He pled guilty."

Finally meeting my eyes, she said, "Mom told me he was framed, that he'd been the perfect big brother to her. Protective. Honest. Upright. All that denial shit. Over the years she talked about how wonderful he was and wanted me to let him meet Bethany as soon as he got out, to let them get to know each other, that every little girl deserved to have a loving uncle. How's that for a laugh?"

I winced. "Why do you think she wanted that?"

Addressing the Clydesdale poster on the wall, she said, "I'm a marketing major, not a shrink, but my guess is that Mom was still trying to convince herself he was innocent, that he never hurt any child. I think she wanted to use some hoped-for relationship with my daughter to prove that he was as normal as she wanted to believe, not the sicko he actually was. But I wasn't having any of it. In fact, I told her that if she ever let him anywhere near Bethany that I'd never speak to her again."

Shana's voice, which had started out strongly enough, was beginning to sound like it was coming through gravel, so I decided to give her a breather. "Pretty horses, aren't they, those Clydesdales?"

She blinked and looked away from the poster. "I guess. I'm just not into horses."

"I used to ride all the time but now I'm too busy."

"Too busy isn't good."

"You should know. I've seen you tend bar."

She brightened. "You ought to see what it's like in an ad agency. I'm an expert at busy."

"Is advertising anything like that old TV program, *Mad Men?*"

"Worse." She laughed again. "And the men aren't as good-looking."

Now that she had calmed, I eased back to the subject, careful to keep it away from her own possible history with Wycoff.

"You're very protective of your children, aren't you?"

"Every mother is."

But not yours, I wanted to say. "When you warned your mom about letting Bethany near your uncle, how'd she take it?"

"Not well."

"Shana, you know I've interviewed her and your father, and I know that she would have taken Bethany out to the Winnebago if Luke hadn't stepped in to stop her."

She looked down at her turquoise rings. "Yeah." Then she looked back up. "Luke told me."

"How did you feel about that?"

Staring at me like I was the biggest idiot in the world, she said, "How do you think I felt? *Still* feel?"

I started to reply, but she shook herself, and said, "Let's forget about my mother. She needs help. Or medication. Or something. But it's over now, thank God, and the creep got what he deserved. But like I said before, there's no way Debbie or even Cyril was responsible. If I were you, I'd start looking at that redheaded lawyer who's staying at Debbie's place."

"You know Nicole Bertran?"

"I've served her margaritas. Her and that other gal, Jacklyn, I think her name is. The biker chick always walking around with a pistol strapped to her hip."

The average person would consider a gun-toting biker chick more prone to commit acts of violence than an attorney, so the fact that Shana had singled out Nicole piqued my interest. "What makes you think Ms. Beltran might have been involved in your uncle's murder?"

"Just something I heard her say."

"Which was?"

Brushing her hair back, she looked down at the Budweiser invoice again. "This is all wrong."

"That invoice or the conversation?"

She actually laughed. "The invoice. But it's wrong for you to suspect Debbie, too. That attorney, here's what she said, and the guys who were sitting in the booth next to hers when she said it will back me up. She said that whoever took him out—my uncle being the 'him' in question—would be doing the world a favor."

I showed my skepticism with my own laugh. "That doesn't exactly boil down to a death threat, Shana. Plenty of people have said the same thing about other pains-in-their-asses, but they never did anything about it."

Eyes narrowing, she leaned forward. "I doubt few of them added that this particular pain-in-the-ass should be castrated prior to being taken out."

There was little more I could get out of Shana after that, so I left Coyote Corral after first giving Red Beard and Burley two twenties as a donation toward replacing Jeff Somebody's washed-away trailer. As I pulled out of the parking lot, I decided Shana had a point. I needed to take a better look at Nicole Bertran. Maybe Brian Wycoff had been in prison when her Candice was taken, but that didn't mean she had no motive. Shana had been right about something else, too. Anyone who had ever had a loved one molested or kidnapped or killed would be good at bearing grudges. Kill-worthy grudges.

And from what I had seen of Nicole, she had enough steel in her spine to act on them.

Cyril Sanders lived in a small adobe house perched halfway up a hill two miles from Debbie's Desert Oasis. Given his reputed drinking problem, I was surprised to see how well the property was kept up. Fresh pink paint on the adobe and matching garage, no cannibalized vehicles on cinder blocks, just an un-rusted chain-link fence to keep two noisy but well-groomed toy poodles from running off to play on I-17. Having had my ankles gnawed on by their kindred before, I respected their warning yips and didn't enter the yard, just yelled at the house.

"Cyril? Roseanne? Anybody home?"

After a few seconds, the snow white door opened and a large woman wearing a flower-print housedress looked out. "Whatcha want?" she yelled back.

I flashed my ID, not that she could read it from this distance. "Lena Jones, private investigator! I'd like to talk to you! And your husband!"

She thought about that for a moment, then yelled again, "This about that dead guy?"

"Yes!" No point in being coy.

"Guess you'll hafta come on in then."

I gestured toward the pint-sized dogs. "They bite?"

"Nobody lately!"

I took a deep breath, opened the gate, and hurried across the yard, trailed by two yipping poodles. "They're not all that fast, are they?" I said, scooting into the house.

Roseanne smirked. "Shoulda told you they don't hardly have any teeth left. Fifteen years old, same litter. When they was pups, they was hell on wheels. You wouldn't a made it halfway across the yard before they brought you down."

The tidiness of the house's exterior was matched by its interior. Spotless mauve carpet, spotless flowered sofa—almost the same print as Roseanne's housedress—spotless matching chairs, magazines arranged in a neat pile on the unscuffed coffee table, no dust bunnies under the mahogany tallboy, a row of well-dusted family photographs perfectly aligned along the far wall. The only thing that didn't appear to belong in this Temple of Clean was the bleary-eyed man slumped in one of the chairs. Yellow-skinned and wizened except for his pot belly, shaggy-haired and five o'clock shadowed, he looked like thirty miles of bad road and smelled like it, which explained the miasma of lemon-scented air freshener that hung about the room.

"Mr. Sanders?" I asked.

"Yer."

I took that to be a yes.

"Don't just stand there gawking, Miss Private Investigator," Roseanne said, plopping her heavy body on the flowered sofa while gesturing to the other chair. "Sit yourself down and ask him what you come here to ask."

"Cyril, did you ever have any trouble with the Genoveses?"

Before answering, he flicked a look at his wife. At her nod, he said, "Naw."

"How about Brian Wycoff?"

"Piece a shit."

His wife nodded again.

"You knew he was in town?"

"Everbody and his dog did. Mario 'n Grace screaming all over the damned bar 'bout it." He sniffed. "Like I said, piece a shit."

"I hear your daughter was abducted once."

Cyril's bleary eyes got blearier.

Before I could remark on it, Roseanne interjected, "We don't talk about that 'round here. B'sides, she's living with her mama now. Out of state."

"But…"

"'But' your ass, Miss Private Investigator. Keep talkin' 'bout that and I'll haul that ass right outta here." She had the heft to do it, too.

I changed tactics. "Mr. Sanders, did you hold any grudges against Mr. Wycoff?"

He waved a blue-veined hand. "Wasn't nothing for me to hold a grudge about."

I shot a nervous glance toward Roseanne, who I now realized was more Cyril's caretaker than his wife. Then I said, "He had, um, problems with children, I hear."

Roseanne made a noise somewhere between a throat-clearing and a growl but otherwise didn't move, so I was still safe.

"Yer. Piece a shit shoulda got strung up years ago."

"I'm with you there," I said.

An agreeing grunt from Roseanne.

"You know anybody who might have had it in for him?"

"Who didn't?"

Well, that was the question, wasn't it? Who *didn't* feel justi-fied in ushering—to quote Cyril, "a piece a shit"—into the next world? Count me among the crowd, although I'd have dispatched Papa Brian without the additional ruffles and flourishes.

"Maybe, in your, ah, travels around town you heard some talk?"

"Naw."

Roseanne, in a kindlier voice than earlier, said, "He gets to drinking, he don't hear much."

"You ever go out with him, maybe? Hear something yourself?"

She gave me a sad look. "I told him when we was first married that he'd have to kill himself without me, so no. I don't never go out with him to any of his bars."

"But you picked him up at the Coyote Corral the night Wycoff was murdered."

"Always do that. Otherwise he'd kill hisself on the road, maybe some other poor soul, too."

"When you picked him up, did Mario or his daughter say anything about maybe one of their customer looking upset and leaving early?"

"Mario didn't. We was too busy pouring Cyril into my car."

"How about Shana? Maybe she heard something while Mario was getting food from the kitchen."

"Shana? Naw. She wasn't there."

Careful not to let my surprise show, I asked, "Do you mean she didn't help get Cyril to your car, or that she wasn't there period?"

Roseanne shrugged. "Don't know for sure, just that I was under the impression she'd already taken off. "

I had to be careful not to alert Roseanne to the fact that the night of Wycoff's murder, I'd seen Shana leaving the Genovese ranch in the pickup truck with Mario. "I was under the impression she drove home with her father."

"Ain't hard for a pretty girl like Shana to catch a ride from one of the customers. They'd be fallin' all over themselves to play Sir Galahad."

And Shana's father would be just as eager to cover up for her. I filed Roseanne's information away for further use.

"One more question. You ever hear anything odd, and I'm including guesses here, about Wycoff's murder from visitors, maybe someone who stopped by just to chat?"

She shook her head. "Don't nobody come to see us, 'cept Cyril's daughter once. She was gonna stay for a week, stayed two days, went on back to Indiana. Couldn't take the memories, I guess. As for the rest of them…" She shrugged. "…they stay away unless they're dragging him home. Don't blame them none, either."

I felt a stab of pity for her. "But you keep a beautiful house."

Her laugh was bitter. "Place is just a house." Then she motioned with a callused hand toward the bleary-eyed wreck in the chair. "That thing over there, wherever he is, that's my home."

Life wasn't fair, I reminded myself as I pulled away from the Sanders' neat little house. Hardly a news bulletin, but I couldn't remember any investigation where one perpetrator—or two, if you counted Norma—had permanently damaged the lives of so many people. Besides me, Wycoff had victimized at least six other foster children: Errol Bidley, Gayle Mitter, Molly Arness, Tamara Clemson, Casey Starr, Magda Wallace, and possibly many more who never summoned up the courage to come forward. And then there was Wycoffs' own family: his sister, Grace, and her husband, Mario; his niece Shana, his attempt on Bethany, stopped only by young Luke. Not to mention Guy DeLucca, the social worker who had…

I slammed on the brakes before shock made me run off the road and send the Jeep tumbling down the hillside. After catching my breath I steered over to the shoulder and sat there thinking.

Guy DeLucca.

When I had talked to him, he said something odd, something that I paid no attention to at the time, but my unconscious mind had glommed onto it and wouldn't let go. We'd been talking about the Wycoffs' other foster children and how they were getting on with life when he said, *"You've done the best of them all."*

Earlier, he'd told me about following my career, which meant he knew about the bullet I still carried in my hip from a botched drug raid, knew about a different perp at a different time shooting me in the shoulder, knew about my almost dying in the desert, and even that I'd been placed in an anger management program after my attack on an abusive mother in a parking lot.

Yet he'd said, *"You've done the best of them all."*

Which meant DeLucca thought I—with all my problems—had done better than Magda Wallace, the beautifully-put-together flight attendant. Better than Casey Starr, dot.com millionaire and seemingly contented husband.

What did DeLucca know that I didn't?

Chapter Twenty-one

As soon as I returned to the butterfly trailer, I called DeLucca. Although he was polite, he pretty much told me to mind my own business.

"Lena, leave Magda and Casey alone. They've had enough problems."

"What kind of problems?"

"Sorry, but I can't help you." His voice was kind but firm as he ended the call.

I had brought my laptop with me but a quick search for Magda Wallace Pierce and Casey Starr revealed little more than the fact that Magda had been married and divorced twice, and that she had a habit of accumulating speeding tickets. As for Starr, he remained pure as the driven snow.

I don't trust pure.

Picking up my cell again, I called Jimmy, who promised to run a more detailed search on Magda and Casey. To cover all my bases I also added the names of Shana Genovese Ferris, and Nicole Beltran. Then I asked, "How's Snowball?"

A chuckle. "Snowball is fine. Your drapes, not so much."

"Do you think he misses me?" The minute the words were out of my mouth I realized how dumb they sounded.

"Let me ask him since he's right here on my lap shredding my jeans. Hey, Snowball, do you miss Lena?" A pause. "Snowball says he misses you and wants you to hurry home."

"Tell him I miss him, too." People can be such fools about animals.

Jimmy didn't laugh as he said, "Snowball, Lena misses you."

I thought I heard a purr. Or maybe it was just the sound of denim ripping.

Later that night as I lay in Monarch's comfy bed, I wondered how I'd wound up with a cat instead of a Rottweiler. Or maybe a German shepherd. Or a Doberman. Something that, given the business I was in, would be more useful. But a cat?

Belatedly, I realized that Casey Starr had a rare gift for manipulation. When he first asked me if I had ever considered having a pet I'd told him the story of Sandy, the stray dog I took in while living with the Wycoffs. Every time I threatened to tell the authorities what was going on, Brian threatened to kill my dog if I did. So I'd told Starr—an equal sufferer under the Wycoffs' regime—I would never own a pet again, would never again allow another creature to have a hold over me.

Yet I'd left the Starr household with a kitten in my arms.

When I woke up the next morning thin rays of sunlight were creeping through Monarch's windows. I checked my watch. Almost six. I climbed out of bed, put on loose running clothes, and headed out with my .38 secured in its fanny pack.

The world looks so hopeful at sunrise. The air is clean, birds sing, frogs hush their complaints, and coyotes stop their slaughter of innocent bunnies and head home to bed. It's all a lie, of course. The world is as vicious in daylight as it is at night.

Brian Wycoff had only raped me during daylight.

As I crested the hill that overlooked the Genovese spread, I saw Luke and his grandfather in the pasture below, giving extra feed to the horses and cattle. From their house, a soft breeze carried the sound of George Strait singing "If You Ain't Lovin' You Ain't Livin'". Such a peaceful country morning.

Following Luke's earlier directions, my run took me to the half-hidden trail Wycoff's killer had taken. The police presence had long since disappeared, but a solitary piece of yellow crime-scene tape remained stuck on a barrel cactus. Like the crime scene techs before me, I scanned the now well-trampled ground, hoping to find something they might have missed. Nothing. Disappointed, I continued down the hillside without finding anything to contradict what appeared to be little more than an innocent footpath. When I reached the bottom of the hill where the trail abutted the far end of the Genovese property, I'd still found nothing other than an additional piece of tape caught in a creosote bush. By now Mario and his grandson had returned to their house and the only sounds from the pasture were the lowing of cattle.

Disappointed, I turned around and jogged back up the hill toward Monarch for a shower and change of clothes. But less than twenty yards from the top, I heard hoof beats, the rattle and clink of bridles, and the soft whuffle of horses' nostrils. A baritone cautioned everyone to form a single file because the trail was about to narrow.

I knew that voice.

Since there was no nearby bush large enough to hide behind, I moved onto the side of the trail and steeled myself for the encounter. Mere seconds later, a Stetson-hatted wrangler topped the rise, leading a mostly female group of tourists on a morning trail ride.

"That's some nice piece of horseflesh you're riding, Dusty," I said.

No lie there. The bay mare the cheating son of a bitch was astride could have won a confirmation class at a statewide quarter horse show, but considering Dusty's spotty employment record, I doubted the mare belonged to him. Probably to the owner of the Red Rock Ranch.

Allowing his shock to show for only a second, Dusty reined in only a couple feet away from me and gestured for the others to stop. "Why, if it isn't Lena Jones! What a delight to meet you here, Hon."

I wanted to point out that I was no longer his "Hon," but there was no point in embarrassing him in front of paying customers.

"Gonna be a hot one, isn't it?" I commented. If nothing else, talking about Arizona's weather was a good conversational default when you couldn't say what you wanted to say.

A blonde and a redhead had not followed his instructions to rein in until they'd maneuvered their horses beside his. Both appeared besotted by their handsome trail guide. Dusty's brief look of annoyance at the two women faded quickly. He was paid to be charming, but the women—in their late forties or early fifties—were on the outer edge of his preferred age range.

"Weather's always hot in August, Lena. So what brings you to Black Canyon City? And don't tell me you're just fishing."

"Then I won't. Haven't you been keeping up with the news?"

He jerked his head toward the other riders as a warning not to say too much. "You know me. Always too busy to read the papers. Especially when the weather's this nice in the mornings."

Another lie from the Prince of Lies. Despite Dusty's "Aw shucks" cowpoke demeanor, I happened to know that he started every day drinking a pot of black coffee—straight, no chaser—while watching CNN. He also read the local newspapers, so there was no doubt in my mind that he knew exactly why I was here. I was about to bid him a polite goodbye and continue my run back to Monarch when he made me an offer that he knew perfectly well I couldn't refuse.

Leaning closer from the saddle, he whispered, "This group's leaving at noon, and the next one doesn't arrive until Saturday. Wanna ride this mare tomorrow morning?"

Instead of cheering, which I felt like doing, I forced a frown. "I doubt your boss would allow a total stranger up on that beauty."

Still whispering, he answered, "Boss, my ass. Arabella's mine, won her in a poker game over in Sedona last year. She took first prize in Western Pleasure at the Tri-State Quarter Horse Show, and her owner got so drunk celebrating, it put him off his game.

So how about it, Hon? This pretty lady's got a canter that'll make you think you've died and gone to heaven."

For a ride on that mare I would even put up with my cheating ex-boyfriend. Sighing, I asked, "What time? And stop calling me 'Hon!'"

A wink. "Be at the barn at six, Hon."

More fishermen and hikers had moved into the other trailers during the night and they were already chowing down in the breakfast room when I arrived, freshly showered. Nicole Beltran was serving up a generous helping of herbed scrambled eggs, cottage fries, and only slightly burned toast. I sat across from one of the hikers, a friendly, sturdy-looking woman who introduced herself as Nancy Miller-Borg. Several times during our conversation, she paused to pick a piece of broken eggshell off her tongue.

"I heard the food here was good," she said, frowning at her plate.

"It usually is but the regular cook is, ah, indisposed." *Like locked up at the Prescott jail.*

Misunderstanding, she said, "Let's hope he or she feels better soon."

"Crossing my fingers."

Miller-Borg must have been raised well because before she grabbed her backpack and headed for the trails, she said to Nicole, "Lovely breakfast. Thank you."

As for myself, I picked my way around pieces of eggshell while berating myself for having a weakness for horses and two-timing cowboys. I was about to call the Red Rock and cancel when my cell rang. Jimmy.

"You're up bright and early," I said. "And what's that noise in the background?"

"Didn't get much sleep. Snowball kept trying to smother me. As for the noise you hear, he's still trying. Either he's draped over my head and playing with my hair like he is now, or he's lying across my face. I can hardly breathe."

"You're still in bed?"

"He bites my nose every time I try to get up. Anyway, as per your request, before I slept in your apartment last night to keep the vicious little thing company, I did some checking on those names you gave me."

"Get anything useful?"

"Only if you think the fact that Magda Pierce, who was once Mrs. Elroy Grice, once ran down a man with her Cadillac Escalade. He just happened to be a convicted child molester."

I almost spit out my burned toast. "Are you serious?!"

"Serious as a heart attack. Hit him with her car while she was living in Dallas, Texas. Luckily enough for her, several witnesses said the guy wasn't in the crosswalk and the lovely Magda had the light, and thus the law, on her side. She also wasn't speeding, wasn't impaired, just braked the Escalade a couple of seconds too late."

I thought about that for a moment, replaying the accident in my mind. It didn't look right. "What was victim's story?"

"He said zip since he was DOA at the hospital. Before you ask, I checked but couldn't find any prior connection between Magda and the squashed-flat-as-a-bug-in-the-proverbial-rug Joseph Fellows."

"When was this?"

"Ten years ago, a week before Magda's husband filed for divorce."

"He divorced her right after the accident?"

"Exactamundo. Now listen to this. Magda's second husband—one James Basker Pierce—divorced her, too, claiming spousal abuse. He made his case well enough that she didn't get one penny from the sale of their house; her share was applied toward his medical expenses. She served thirty days, he still walks with a limp."

"Holy shit!"

"I'm guessing that's what Mr. Pierce said when he saw the hospital bill."

So the seemingly together flight attendant had serious anger management issues, and had once run down a convicted child molester. Boy, do I hate coincidences.

"Then there is Shana Genovese Ferris," Jimmy continued. "Quite the gal, it appears, our Shana." A long pause.

"Don't be coy with me, Jimmy. Spit it out."

"Before she married her now ex-husband, she received two citations for prostitution, both in Scottsdale. Seems she catered to the upscale crowd."

Since private investigators are not unacquainted with life's dirty underbelly, I don't know why I was surprised, but I was. On the other hand, given the behavior of her disturbed mother, her childhood must have been less than idyllic. In fact, I'd have bet my Jeep against a hip-switching Chevy Corvair that Wycoff had molested Shana, too.

"That's bad," was all I could say.

As he always is where women are concerned, Jimmy was quick to leap to Shana's defense. "Both citations came right after two hospitalizations for injuries suffered at the hands of her boyfriend. He was a druggie and didn't care how he got his drug money, even if it meant prostituting the love of his life. The second hospitalization turned out to be the charm, because that's when Ms. Ferris fled to a women's shelter, then began taking classes at ASU, where she met her future husband. They opened an ad agency together, and everything seemed to be coming up roses for her until he began taking an interest in the female employees. She eventually took the kids and moved back in with her parents, where I take it she still resides?" He ended the last in the form of a question.

"Yeah, she's up here in Black Canyon City with them and is working at their restaurant. Temporarily, she says. Now what about Casey Starr?"

"Nothing."

Somehow that surprised me more than any of the other information. "Did you dig? I mean, *really* dig?"

He sounded vaguely offended when he said, "Dug my way to China and came up with nothing but a battered copy of Chairman Mao's *Little Red Book*. Oh, by the way, as soon as Casey turned eighteen, he changed his name from Richfield to Starr. Didn't want to be associated with his parents, I guess. Other than his encounter with the legal system at Wycoff's trial, your boy's clean."

"Try again."

A long silence. Then, "Sure. I've got plenty of time to waste." With that, he ended the call.

Temporarily stymied, I sat there for a while thinking as the breakfast room emptied out. Everything about this investigation seemed off. Madga Pierce, one of Wycoff's victims, had killed a child molester, whether accidentally or not. Magda also had a record for domestic violence. Shana Genovese may or may not have been at the Coyote Corral when he was murdered. Yet Debbie Margules, who suspected Wycoff of abducting her long-disappeared daughter, hit the murder trifecta with motive, method, and opportunity. As much as I liked Debbie, maybe she had killed him, after all.

But if I could find anything to weaken the case against her, I would.

I sat there and thought some more. Almost an hour later, all that thinking had availed me little but one idea had insinuated itself into my exhausted brain. I picked up my phone again.

"What now?" Jimmy sounded annoyed, as well he should.

"Run a check on Casey Starr's wife."

"Kay Starr? Why?"

"Just a hunch."

"Lena, you do realize Mrs. Starr heads up the Engineering Department at Phoenix College, and you don't attain that kind of position with a criminal record."

"It never pays to ignore a hunch, okay?"

A sigh, then a click.

Feeling guilty about piling another set of background checks on my work-swamped partner, I went into the kitchen to ask Nicole if she needed help with the dishes.

Despite her glowing skin, Nicole didn't appear happy, which wasn't surprising since she had more dishes than the dishwasher had room for. "This is the first time in years I've had to do this."

"You must eat off paper plates."

She gave me an odd look. "Of course not. I just stack everything in the dishwasher and run it every few days."

"You're more domestic than me, then." I eyed a dish towel hanging from a peg above the sink. "Want me to dry?"

"As long as you know how."

We worked in amiable silence for the next few minutes, but when we reached the last skillet, Nicole turned to me and said, "How would you feel if I asked you to help me straighten out a couple of trailers?"

I smiled my answer.

The job turned out not to be as onerous as I'd expected. Nancy Miller-Borg, the hiker in Mustang, was a neat type who made her own bed, and the two guys in Fishin' Frenzy were cleaner than fishermen had a right to be. Since Debbie enforced a non-smoking policy for each of the trailers, we didn't have to sanitize the hell out of them, just empty the garbage, change the linens, clean the toilet, and spritz a little air freshener around.

"You look quite the professional," Nicole said to me as we carried a heap of dirty towels through the trees toward the yellow house.

I smiled. "You, too. There's something about mindless activity that's rather relaxing, isn't there?"

"Almost as good as yoga."

"I'm not sure I'd go that far." I'd tried yoga once, but my hyperactive mind refused to let me torture my body as much as the instructor demanded. As for relaxing, applying liniment to my aching muscles after that first and only yoga session had mitigated the so-called relaxation.

This was what I needed. Nature's balm. Above us, the sky was a clear blue and birds were in full song. Other than the crunch of a car's tires traveling the gravel road at the edge of Debbie's property, the pine-scented morning was uninterrupted by the usual noise pollution of modern life. How had I let myself get so far away from it?

"What do you think that's supposed to be?"

Nicole's voice startled me out of my reverie. We were just crossing the small meadow where one of Debbie's larger sculptures stood, the six feet-and-something conglomeration of iron, bronze, pipe fittings, and rocks. As I'd noted before, the piece didn't seem to be representative of anything, and the bronze plate on its stone base merely said MEMORY. An aura of sadness enveloped it.

In answer to Nicole's question, I said, "No clue, but one of my foster mothers, an artist, taught me that when it comes to art, we don't have to 'understand' a piece in order to like it."

Obviously not sharing my reaction to MEMORY, Nicole grimaced. "Non-objective art isn't my cup of…"

A spurt of dust kicked up a few feet in front of us. A nanosecond later I heard a loud pop.

Instinctively, I dropped the pile of laundry I was holding and grabbed Nicole. Not recognizing the noise, she stood stock-still, looking toward the origin of the sound. Ignoring her protests, I pulled her with me to the ground behind MEMORY.

"Lena, what…?"

I put my mouth close to her ear. "Duck your head and be quiet."

When she started to speak again, I clamped my hand over her mouth, hoping she wouldn't bite me. She didn't, but began to struggle, so I tightened my hold on her.

Nicole continued to struggle even when she saw two more dust spurts rise from the ground, followed quickly by two more pops. City girl.

"Someone's shooting at us," I whispered in her ear.

Fear has a smell. Sharp. Acrid. It rose off her in rank waves, but she stopped struggling. Having been through this sort of thing several times during my career, I stopped worrying and slipped my .38 out of my pocket holster.

Due to the dense vegetation, I could see nothing. The tree line was approximately five yards away, interspersed with clusters of creosote, sage, and other brush. It provided cover for the shooter, leaving us only MEMORY, and as large as the sculpture was, it wasn't enough. Although I hated the idea of a firefight with the unarmed Nicole beside me, I had no choice. At least I could draw the shooter's fire away.

"Stay quiet and no matter what happens, don't move," I whispered to Nicole.

Her eyes remained wide in fear, but she didn't make a sound, just nodded. With that, I bent myself double and rushed toward the trees, expecting at any moment to receive a bullet in my back for my trouble. It didn't happen. I reached the cover of the trees unscathed, but to my dismay, the woods that had seemed so peaceful earlier now seemed to broadcast every step I took. Because of the monsoon the other night, the forest floor was littered with debris, and there was simply no step I could take without rustling leaves or snapping a twig. Where was all that birdsong now that I needed it? Even the hum of insects might have helped, but it seemed as if the entire world had fallen silent at the shooter's intrusion.

Well-hidden now, I snapped off two quick shots toward the shooter's last location.

No returned fire. No cry of pain.

I looked over at MEMORY. Nicole had followed my instructions, and although I could see the edge of her sleeve, most of her body remained hidden behind the sculpture.

Guessing that he—at least I surmised the shooter was a he—had arrived in the car I'd heard earlier, I inched in the direction of the road, hoping to circle around him.

Then, just as I was tippy-toeing past a stunted pine, I heard the sound of running feet.

A car door slam.

Tires on gravel.

Noise be damned now, I crashed through the underbrush with all the delicacy of a bull elephant and reached the road just in time to see the tail end of a white sedan disappear around the bend at the bottom of the hill. Not only hadn't I managed to get the license plate number, I wasn't even certain the car bore an Arizona plate. Still, I holstered my .38 and grabbed my cell from my other pocket. Breathing heavily, I hit 9-1-1 and within seconds I was talking to a dispatcher. I duly made my report. Once assured a patrol car was on the way, I went back to the meadow to check on Nicole, who by then had emerged from behind MEMORY, her fear transformed into fury.

"Someone shot at us! Three times!"

My pulse had returned to normal, and I tried to calm her. "Whoever it was is gone now and the important thing is that we're okay."

"Fucking hunters!"

I shook my head. "That was no hunter."

Chapter Twenty-two

Not as many officers showed up at the Desert Oasis as had at the scene of Wycoff's murder, but enough rolled in to ensure me that my 9-1-1 call was being taken seriously. In fact, Detective Eastman was serious enough to forgo her usual rendition of "Maria." While she interviewed Nicole and me in the kitchen of the yellow house, two crime techs dug around in the dirt by MEMORY.

"You say you never saw the shooter?" Eastman asked.

"Afraid not."

"Ms. Beltran? How about you?"

"Sorry, Detective. I was too busy ducking to get a good look." Attorneys are made of tough stuff, so Nicole had already regained her calm. Color was back in that beautiful complexion and she even managed a smile.

Eastman wasn't smiling. "The car, Ms. Jones. Any idea of the make?"

"Sorry. It was too far away by the time I made it to the road."

"Do you know how many white sedans there are in Arizona?"

"Most popular car color here since white reflects heat."

She tsk-tsked. "Could you at least tell if it had an Arizona plate?"

"The sedan was kicking up enough dust that I couldn't even see the color."

"Did you…?"

Her question was interrupted by the entrance of a crime tech. "Got a couple," the woman said. "Impact was pretty clean, no rocks, just dirt. Looks like a .22LR, but ballistics can tell us for sure." With that, she bustled off.

A rifle.

Eastman shot a quick look at my handgun, which I'd unloaded and set on the table. I had been concerned she might commandeer the .38—I had, after all, fired it—but the tech's information made me breathe easier. I breathed even easier when she thanked us for our information and left.

Being shot at raises your adrenaline level. Energized, I spent the next few hours in Monarch making phone calls and typing up new case notes.

What, besides gunshots, had I heard? Just branches snapping as the shooter fled. No coughs, no muttered words.

What had I seen? Nothing. Just trees and brush. And that damned white sedan snaking out of sight.

Nothing, in fact, that would be of any use to me or Detective Eastman. No wonder she had looked so disgusted as she drove away.

Typing done, I shut down my laptop and went out for a late afternoon run to burn off the rest of the adrenalin. It didn't go well because by then the temps were high enough that every step was a struggle. To make matters worse, on the way back I skidded on a rock, almost twisting my ankle, and when I finally limped back to the Oasis I felt as disgusted as Eastman. This case was going nowhere, and to top things off, I'd almost gotten myself killed for my trouble, and now I had a swollen ankle.

A half hour and an ice pack later, my ankle and my mood had eased. Finally relaxed, I sat on the trailer steps listening to birdsong and the creek burbling below. From the human voices that floated to me on the wind, I was aware of the Oasis' other guests returning. From their soft laughter and easy banter, I surmised that word about the shooting hadn't yet gone out.

I spent the rest of the day on the steps, enjoying the smell of pine, rushing water, and leafing through a book on Arizona butterflies I found in the nightstand. It included monarchs, of course, those big, beautiful gold and brown things, but also hundreds of other colorful-winged specimens whose Latin names I couldn't even pronounce. *Limenitis arthemis astyanax. Helico-niinae. Speyeria coronis. Euptoieta claudia.* Their brilliance dazzled my eyes, reminding me that I really needed to get out more.

By dinner time I remembered that I hadn't eaten lunch, so I drove over to the Coyote Corral for a couple of tacos. I would have liked to talk to Shana again and ask her some more questions, but the minute she saw me come through the door, she made herself scarce.

I finished my meal and left.

"Why're you lookin' so jumpy, darlin'?" Dusty asked the next morning, as our horses picked their way along the bank of Black Canyon Creek.

"I didn't sleep well last night."

"You know what's good for that, don't you?" He had a sly smile. Before I could answer, he said, "Meditation."

It being a Saturday, I'd expected to be safe from temptation among a trail-riding crowd of tourists, but Dusty had pulled another fast one. The Red Rock Ranch trail ride didn't begin until eight, so I was all alone with one of the most seductive men I'd ever known.

As we rode along, the world woke up.

Knowing Dusty's penchant for gossip, I had decided not to tell him about the gunfight. He would find out about it eventually—but by then I would be back in Scottsdale. In fact, I had originally been tempted to return as soon as Eastman finished interviewing Nicole and me, but the memory of Arabella, Dusty's bay mare, had kept me here. Besides, the clip-clop of horses' hooves is as calming as a kitten's purrs.

How had I become so busy that I'd forgotten the joy being outside with a horse could bring?

The day was perfect. The breeze was soft and pure. Early birds were out getting their worms, and hungry fish were leaping at flies swooping too low near the creek. I needed more of this, but given my schedule, I didn't know how I could manage it. Due to the ongoing spread of development in the outer Phoenix area, riding stables and dude ranches have been pushed further and further away, many of them almost as far as Black Canyon City. But oh, God, what a wonderful thing a horse was! There was something about a horse that renewed my spirit.

Not for the first time it occurred to me that I could purchase my own horse and board her on the Rez. Maybe even buy a horse trailer so we could explore the forests up north, the canyons to the east, the…

"Thinking of me?" Dusty's horse, a buckskin gelding, was nice enough, but nowhere near Arabella's class.

I scowled. "This is a trail ride, not a date."

"Whatever you say." He winked.

The man was incorrigible, but he had his charms. Still, to keep from falling under his spell again, I forced myself to remember his Las Vegas-acquired wife shooting up my apartment, and how much it had cost to replace all that drywall.

Arabella's gaits were as beautiful as her glistening coat, her jog easy to sit to, her canter smooth. Riding her was like sitting on a cloud.

"What are you smiling about now, Hon?"

"I didn't know I was smiling. And don't…"

"Don't call me 'Hon,'" he mimicked. And smiled.

Oh, how could any woman ever refuse this man?

By the time I returned from my ride, I discovered that everything had changed at Debbie's Desert Oasis.

Not only had the sheriff's office returned the backpack they had commandeered from me right after Wycoff's murder, they returned something else, too.

Debbie.

Ballistics tests had confirmed that the bullets the crime scene techs sifted from the dirt in front of MEMORY were a match for the bullets dug out of Norma Wycoff's brain. Unfortunately, ballistics had not been able to match the spent .22 LR bullets to any rifle in the system. As soon as the guilt-ridden Detective Eastman called the Oasis with these good tidings, Nicole—fully recovered from yesterday's scare—had filed a motion to have her friend released. The sheriff joyfully complied.

Still smelling like horse, I joined Nicole and Debbie in their get-out-of-jail-free celebration in the yellow house. Arrayed on the kitchen table in front of us were a Bible, five paperback romances, a box of Godiva chocolates, a giant bag of BBQ-flavored potato chips, numerous Slim Jims, and a homemade red velvet cake with cream cheese frosting.

My third chocolate, a tasty Godiva morsel named Almond Praline Raindrop, almost held its own against the superb red velvet cake.

"This cake's fantastic," Nicole's voice was little more than a mumble since her mouth was stuffed with the red stuff.

I was feeling guilty for even considering the fact that Nicole might have killed the Wycoffs. After all, she'd been shot at along with me. Then again, Nicole had once been a criminal defense attorney and probably still had contacts in that world. Deciding to worry about that later, I turned to Debbie and asked, "Sure you don't want a piece of chocolate? I saved the Raspberry Ganache Twirl for you."

Looking more refreshed than you would expect for a woman who had just spent two days in the slammer, Debbie shook her head.

"That's my second Godiva box. I already scarfed up the one Sheriff Headley gave me right after I got booked. By the way, did you know that good chocolate is more uplifting than cocaine? I sure had a buzz on in that cell, but I'd better settle down now or I won't get any sleep tonight." She took another sip of her chamomile tea.

Since Brian Wycoff was universally loathed, the authorities hadn't wanted to arrest Debbie in the first place, so to make up for doing their lawful duty, gift-bearing visitors would sometimes sneak illicit gifts into her holding cell. The Godivas came from Detective "Maria" Eastman. The Bible, courtesy of the swing shift dispatch officer. The red velvet cake had been baked from scratch by the sheriff's wife, who also passed along the romance novels. The rest of the haul came from other law-breaking officers of the law.

Nicole and I had already packed up for our return to the Valley, the attorney's inn-keeping duties now no longer necessary, but Debbie had insisted that we join her calorie-laden celebration first.

"Good as that cake is, I can't eat it all by myself," she said. "Take some with you."

Not wanting to appear greedy, I demurred. Nicole felt no such delicacy, and when I finally headed out the door to my Jeep, she was wrapping a huge slice of cake to take with her on her own drive back to Scottsdale.

As I drove south toward Phoenix and saguaros replaced scrub pine along I-17, I refused to think about Dusty and my growing desire to rekindle our romance. Instead, I made myself focus on the Wycoff case.

Thanks to my interview with Cyril and his wife, Shana Genovese Ferris' alibi was no longer as tight as before. Despite what Mario Genovese had told me, Shana hadn't helped her father pour the drunken Cyril into Roseanne's car. But Mario Genovese's alibi remained firm. He was definitely still at the bar when Wycoff was murdered. Of course, Roseanne could have been lying, but why would she? The only thing she cared about besides her well-kept home was an alcoholic husband who had been too drunk to squash a cockroach, let alone slowly torture a man to death.

And then there was the handsome, manipulative, too-good-to-be-true Casey Starr. Guy DeLucca, my old social worker, had said to me, "*You've done the best of them all.*" Jimmy had checked him out and he'd come up clean, but what if…?

I shook my head. Impossible.

But maybe not.

I worried about it all the way to Scottsdale, where to my surprise, I found Jimmy bent over his computer, typing furiously away. He greeted me with a smile.

"The traveler returns!"

After driving around in my open-air Jeep in the heat, the air-conditioned office felt like the inside of a glacier. Ignoring the rapidly-rising goosebumps on my arms, I said, "What are you doing here on a Saturday?"

"Making up for the time I spent up at the pow wow."

"Good. Then would you do me a favor and look up Casey Starr again?"

"As I told you before, Lena, I ran the usual check on Casey Starr and the guy's clean. I'm working on his wife now."

"But you know what we forgot? Starr's a major computer whiz, owns an Internet security company. What if he was able to erase his records? Can that be done?"

His smile vanished. "In certain circumstances. Even high school kids have been known to use their computer skills to change their grades, but they leave a trail that's pretty easy to follow back to the originator. If someone on the level of Starr wiped his records, though, there's a good chance those records are gone forever. With no telltale markers."

"Try."

A frown.

"I mean, as soon as you get a chance. I can see you're busy. But in the meantime, could you just get me the address of every place Casey Starr ever lived, starting with the time his daddy got his mommy pregnant?"

An almost canine growl. "Don't want much, do you?"

Abashed, I apologized. ""I just want to make sure Debbie doesn't wind up arrested again. Or Nicole. Now, if you'll excuse me, I'm going to go upstairs and take a cold shower. There was a dust devil crossing I-17 up by Anthem, and the Jeep got the brunt of it."

Actually, I wanted to see how Snowball was doing.

An hour later, dust-free, wearing clean clothes, and sipping on a Tab while a little white kitten purred in my lap, I was still thinking about the case. With Debbie in the clear—for now, anyway—I could in all good conscience walk away from it. I didn't care who'd killed Brian Wycoff. No one cared. My feelings were the same for Norma, his purposely see-no-evil wife. But getting shot at had changed things. The case was now personal.

I had realized during the drive from Black Canyon City, that I should have stopped at the Coyote Corral and re-interviewed Shana, but I hadn't. Speaking of bars, it also occurred to me that I had never interviewed Jacklyn Archerd, the biker chick who supposedly had been bunking in the Mustang trailer when both killings went down. Unlike Nicole, who had stayed to help out at the B&B in Debbie's absence, Jacklyn had pled work obligations and returned to the Valley.

Like so many others, Jacklyn had a motive to kill the Wycoffs since her own son had been kidnapped and God only knows what else had been done to him. Besides that, her holstered Glock proved she was no stranger to firearms. Maybe I should…

My landline rang.

"I've got those addresses for you," Jimmy said. "and it's quite a list. Looks like CPS moved Starr around a lot after his placement with the Wycoffs. That could be a sign of serious behavior problems."

I remembered my own childhood behavior problems, which included breaking a bullying classmate's nose and pouring vinegar into a harsh geometry teacher's Coke. Some incidents were even more serious, so much so it was a miracle I hadn't wound up in a correctional facility. And Casey Starr and I had both endured the same horrors.

"I'll be right down," I told Jimmy, killing the call.

I gave Snowball a final nuzzle and sat him down on the floor. He scampered over to what was left of my drapes and began climbing them again. He liked heights.

When I walked into my office downstairs, Jimmy handed an odd-looking object to me. From the amused expression on his face he'd recovered from his earlier bad temper. My partner never could hold a grudge.

"What's that?" I asked.

"It's called a Sticky Buddy. Pet hair remover. I bought one for myself when I started babysitting Snowball. It's my guess you're about to leave for an interview, and you can't go around looking like that."

I looked down at my black cargo pants and tee shirt. Or rather, *formerly* black cargo pants and tee shirt. They were now covered with fine white cat hairs. "Oh."

"Yeah, oh. Snowball's also why I'm wearing beige, in case you didn't notice."

He was right. I hadn't noticed. His snug-fitting beige tee shirt and beige khakis made a nice contrast to his terra cotta-colored skin, not to mention showcasing his ripped abs and pecs. Forcing myself not to stare at this vision of male perfection, I got busy with the Sticky Buddy. A few minutes later, I said, "How's this?"

"Looks good. Now turn around."

A chortle let me know that I'd forgotten to Sticky Buddy my ass, so I rolled that, too. "Better?"

"All good. Now here's those addresses you wanted, all the foster parents he went through. One additional thing. I tracked down Casey Starr's mother's name. Or names, plural."

I lifted my eyebrows.

"Maiden name, Etta Mae Eloise White. At the age of sixteen, she gave birth to a little girl, father unknown, and gave the baby up for adoption. A couple years later she married a guy named Pete Craddock and had another baby—a son, this time—but kept the kid until CPS stepped in and took it away. She claimed her husband was the one who broke the baby's arm and leg, he said she did it. The upshot of the deal was that they relinquished parental rights, and he was adopted out, too."

"That kid was Casey Starr?"

Jimmy shook his head. "Nope. Turns out, Etta Mae was quite the prolific mama. After losing custody of another child to CPS—her second girl, by the way—she and Craddock wound up divorced. She took back her maiden name and married a few more times, giving birth to three more children by two different husbands and one boyfriend. Names on those birth certificates were, in order, Seth Jepson, Ramsey Heat, and our old buddy Casey Fairfield/Starr. After Baby Jepson died under suspicious circumstances, the next two babies were both removed from her custody at birth."

"Jesus!"

"Yeah, gotta have a license to drive a car, but anyone can be a parent."

"Where's Etta Mae-nee-White now?" I asked.

"OD'ed a year after her last kid was born. She was pregnant at the time."

Jesus was probably tired of getting his name evoked under such circumstances but I did it again.

Indians don't curse, so Jimmy just said, "What a world, huh?"

"Not gonna disagree with you there."

"As to the last kid. Casey. He already had a couple of broken ribs by the time CPS got to him."

I winced. "So Casey's father of record was definitely Richard Fairfield?"

"Etta Mae got around, so without a DNA test, Casey could be anybody's. By the way, Richard Fairfield, better known as Dick, has a lengthy criminal record, including armed robbery and assault. Pistol-whipped some guy during a gas station heist, sentenced to twenty years, released early for good behavior, nothing nasty on his record since. A year after his release he married a woman named Ada. Before you ask, the current Mrs. Fairfield has no record other than a parking ticket, and that was on the day she reported for jury duty and couldn't find an all-day spot.

Dick and Ada have a couple kids—Richard, Jr. and Avalon, female. Twelve and ten, respectively."

After digesting this, I said, "So it looks like Casey Starr wiped his past, but for some reason, left the record of his crappy parentage intact. I wonder why."

Jimmy shrugged. "Prepping for an 'I-had-an-abusive-child-hood-so-that's-why-I'm-a-serial-killer' defense? Who knows what evil lurks in the hearts of men."

"From *The Shadow*. I didn't know you liked old radio shows."

"And the 1994 film remake starring Alec Baldwin. I like a lot of things you don't know about, Lena."

"Apparently so. Did you by any chance come up with Richard Fairfield's last known address?"

He hit the PRINT command, and Fairfield's address, along with several others, slithered out of the printer. Glendale. Where Jacklyn Archerd lived and worked.

Wondering if there was any connection, I put my .38 in its pocket holster, picked up my tote, and left.

Chapter Twenty-three

Casey Starr's supposed biological father lived in a trailer park on the rougher side of Glendale. No charming Debbie's Desert Oasis, Sunrise Acres looked like a place where those who had given up all hope went to die, so it was disconcerting to see a couple of heatstroke-daring children playing on the trailer court's decrepit swing set.

The new Fairfield brood lived at No. 83, a double-wide defaced by several years of rust and wear. I parked the Jeep next to a paint-peeling Dodge Shadow, and rapped on the trailer's door.

The woman who answered wasn't what I expected. Hispanic, somewhere in her forties, she wore an orange fast-food uniform; her nametag announced her as ADA. No beauty, but with her soft brown eyes a shade darker than her lush brown hair, she'd been good-looking enough to attract an ex-con.

"Yes?" she smiled, revealing crooked but white teeth. "What can I do for you?"

The smile faded when I handed her my card and told her the reason for my visit. "Oh. Casey. We haven't seen him in months, God love him. But you might as well come in, not that either of us will be of any help."

You can't tell a book by its cover, and you can't tell a double-wide from its rusting shell. While no Versailles, the living room was spotless and the heavenly scent of homemade chili emanated from the open-plan kitchen. Bright throws cheered up an old leather sofa and matching chairs, and the big coffee table was buried under a mound of library books. The one on top was titled *Nightwatch: A Practical Guide to Viewing the Universe.* That's when I noticed the telescope in the corner.

"I just got home from work," Ada Fairfield explained, "so sorry about the mess."

"What mess?"

She looked around. "The kids haven't been too bad today, have they? Here, have a seat and I'll go get Richard."

Ada waved me to one of the chairs and headed down a narrow hall.

While she was gone, I sifted through the books on the coffee table. Harper Lee's *To Kill a Mockingbird.* Bill Bryson's *A Short History of Nearly Everything.* Diana Gabaldon's *Outlander.* A Julia Child cookbook, a *National Geographic*, a *Scientific American,* and several other science-based magazines. Someone in this trailer was smarter than the average-type bear.

A series of clanks and thumps from the hallway tore me away from my snooping. I looked up to see a tall man dressed for the weather in a Led Zeppelin concert tee shirt and denim cutoffs. He favored his right leg, which was encased in a brace from the ankle to just above the knee. As he drew closer, I could see a flattened nose and a half-gone ear. Prison can be rough on a man's looks. He looked closer to seventy than sixty.

Without preamble, he demanded, "You accusing my son of killing that son of a bitch?"

"Just a few routine questions."

He snatched my card from his wife and scowled at it. "Just routine, my ass." A bitter laugh. "Hold your horses while I go stir the damned chili, then I'll come back and properly tell you to mind your own business. Not gonna ask you to stay for dinner, neither."

"Dick," Ada reproved, "don't be rude."

He turned to her, a fierce look on his battered face. "And don't you..." At her expression, the fierceness faded into shame. "Sorry." Turning to me again, he muttered, "Sorry to you, too. Want some chili? Made enough to feed an army."

"No thanks."

He looked relieved. "Be right back."

While Fairfield fussed with the chili, Ada sat on the chair next to mine and leaned forward. "His leg's bothering him, and that makes him cranky, but we've agreed he will not take pain-killers. He's going in for an acupuncture treatment tomorrow and that should help some."

Sharing the usual cop's cynicism toward "reformed" criminals and the women who made excuses for them, I merely nodded.

Chili stirred, Fairfield clanked back into the living room area and collapsed on the sofa, his braced leg sticking straight out. "Okay, Miss Jones. What you want to know?"

"Tell me about Casey."

A hint of pride entered his voice. "My boy's doing great. Brains oozing out of his ears."

"Like both of Dick's other children," Ada interjected.

"I know how successful Casey is, but what about when he was younger and in foster care?"

Fairfield paused, then said, "All kids go through a stage."

"Can't argue with that. What kind of a stage did Casey go through?"

"Damned if…Uh, darned if I know, seeing how I was in prison through most of the time he was fostered out."

"Even in prison you must have heard things."

When he shrugged, his wife gave him a worried look. "Only that he borrowed a couple of cars for some joy-riding. Nothing serious."

No car thefts had appeared on Casey Starr's juvenile record, thus proving my suspicion that he'd used his hacker skills to wipe it clean. "Anything else? Violence, for instance?"

"Nah." Fairfield shot a quick look toward his wife, who suddenly found something of interest on the perfectly vacuumed carpet.

"He had a bad time in foster care, didn't he?" *Such as being raped by Brian Wycoff.*

A shame-faced expression was Fairfield's only reply.

"Tell me about your ex-wife."

"Etta Mae? Crack addict, not that I have any right to judge. Still, I shoulda divorced her earlier. Come to that, I never shoulda got mixed up with her in the first place. Paid too much attention to how good-looking she was."

"Pretty is as pretty does," Ada said, her face rigid with disapproval.

I agreed with her. "When did you find out Etta Mae was abusing Casey?"

"When he got taken away."

"You didn't notice before?"

He looked like he was about to cry. "Etta Mae said he was clumsy, always falling over things. And me, I had my own problems going right about then."

Such as a heavy meth habit. "Did you ever try to get your son back?"

"Told you. I was in prison."

"How'd you feel when you found out he'd changed his last name?"

He shrugged. "Can't say I blame him. Who wants to walk around named after an ex-con? Kid needed a fresh start."

"You felt no resentment about that?"

"When I walked out of the prison, guess who was waiting for me in a brand new Cadillac? My boy, that's who." He cleared his throat, then clanked to his feet. "Now excuse me, 'cause I gotta go stir the chili again. And check on the rice and the corn. Complete protein's important for growing kids. Gonna finish up the cornbread, too, and get started on the salad."

"Dick's a wonderful cook," Ada offered as her husband clanked into the kitchen. "Last night we had chicken crepes for a main dish and peach crepes for dessert. But the kids…"

The door to the trailer opened and two neatly dressed children walked in. The boy, a handsome younger version of Fairfield, was lugging a stack of library books and vanished with them down the hall without so much as a look around. The girl headed straight for the telescope and began fiddling with it.

"Super moon's tonight," she said to her mother. "Dad said he'll drive me further out in the desert where the city lights won't bother us. We want to take a better look at the Copernicus Crater, see if I can tell…" Belatedly she noticed me. "Oh. Hello. I'm Avalon. And you are?"

"Lena Jones, I'm a…"

"Private detective. Saw you on the news once, you took down some guy after he'd murdered three people. Major *cajones*, you!"

"Language!" Ada reproved.

"Sorry," the girl said, not sorry at all. "But why're you here? Is Casey in trouble again?"

"Avalon!" her father yelled from the kitchen. "What did I tell you?"

The girl grinned. "Oops." To her father, she said, "Chili night, right?"

Fairfield clanked back into the living area. "Chili it is, with homemade jalapeño cornbread. Now go clean up."

"But I already…"

"Obey your father," Ada said.

After throwing her mother a dirty look, the girl skulked off down the hall.

"What did she mean when she said Casey was 'in trouble again'?" I asked Fairfield.

"Avalon's got an over-active imagination. Both kids do. Now, uh, sorry, but I'm going to have to ask you to leave. Dinner's done and we're getting ready to eat."

With that, he politely but firmly steered me to the door before I could ask him if he knew a biker chick named Jacklyn Archerd.

Jacklyn Archerd worked the day shift at a bar called the Iron Cross, and I doubted she'd be home yet, so I decided to talk to her at her place of business. You learn a lot when you catch people at work.

The Iron Cross was on Glendale Boulevard, across town from the Fairfields' trailer, tucked away in a strip mall that had seen better days. There were more Harleys in the parking lot than cars, so my senses went on high alert. As I entered the bar, a wall of sound and smell hit me. Bob Seger's "Against the Wind" played at an ear-bleeding level on a cheap sound system. The acrid odor of sour beer and sweat was almost, but not quite, overpowered by the tang of Lysol. It took a few moments for my eyes to adjust to the bar's dark interior, but when I did, I saw several rough-looking men clustered around a pool table, at least a dozen more at the tables. Most shared pitchers of beer, but a few holdouts clutched longnecks. The jackets hanging on the chairs had the name MOGULS emblazoned on the back.

Jacklyn Archerd appeared to be the only woman in the place, unless you counted the naked pole dancer grinding away to Seger's raspy baritone. Her eyeliner was black and so was her lipstick. She didn't look happy to see me, but then neither did anyone else. As I crossed the room, all conversation stopped— never a good sign.

"You shouldn't be in here," Jacklyn said when I reached the bar. She was in black leather again, which looked more appropriate at the Iron Cross than it had at Daisy's Desert Oasis. She still wore her Glock on her hip. I wondered if she wore it in bed, too.

I could hardly hear her over Seger's yowls, so I said, "Is there someplace we can talk in private? Someplace quieter?"

She waved a tattooed arm, taking in the crowded room. "This is it, other than the john or the stockroom, but I can't leave the bar, anyway."

"You the only one here?"

She gave me an incredulous look. "Do I look like I have a death wish? Rollo and Gus are in the stockroom taking inventory."

"What time do you get off?"

Checking her watch, she said, "In forty-five minutes, and I'm going straight home. Didn't get much sleep last night, what with…" Then she thought better of what she was about to say and made a sharp segue. "I live at…"

It's never wise to let someone know you've already been checking them out, I let her finish giving me her address, and told her I'd meet her there in an hour and a half. It would give her time to shower off Eau de Iron Cross.

I had been starved ever since smelling Fairfield's chili, so I killed time at a Mexican eatery on Glendale Boulevard about a stone's throw from Jacklyn's house. The beef enchiladas were a cardiologist's nightmare, smothered in cheese and served with a huge helping of cheese-covered refried beans. To make the meal more heart-healthy, I dug deep into the fresh tomato salsa with greasy tortilla chips.

My mouth was full of enchilada when my cell buzzed. Jimmy.

"Got some info for you."

"Mph," I said.

"You eating?"

"Mph."

"Here goes, then, and you don't have to talk back. Nicole Beltran, that real estate attorney you wanted me to look up? Clean record, of course, since the ABA isn't big on admitting felons. No minor infractions, either, other than a couple of speeding tickets, both on that speed trap over on Lincoln. You know, that spot where the radar cameras are lined up like the Radio City Rockettes. I did find something interesting, though."

"Mph?"

"Ms. Beltran started out as a criminal defense attorney but only lasted three years. Then she went back to school and got certified in commercial real estate. Worked for a big RE firm for a while, you might have heard of it—Jacobson, Schaffner, and Ross, they specialize in high-end malls—then struck out on her own. Has an office near Hayden and Indian Bend. House is close by, in McCormick Ranch. Lakefront, so she's not doing too shabby."

I swallowed a lump of spicy beef. "Give me the address."

"The office? Attorneys work late."

"House. She's on vacation. Maybe I'll just drop by."

A grunt. "Then I'd better feed Snowball."

We said amiable goodbyes and I went back to my enchiladas. I was halfway through when my phone buzzed again. Expecting another call from Jimmy I almost answered it, but at the last moment I noticed the display.

Dusty's picture smiled out at me.

I put the phone back down as quickly as if I'd picked up a rattlesnake.

Six o'clock found me driving up to Jacklyn's tiny stucco, a house she had inherited from her mother two years before her son vanished into thin air. The blue-collar neighborhood seemed quiet, but several signs posted in windows along the street announced that the residents were members of the local Neighborhood Watch. Some of the vehicles in the driveways—mostly pickup trucks—sported bumper stickers that warned PROTECTED BY SMITH & WESSON.

Jacklyn greeted me at her door, freshly showered and changed into an ankle-length sundress. No Glock. Her hard makeup had been scrubbed off, replaced by only lip gloss. She looked ten years younger.

Her house's décor also came as a surprise. The walls—all of them decorated by studio portraits of the same gap-toothed boy—were pale blue, and the carpet a deeper shade of blue. A hand-knitted afghan covered a baby-blue velvet sofa, and blue-patterned pillows leaned against the backs of two elegant Queen Anne-style chairs.

"Stevie loved blue," Jacklyn said, seeing me look around.

Stevie, her seven-year-old son who had disappeared from El Camino Park nine years earlier. Stevie, who had been insured for five thousand dollars.

Jimmy's check on Jacklyn had revealed that after seven years, she had her son declared dead. The insurance company subsequently paid up, but not without a fight.

The Iron Cross had been so dark I hadn't been able to see much, but here in Jacklyn's brightly lit house I could once more see the two-inch-high STEVIE tattoo that stretched from collarbone to collarbone. A mother's reminder to never forget, or an act for the cops?

She broke into my suspicions by asking, "Would you like to see his room?"

"Of course," I answered, even though I dreaded it.

The room wasn't a room, it was a shrine. Painted the same blue as the rest of the house, it looked like the room of a boy who was expected back home any minute for dinner. Sitting on the blue print bedspread was a collection of teddy bears, one of which had the name STEVIE embroidered across its chest. Above the bed hung several sports banners testifying to Stevie's love for the Arizona Diamondbacks, the Arizona Cardinals, and the Phoenix Suns. On another wall, Stevie himself smiled from a dozen framed snapshots.

Thank God none of us can see the future.

Back in the living room Jacklyn bucked the Arizona habit by serving me hot, not iced, chamomile tea. "I read in *Modern Health* that you cool off faster if you drink hot beverages," she explained.

I'd read the same article and wondered if its author had ever lived through Arizona's one hundred-fifteen-degree Augusts. Probably not. I sipped my tea anyway. On my way home I could always stop at a Circle K for a cold Thirst Buster.

"Go ahead and tell me what this is about," she asked, setting her tea cup down. "Nicole called and said Debbie had been released from jail, so shouldn't that be it? I mean, who cares who killed that creepoid? As far as I'm concerned, they deserve a medal."

"Did Nicole also tell you someone tried to kill us?"

The color drained from her face. "What are you talking about?"

She was either an Oscar-worthy actress, or she really didn't know.

I told her what had happened, then asked, "Do you have any firearms other than your Glock?"

"If you have a Glock you don't need anything else."

"Mind telling me where you were at ten o'clock yesterday morning?"

Her eyes narrowed as the grieving mother disappeared, replaced by the toughened biker chick. "None of your business."

"Maybe you were you at work. I can find out easy enough."

"What did I just tell you?"

"That it's none of my business. And you're wrong there. When someone shoots at me—and Nicole, too, by the way—it becomes my business."

Since Jacklyn liked Nicole better than she liked me, it worked. She closed her eyes for a moment, then said, "I was at the Iron Cross. Just like today. Around thirty Moguls can testify to that."

Before I could refute the veracity of one of the state's most notorious biker gangs, she added, "And I punch a time clock. In at ten, out at six. Theoretically. Yesterday I pulled a double shift. Hell, all I fucking do these days is work."

"The police can get a warrant," I bluffed. "They can come down to the Iron Cross and collect the time clock for evidence."

Her smile had little humor in it. "That would be fun to watch. The Moguls play rough. So do I."

I believed her.

All my other questions elicited negative answers, so I wrapped up the interview and headed for the door. Just before I reached it, I asked one more question.

"Jacklyn, do you know a man by the name of Richard Fairfield?"

She shook her head.

But she couldn't hide the shock in her eyes.

Chapter Twenty-four

By the time I made it back to Scottsdale it was almost eight, a little late to just drop in on an attorney. Besides, the area of McCormick Ranch where Nicole Beltran lived was gated, with a guard shack by the gate to make certain you didn't try any funny stuff.

So I called.

"Missing me already?" she quipped, picking up.

"Something like that. I need to talk to you."

"Sounds serious."

"Not at all, but hey, you're not that far from me, so if you're not busy right now, I could swing over there."

There was a long silence, and just as I was about to reframe my request, she said, "I'll tell the guard to let you in."

McCormick Ranch is one of Scottsdale's prettiest neighborhoods. Once a working Arabian horse ranch owned by the grandson of Nelson D. Rockefeller, most of the acreage had been subdivided in the seventies. It was now an upscale community that sported seven artificial lakes, two championship golf courses, and lots and lots of green, a color relatively rare in this desert city. But I could see little of the lush landscaping when the guard let me through the gate, just lights reflected in water.

Nicole's house, a triple-decker Mediterranean, sat on an artificial island among other large homes, all reached by driving over a short causeway. As I parked my Jeep between a Bentley and an Aston Martin—I guessed their owners were attending the noisy party down the street—I wondered if Nicole had an additional source of income other than her real estate interests. Nice homes weren't unusual in Scottsdale, but her mini-mansion wasn't all that mini, a splashy choice for a single woman with no children.

At least no known *living* children.

My puzzlement must have shown on my face, because when she greeted me at the door, she smiled and said, "Relax. I'm not the mouthpiece for the Sinaloa Drug Cartel."

I pretended to buy it.

Which made her smile again, but this time it was a sad one. "This was originally my mom and dad's house, but I raised Candice here. Yeah, it's too big for one person but I can't move in case…"

"In case she comes back."

A nod.

She had changed out of the jeans she wore at Debbie's Oasis, and was now garbed in yoga pants and a tank top. Barefoot. No visible tattoos.

Saying nothing else, she led me into a barn-sized living room where a glass wall looked out on the development's largest lake. Decorative streetlamps lined the shore, giving the water such a fairy-tale beauty I half expected Tinkerbell to fly by waving her tiny wand. Instead of matching the lake's dark elegance, the house's furnishings were dated and worn. The room looked like a museum exhibit dedicated to the design choices of the Eighties, right down to the Thomas Kinkaide landscapes on the wall. Originals, not prints.

"So what's up?" Nicole asked, gesturing me to a flower-print chair. "I'll admit I'm a bit surprised to see you again so soon. Not that it isn't pleasant, but I'd think you'd be tossing back a few brews, trying to forget about almost getting killed."

When I sat, I half-expected to see a cloud of dust shoot into the air. It didn't. Maybe she had a maid tucked away somewhere.

"Happens all the time in my line of work. When did you arrive at Debbie's?" I asked.

She raised her eyebrows. "Boy, you're abrupt. Want some tea? Fresh made."

"Thanks, but I stopped at Circle K and had a Thirst Buster on the way over. Don't you want to answer my question?"

She stood up again, to throw me out, I guessed, but no, she waved for me to follow her up a dark oak staircase to the next floor, then down a spacious hall to another room that overlooked the lake.

"This was Candice's room," Nicole explained.

Another shrine to a vanished child. Did all grieving mothers do this? Or just some?

Everything in Candice's room was pink, except for the plush animals heaped on the pink canopy bed. I saw a stuffed elephant, a giraffe, a cheetah, several monkeys, and God only knew what else was under the pile. More stuffed animals were arrayed on a window seat overlooking the light-reflecting lake.

"Candice wanted to be a veterinarian, go to Africa, treat animals wounded by poachers."

Something else wasn't pink. In back of the pink-dressed blond girl in the life-sized painting above the bed, the trees were green with lilac flowers.

Seeing all this, so soon after Jacklyn's shrine to her Stevie, reminded me of something. "I didn't see anything like this up at Debbie's. Doesn't she…?"

She cut me off. "We all grieve in different ways. Debbie wants to forget, I want to remember, to believe that Candice will find her way home someday. That's why I continue to live in a house that's too big for me, so when she comes back I'll be right here waiting for her. She used to sit in that window seat, watching the birds in the lake. Herons. Egrets. Plovers. Canada geese, six different species of ducks. She'd even given some of them names, like the little cinnamon teal that was missing a foot. Peg Leg, she named him. One of the herons was named Estelle, but heaven only knows why. I had plenty of time to kill Norma before I drove up to Black Canyon City."

She wasn't even looking at me, just at the portrait.

"Did you?"

"If I were a stronger woman, I would have. I would have killed Wycoff, too, burned those marks all up and down both legs and both arms and..." She cleared her throat. "But I'm not that strong."

I know truth when I hear it.

"You know what? I'll take that tea now."

Back at my apartment I opened the bankers' box again and took out the pictures of my bloodstained dress, now lying next to my Vindicator.

I left the knife where it was—its time was past—but I picked up the photograph of the dress.

Closed my eyes.

Whispered the names of the children.

Candice.

Lindsey.

Stevie.

And all the other missing children out there whose mothers couldn't forget them, mothers still waiting for them to come home.

Was my mother waiting for me?

Chapter Twenty-five

When I woke up the next morning, Snowball was lying on my chest, purring. It sounded peaceful.

And peaceful wasn't a condition I was used to.

I've had conversations with worse creatures than kittens, so I asked, "Does Snowball want breakfast?"

He purred louder.

"Coming right up, then."

Gently moving him aside, I crawled out of bed and staggered to the kitchen with him trailing behind me. I opened a can of Fancy Feast, and ladled it into his bowl. After watching Snowball eat for a while, I went into the living room and surveyed the damage. Ruined drapes, ruined sofa cushions, scratched-up coffee table. For some reasons known only to his little cat brain, he had spared the black satin pillow emblazoned with WELCOME TO THE PHILIPPINES that I'd stolen from one of my first foster families. They were good people and I'd wanted something to remember them by.

But maybe it was time to return it.

Andrew and Bernice Preston lived in Leisure World in Mesa, a gated retirement community just a little over twenty miles east of Scottsdale. The Prestons had been forced to give me up when Andrew lost his job at a car dealership that went bust under during one of the Valley's economy slumps, necessitating him to take a job at his brother's John Deere franchise in Kansas. That was more than, what, thirty years ago? A couple of years ago they moved back to Mesa, where two of their own children and several grandchildren lived. Through some miracle, they had seen me being interviewed on television after the bloody end of one of my cases and managed to track me down. We had kept in touch ever since.

Like many of the Leisure World residents, the now-retired Prestons opted for a maintenance-free condo. Theirs overlooked the golf course, which came in handy for Andrew since he loved spending time on the links. As for Bernice, she spent most of her days quilting and visiting with family and friends, every now and then paying homage to the God of Exercise by losing tennis matches. If it hadn't been for the Prestons, I might never have known normal families existed.

I parked my Jeep in the visitor's lot and hiked through the heat to their condo, where Andrew, a young-looking seventy, immediately invited me in. Like many Arizona homes, the Prestons' décor paid homage to various Indian tribes. As I took a seat on the butternut-colored sofa, I spotted two Navajo sand paintings, several Hopi Kachinas, a Yaqui mask, a Zuni pot, and even several Northwest Indian carvings—Tlingit, I think.

Bernice, still lovely although her hair was now entirely silver, waved away my apology when I tried to hand over the WELCOME TO THE PHILIPPINES pillow. "You didn't have to drive this all the way out here, Sweetheart. If I've lived without it this long, we can go on without it."

"But I stole it," I muttered, red-faced.

Andrew, always genial, grinned. "When I was seven, I stole a package of Fleer's Double Bubble from the corner grocery store. 'Course, my father made me take it back."

I thrust the pillow at them again. "But the pillow's life is threatened. I have a cat now."

"Cats love pillows." Andrew shoved it back.

Bernice ended the shoving match by plucking the pillow out of her husband's hands during a too-slow transfer. "We'll put it on the bed in the guest room. Thank you, Lena. That's a very kind thing to do, returning this, but we always understood why you took Andrew's pillow. You hated to say goodbye, so it was something of ours you'd always have with you."

Since they had returned to the Valley, we had discussed our tearful parting several times. Long ago I'd forgiven them for leaving me behind. CPS rules forbade a foster parent taking a "client," as we children were called, permanently out of state. But even adults had to eat, and the Prestons had to go where the jobs were.

"Iced tea, Lena?" Bernice asked, after she'd returned from taking the pillow into the guest bedroom. "You're all sweaty."

"Still around a hundred-ten out there. Maybe we'll get lucky and a monsoon will roll in."

We discussed the weather—hot and getting hotter—while we sat at the dining room table, sipping our tea. Bernice always snuck sugar into hers, and while it was too sweet for me, I drank it anyway.

"Oh, by the way, did I tell you I found a stack of my old journals when I was cleaning out our Wichita house before we moved back?"

Andrew frowned. "Bernice, maybe you shouldn't…"

She shushed him. "You worry too much."

Journals? I've never understood people's need to record their lives. *Had brunch with Estelle today. Saw Star Wars, it was great. Dreamed about frogs last night, wonder why. Dog barfed on the kitchen floor this morning…* Over the years several therapists had advised to me to keep a journal, but given the nature of my memories I wanted to forget them, not record them. But since Bernice seemed enthused about her find, I faked interest. "Old journals? How fascinating."

"One of them was exclusively about you."

Uh oh. "I didn't do well in school, did I?"

"Your grades were fine, but your behavior worried your teachers. I saved some of their notes and tucked them into the pages of the journal. Want to see them?"

Did I want to see teacher's notes describing my violence in the classroom? The time I'd slapped Cheryllee for taking my pencil? The time I'd kick Ralphie in the balls for pinching my butt? The time I'd bit Mrs. Robinson when she tried to drag me off Carmen because Carmen had called me a homeless little tramp nobody wanted?

"I'll pass." I said.

Andrew was still frowning. "Listen to the girl, Bernice."

As usual, Bernice ignored him, but when she spoke, her tone was gentle. Come to think of it, in the two years I'd lived with them, she'd never once raised her voice to me. "You're still running away from your memories, aren't you, Lena?"

"With only sporadic success." I tried not to sound bitter.

After looking at me for a long moment, she said, "I'll be right back," then headed down the hallway. Andrew muttered something about headstrong women.

A couple of minutes later Bernice returned with a notebook in her hand. Not one of those little blue notebooks I'd used in school, but large, with a paisley print cover. A journal. She sat down next to me and opened it to a bookmarked page.

"There's remembering, which is healthy, and wallowing, which isn't," she said. "Who was Golden Boy?"

When I could breathe again, I said, "I…I'm not ready to talk about that."

She gave me a searching look. "Whoever, or whatever, he was, you dreamed about him all the time. They weren't good dreams."

"Most of mine aren't."

"Whenever you dreamed about this Golden Boy, you'd wake up screaming."

Andrew, bless him, said, "Bernice, is this necessary?"

"I think it's time, Lena. How much do you remember?"

I remembered the shots, the screams, the children's bodies being thrown into the mineshaft. I still woke up nights echoing their screams as they died. Was I already dreaming about Golden Boy when I lived with the Prestons?

"Lena?"

I snapped back to attention.

"After a couple of those screaming episodes—and they were horrific—we took you to a child psychologist. Do you remember that?"

"No."

The expression on her face told me she had expected my answer. "Understandable. You had serious memory issues at the time. The psychologist told us that you couldn't remember anything consciously, but that your dreams…" She paused a moment, then continued. "Once you woke up, you couldn't remember them so she was unable to follow up on what terrified you so much. Lena, please know that we did everything we could to help you."

"Of course you did." The Prestons had been more than kind.

"Now it's time for you to help yourself." Bernice placed the paisley-print journal in my hands. "I recorded those bad nights in here, every word you screamed."

The journal lay on my coffee table the rest of the day while I did everything possible to avoid it. I played with Snowball. I mopped the kitchen floor. I scrubbed the toilet. I returned Dusty's phone call. He invited me out for another trail ride on Monday, but accepted my excuse that I was too busy. No lie, there, but I assured him that once I'd cleared the Wycoff case we would get together again.

"Clear that thing fast, Hon," he said, "because I'm getting' awful lonely up here."

When I ended the call, I immediately regretted postponing his invitation. One night in his arms, just one night…

Although I knew it was a cliché, I had always gone for the bad boys. In a way, they were safest boys of all. Knowing a boy was "bad" allowed you to hold back, not let yourself get in too deep. That way, when they finally got around to doing something outrageously bad—like getting married and forgetting to tell you about it—you had an excuse to kick him out of your life, to shut the whole thing down.

Bad boys were so much safer that the good boys, the soft-eyed boys who never gave you cause to doubt them, the boys who hung in there until you wanted to scream, "Get this over with already, end this, because that's what happens, that's the way it always works!"

Black garbage bag "suitcases" dragging behind me as CPS forced me from one "home" to another to another to…

People disappeared on you. I remembered the waiting—almost holding my breath with the fearful waiting—for those endings to happen, the feeling of almost relief when they did, because I had no choice over the matter, no power over the endings, the endings that always came. Ah, but with bad boys you had the power to end it yourself, because bad boys always gave you a reason to end it before you began to care too much. Then the bad boys were the ones who had to drag their dirty black garbage bags to the door.

No wonder the only male relationship I'd maintained at length was with Jimmy, my business partner.

And Dusty.

With my apartment cleaner than it had ever been, I headed to the gym and worked out for an hour and a half. Someone had left a copy of the *New Times* in the dressing room, and after browsing through the film section, decided to kill more time at the local Cineplex. The latest *Star Wars* movie helped me lose myself in the action for a while, but the image of Golden Boy returned the second the credits started rolling. Out of desperation, as soon as I left the Cineplex I called Jimmy. Work. That would settle me down. It always did.

"What have you learned about Casey Starr?" I asked, as soon as he said hello.

"Hello to you, too, Lena. You do realize that it's Sunday, right? The one day I'd planned to take off?"

"Sunday? That must be why the Cineplex was so crowded." This is what happens when you get into a tizzy over your so-called love life; you forget that other people have lives, too. "Sorry, Jimmy, it's just that…" I caught myself again. "Uh, everything okay with you and the cousins? How's the new building project coming along?"

A chuckle. "Everyone and everything is A-okay, and thanks for asking. As for Casey Starr, that guy's A-okay, too, at least as far as the Net is concerned. Everything, and I mean *everything* about him until he started Cyber-Sec, has been erased." There was more than a touch of admiration in his voice.

"One other thing."

"There always is."

I took a chance. "Say, uh, I'm thinking about dropping by the Tempe Improv tonight. *New Times* says Janeane Garofolo's appearing. Wanna go with?"

There was a long pause before he answered. "Sorry, but my cousin's expecting me for dinner. It's our usual family evening."

"Oh."

"Maybe some other time? I know how much you like hanging out on the Rez."

"Yeah. Some other time."

I ended the call.

I didn't want to go to the Improv by myself, but I still didn't feel ready to return to my apartment where Bernice Preston's paisley journal awaited me. Instead, I drove out to Cave Creek and ate barbequed chicken at the Horny Toad, where I listened to a flashy, Stetson-wearing woman sing about cheating men and cows. After one set, I drove into Phoenix and stopped by Char's Has the Blues, where a guy dressed like a biker down on his luck sang about cheating women and cruel bosses. Then I went to the movies again—different Cineplex—to see the latest *Hangover* retread. It made me glad I didn't drink.

It was Freud, I think, who proposed that the way to recover from trauma was to face up to it, to name it. Name a scary hobgoblin and it'll disappear, just like magic. I wasn't sure I agreed. If you call a chair a chair, does that make the chair go away? No. the damned chair keeps sitting there, staring you in the face, sneering. So screw Freud. If you don't like the chair, don't keep looking at it. Same for memories. Ignore them. Every time I uncovered a new memory, it ruined my day. Why seek out more? Why should I read that damn journal?

In the end, though, I had to stop driving around the city, stopping in bars, and watching movies I hadn't wanted to see in the first place. I went home because Snowball needed to be fed. Love will kick you in the ass every time.

"Look at the trouble you've caused me," I told Snowball as he lay curled on my lap. "If it hadn't been for you, I could have stayed out all night, maybe drove out to the desert and looked at the stars. And I wouldn't have had to take that pillow back, either. Then I wouldn't have to…"

I eyed the paisley journal, sitting untouched on the coffee table.

Wasn't there a saying, something like, "Sufficient unto the day is the evil thereof"? Shakespeare, maybe. Or the Bible. Supposedly the Elizabethan gobbledygook meant, "Don't eat your heart out over the past and don't worry about the future, because today is already shitty enough."

I eased Snowball off my lap and took a long hot shower. Then, pointedly refusing to look at the journal, I went to bed.

At three I was still awake. Not because Snowball lay purring on my chest, he was light as a feather, but because every time I shut my eyes I could see that damned journal.

And because I was afraid to dream.

No, not afraid.

Terrified.

Even thinking about what might be in those pages had started my hands shaking again.

But did I really want to wake up screaming for the rest of my life? Maybe Bernice was right, that it was time I remembered what I didn't want to remember.

Tucking Snowball under my arm, I crawled out of bed and shuffled into the living room.

Grabbed the journal and began to read.

A bad night. Lena woke up screaming twice. Poor
little girl, what's she going to do when she learns that
CPS won't let us take her to Wichita? It'll only make
her worse, and she's already acting out in so many
violent ways. Something terrible happened to her,
something concerning her parents. She thinks her
mother shot her, but I find that hard to believe. What
kind of mother would shoot her own child?

Bernice had been right about that, too. What kind of mother
would shoot her own child? Not mine. Over the years I had
remembered enough to know my mother had been trying to
save me, not shoot me. She'd aimed the gun a couple of inches
to the left of my head, but then someone knocked her hand
two inches to the right. Almost simultaneously as I heard the
noise, I felt my mother's foot against my chest, and when the
gun screamed in concert with my mother, I flew through the
air, through the door of the white bus and onto the street below.

I saw nothing else until I woke up two months later in Phoenix Children's Hospital, my memory wiped clean.

I kept reading.

Last night's dream was Lena's worst so far. By the time
I made it to her bedroom, she was sitting up in the
bed, and even though she was awake, she was still
screaming. Over and over again, "Golden Boy killed
Daddy! And then he killed Jamie!"

As Snowball purred in my lap, I closed my eyes.
Jamie.
My baby brother's name was Jamie.
Jamie.
Red hair like my father's. Blue eyes like my mother's.
A sweet, powder-smelling lump of love.
Jamie.
I buried my face in Snowball's soft fur.

Chapter Twenty-six

"Rough night?" Jimmy asked when he entered Desert Investigations at seven the next morning and found me already there.

"Something like that."

Remembering Jamie.

Jamie.

Jamie.

Jamie.

I missed my mother.

I missed my father.

I missed my baby brother.

I...

No. Stop remembering the past. It couldn't be changed, couldn't be fixed. Stay in the here and now and do what you can to fix today's wrongs.

I straightened my back. "You know what I need, Jimmy?"

"Let me guess. You want me to run a search on somebody else."

"You're sure on top of things today. You remember Nicole Beltran?"

"How could I forget? After I ran her through the system, I know pretty much everything about her, right down to her favorite game in kindergarten. She was into dominoes."

"Now look up her parents."

"Mob dons? Terrorists plotting to bring down the U.S. government?"

Ignoring the sarcasm, I said, "I don't know their names and they might even be dead, but that big house of hers—she says it belonged to her parents—is weird."

"Nosey, aren't you?"

"Call it that, if you want."

He grunted, then fired up his computer. It sprang to life with a recording of Cree war chants.

I hated paperwork, but for now it helped take my mind off the memories Bernice's journal had unleashed. For a while I worked on our billing, noting with satisfaction that our receivables, worryingly low last month, had risen again. Paranoia, whether in the office or on the home front, pays. Running background checks on job applicants and/or future domestic partners may be a dirty job, but someone had to do it, and luckily, that someone was often Desert Investigations. At least, billing the paranoid kept my mind off what had happened in that long-ago forest.

I lost myself in a flurry of case hours until Jimmy called over to me.

"Got 'em!"

"Got what?"

"Nicole Beltran's parents, and I didn't have to do much to find them. Geoffrey Winslow, her father, founded Renee's Miracle Beauty Spas—thirty-two of them across the U.S.—after his wife, Renee, a chemist, created Renee's Miracle Glow, some super skin cream. From the blurbs I'm reading from satisfied customers, seems the stuff actually works. Reduces wrinkles and pores, or something like that. Anyway, they made a heap of money and were flying in their own jet to the opening of their newest spa in Boca Raton when the Cessna went down over Texas. No survivors. Must be tough, losing two parents at once."

And then your child.

That house wasn't a house. It was a mausoleum.

But now I knew why, with all the grief in her life, Nicole's skin had remained so beautiful. She used her parents' products.

"Good work, Almost Brother."

"There's something else. While I was poking around I came up with the name of Nicole's ex-husband. You know, the father of the little girl that went missing. It's Sean Beltran."

I recognized the name. Sean Beltran was a hotshot local architect, and a fervent gun enthusiast. An article on him in *Phoenix Magazine* swooned over his collection of firearms, many antique, some new, everything from little .22 varmint rifles to a rumored big-ass rocket launcher.

Jimmy gave me a look. "I know what you're thinking, but remember, Wycoff wasn't shot."

"Norma was."

He shook his head. "The timing isn't right. Candice Beltran disappeared eight years ago while Wycoff was still in prison."

"True, but not having the actual kidnapper to take revenge on, Beltran might have decided Wycoff would make a nice substitution. Revenge by proxy, if you will." It would be a tidy solution to a messy case.

"A little far-fetched, don't you think? Oh, and by the way, I came across something else you might want to think about. You told me Nicole said she'd practiced criminal defense law before she got into real estate law, correct?"

Wondering what that had to do with anything, I said, "I was under the impression that was a long time ago."

"It was right after she was admitted to the bar, as matter of fact, a few years before she married and gave birth to Candice. I got a little curious about that abrupt change in specialization. When I started poking around, I discovered that the last criminal case she handled was when she served as second chair in the defense of a man charged in the attempted abduction of a child. She and the lead attorney got the guy off on a technicality, although it was pretty obvious to everyone he hadn't planned to take the little girl for a treat at the nearest Baskin-Robbins."

I had a hunch I was about to hear something I wouldn't like. "And?"

"Six months after going scot-free, he was back in police custody. Not only had he abducted another little girl, but this time

he'd raped and strangled her. Name's Jeffrey Simpson Carmichael, now goes by the handle of Death Row Inmate #783-3761."

I did the math. Less than five years later, Nicole's own
daughter was abducted, possibly by someone much like Jeffrey
Simpson Carmichael.

"Guilt can be a great motivator, Lena."

I didn't say anything. I couldn't.

For a while I tried to continue with the billing, but I felt too
restless. My skin actually itched from anxiety. I liked Nicole,
and despite her ex-husband's over-the-top arsenal, I liked the
homes he built, too. Of all the houses in the Valley of the Sun,
his came closest to looking like they actually belonged in the
desert, unlike those mini-mansion transplants from Italy.

Setting the billing aside for a moment, I stood up and walked
over to the coffeemaker. Surprise, surprise, I'd already gone
through an entire pot, and it was only eight o'clock. If I had any
sense, I'd switch to decaf. I started to make another pot, then
stopped myself. Did I need to be more wired than I already was?
Answering my own question, I went back to my desk, then stood
there for a moment. With a sigh, I removed my holstered .38 from
the bottom drawer and slipped it into my cargo pants pocket.

"Jimmy?"

He peeped over the top of his computer. "What now?"

"You sure you couldn't find anything dirty on Casey Starr?"

He made a disgusted sound. "Like I told you, not even a
traffic ticket. Yeah, I agree that he's cleaner than any human
being has a right to be after forty-plus years on this Earth, but
if the guy's wiped his past, it's down the rabbit hole and I can't
make it reappear."

"That leaves us with only one option."

"Which is?"

"We'll have to do this the old-fashioned way."

Jimmy, no slouch, got it immediately. "Good thing gas is
cheap these days, huh?"

"Considering my gas-guzzling Jeep, yeah. At least all the addresses you came up with are in Maricopa County."

"And that only encompasses something like nine thousand square miles."

Leave it to Jimmy to state the obvious.

Since I like to show up at people's houses before they leave for work, around eight I was ringing the doorbell at Hallie and Merrrill Polov's rambling faux-adobe located in the shadow of Scottsdale Fashion Square. The maid who answered had never heard of the Polovs.

"The Morgans live here now," she said.

"For how long?"

She frowned. "How long what?"

"How long have the Morgans lived here?"

"Ten year. Go away." She shut the door in my face.

It had been my experience that the residents of older neighborhoods like this one usually stayed around, so after striking out at the Morgans', I went up the walk to the house next door, another faux adobe. Before I could lift my finger to the doorbell, the door opened and an elderly man bent almost double by arthritis said, "If you're selling, Honey, I might be buying."

At the expression on my face, he added, "Hey, just kidding, so don't go all femi-Nazi on me. You taking one of those polls? By the way, that's a pretty nifty Jeep you drove up in. Tricked-out '45-'46?"

"Nailed it." I smiled. Despite his physical condition, he was a sharp observer. And lonely. Hopeful, I flashed my ID. "Do you remember the Polov family?"

"Couldn't forget those folks, now, could I? Hey, Miss Lena, why don't you come in and have some ice tea?"

I accepted his invitation and entered a house that could have doubled as a museum devoted to the Old West. Paintings of cowboys and Indians lined the walls, some old, some contemporary. Among them I spotted what might have been a

Frederic Remington, and another which was most certainly a Fritz Scholder. Each table in the sunken living room—and there were a lot of tables—supported bronze castings of Indians killing buffalo, cowboys roping steers, and horses, horses, horses. I decided to like the sexist old coot.

"Great house," I said, meaning it.

"Been collecting for a while. Sugar in your tea?"

"I like it straight."

"Like your whiskey and your men, huh?" He grinned wickedly.

Playing along, I said, "Absolutely."

Gratified, he ignored my offer of help and told me to take a seat on a horse-hair-covered sofa. Then he hobbled into the kitchen. A few minutes later he returned with ice tea poured into matching glasses etched on the sides with the face of John Wayne. After handing me one he eased himself into a chair covered in brown- and white-spotted cowhide.

"Not as young as I used to be."

"None of us are." I curled my hand around the Duke's face and sipped at the tea.

"So. What kind of dirt you want on the Polovs?"

"Maybe you could start by introducing yourself."

He laughed, a raspy, creaking sound. "Here I've been so excited about luring a pretty woman into my abode that I forgot basic manners. I'm Manfred Stephen Chapman the Fourth, but everybody calls me Manny."

"Pleased to meet you, Manny, and you didn't forget your manners. This tea is delicious. Now, about the Polovs. Do you know where they live now?"

"Holy Cross Cemetery. I warned Merrill that TR6 of his was a death trap, but did he listen, hell no, so he and Hallie got themselves splattered all over I-17 up by the Carefree Highway off-ramp."

I made a face. "Tough."

Chapman looked down his long nose. "Could of been worse. At least the EMTs were able to scrape up enough to bury."

I avoided picturing that. "Did you know they were foster parents for a while?"

He sniffed. "Couple of do-gooders, didn't need the money."

"Did you ever have any trouble with the kids?"

"Just the one."

"Which one was that?"

"Cass. Cory. Casey. Something like that. Only eleven years old, but what a little shit. Give a man a fishing rod and he'll eat for a year, give an eleven-year-old boy a can of spray paint and you've got a purple and green garage."

"Casey spray-painted your garage?" That didn't sound too serious, just the usual kid hijinks, more annoying than destructive. Well, except for the repair bill.

"Isn't that what I said? Not only mine, but the Ebersons' and the Wachetzes' garages, too. 'Course, Merrill being the kind of man he was, he coughed up the money for all the repaints, but still."

"What happened after that?"

"Merrill kept him on a tighter leash, not that it worked. Kid was bad to the bone."

People used to say the same thing about me, same as I said about the men in my life. "Define 'bad.'"

"Just what I said."

"Maybe you could give me an example."

"He broke little Rosa's arm, poor little thing."

That shook me. "Casey beat up a girl?"

"Slammed her arm in a car door and pretended it was an accident, but that was no accident. I was watching when it happened and he did it deliberate."

It sounded like another fish story to me. "You were watching at that very moment? Or was the arm-breaking incident something you just heard about?"

He sniffed. "I made it my business to be on the alert when the brat was out and about, so I saw him lure Rosa into the Polovs' Buick. I was on my way out there to keep them from getting in—it was summer and hot and you know what happens when kids get locked in cars—but before I made it halfway down the walk it was already too late. After the 'incident,' as you called it, I grabbed Rosa and carried her across the street to her parents' house, then went and told Merrill what the little monster had done, but I don't think he believed me."

I'm not sure I did, either. From my own experience, I knew that people tended to blame foster kids for everything that went wrong, from destructive oceanic tides to total eclipses of the sun, and tailored what they saw accordingly.

The next three stops didn't pan out. The Atkinsons had long since moved away from their Tempe home and none of the neighbors remembered them. Same story with the Gaults in Mesa. Another foster family, the Morrises, had died in a Queen Creek house fire, but the only person who semi-remembered the fire was in the early stages of Alzheimer's and had trouble remembering his own name. He was also convinced I was his daughter. The long drive from Queen Creek to Maryvale also turned up nothing, although Fairfield/Starr had lived with two different sets of foster parents in the area. Casey's former foster parents were long gone, as was everyone who knew them.

Most people don't realize how transitory the Phoenix area is. We're a magnet for frostbite victims fleeing the northeast winters, as well as for people running away from bad relationships and/ or criminal acts in other states. It's not unusual for a newcomer to run through several different addresses here before giving up and moving on to California to try their luck there. Foster parents, though, were usually more settled, so I was surprised at my run of bad luck. Surely someone else remembered the kid.

My luck changed when I circled back east and to the Phoenix suburb of Gilbert. Bill and Edith Larson lived in a two-story brick house that looked like it belonged in Wisconsin, not Arizona. The lush green lawn belonged back East, too, and made me wonder about the occupants' water bill. Growing grass in the desert is an expensive proposition.

After I'd identified myself to the fifty-something woman who answered the door, she informed me that her parents were at

Bonny Glen, a nearby assisted living facility. Her mother, she said, had suffered a near-fatal stroke and was no longer verbal. Her father's mind, however, remained unaffected by the rheumatoid arthritis that kept him in a wheelchair.

"What did you want to talk to them about?" the woman who introduced herself as Beth asked. She was in the middle of "freshening up" the house, as she put it, before the realtor arrived. In contrast to her expensive salon hair, she wore baggy jeans, an oversized man's shirt, and clutched a filthy dust rag in her hands.

"I'm interested in hearing about their time as foster parents."

She gave me a bemused look that struggled with the Botox in her face. "Good luck getting Dad to discuss that."

I made a quick mental calculation. At the time Casey Fairfield/Starr had been fostered by the Larsens, Beth would have been somewhere in her early teens. "How did you feel about sharing the house with foster kids?"

"Probably the same thing any young girl would feel."

"Which would be?"

"Irritated. Maybe a little jealous."

"Nothing else?"

"I had my own life. Puppy loves, that sort of thing. If I remember correctly, at the time I was mooning over some boy named Kevin, or maybe it was Keith, or Kenny, whatever, and when I wasn't breaking my heart over him, I was hanging out with my girlfriends. I didn't pay much attention to what was going on at home."

Her tone was chipper but she was twisting the holy hell out of that dust rag.

"Do you remember a boy named Casey?"

She didn't answer right away, just twisted the dust rag some more. Finally, she said, "You'd better come in. But we need to make this fast because the realtor is due here in a half hour and I still have to drag more stuff out to the garage. Old people, you know, they never throw anything away."

When I stepped inside, I saw a living room that had been pretty much gutted. No family pictures, no books, no knickknacks, just furniture that could have been shipped on Noah's ark. Many of the Larsens' personal things had taken up residence in the six large cardboard boxes sitting in the middle of the room. After settling myself onto an ugly green sofa, I got straight to the point. "What do you remember about Casey?"

Beth, sitting across from me in a matching chair, raised her already surgically lifted eyebrows even further. "Not much, really. Just that after him, my folks didn't take in any more fosters."

If that dust rag had been a chicken, it would have a broken neck.

"Did Casey cause problems?"

"Most foster kids had crappy lives, which is why they wound up in foster care in the first place."

Not exactly an answer to my question, but a hint that something was already off about Casey. Remembering the name change from Fairfield to Starr, and that his identity was more or less protected, I decided to take a chance.

"I'm investigating a suspicious death," I told her, "so anything you can remember, however small, might be helpful."

Beth's face went white. "A death that involved Casey? But… but wouldn't the police…?"

"How long did Casey live with your parents?"

"Less than a year."

"How old was he at the time?"

"Ten, I think. Maybe nine, eight, I'm not sure. Why do you want to know, anyway?"

"Just following up leads. Talking to a lot of people about a lot of people, and Casey is only one of them."

"So you don't actually suspect him of anything."

I shook my head.

"Then why does this sound like you do?"

I tried a reassuring smile, for myself as much as her. "How about any of the other children your parents fostered. Any trouble with them?"

"Just Casey. He…" She caught herself too late. "I shouldn't have said that."

I always like it when I can interject an element of truth into an interview. My own aggressive behavior is what had led to my prolonged trek through the CPS foster care system, so I said, "All kids get into a little trouble at some point," I soothed.

Beth was eager to agree. "It was just small stuff. Casey tried to shoplift some gum from the Circle K down the street but got caught. And every now and then, something would come up missing around the house. A little money, some of mother's costume jewelry, you know, things like that. But his grades, hey, the kid got straight-A's. Mom was always talking about how smart Casey was. Me, I was lucky to get C's. Too hung up on boys."

She and I both. "Anything else?"

"About Casey? Nothing…" She paused, then added, "Well, there was some concern about a couple of sheds that caught fire in the neighborhood."

"Concern? What do you mean?"

She shrugged. "One of the neighbors said he'd seen Casey fooling around his shed before it burned down, but he was one of those weird guys into conspiracy theories, convinced the government was spying on him from cameras they'd hidden in his light bulbs, so nobody paid any attention to him. Especially since he hated kids in the first place."

"I'd like to talk to him."

"Good luck there, since he died something like twenty, thirty years ago."

I didn't like the sound of the fires, never a good sign for a troubled boy. And remembering Manfred Stephen Chapman the Fourth's accusation that Casey had purposefully broken a little girl's arm, I pressed on. "As you said, most foster children led crappy lives before they wound up in the system, and it's not unusual for unhappy children to act out in physical ways. Do you remember anything like that?"

"Like fights? Not that I know of."

"You said that Casey was the last foster your parents took in. What made them change their minds about the program?"

"I don't…I don't…"

"Beth, this could be important."

She cleared her throat before replying. "Well, there was Sprinkles. Not that it was ever proven."

"Sprinkles?"

"My kitten. Dad found her half-buried behind the garden shed in back. Someone had, um, it looked like they had, um, *operated* on her."

I thought about Snowball. His trusting eyes. His soft purr. It took me a few seconds to respond, and when I did, I had trouble controlling the quaver in my voice. "Is that when your folks withdrew from the foster care program?"

"They, um, they returned Casey to CPS right after that, but it doesn't mean anything, does it?"

I had to make myself stop thinking about Snowball. About his tiny sisters and brothers. And his sweet-faced mother. Clearing my throat, I said, "Do you know if CPS provided psychiatric treatment while Casey was with your family?"

The question touched another nerve. With a bitter laugh, she answered, "Are you kidding me? Not in *this* state! A kid could be drooling, flat-out psycho in Arizona, running around with knives or guns or who knows what else, and the powers-that-be would just go 'so sad, too bad' and do squat-all—until he finally killed somebody. Whatever psychiatric help those foster kids got, my parents paid for out of their own pocket."

The dust rag, in pieces now, fell to the floor.

Beth bent over and picked them up. When she raised her head again, her face was flushed. "So if Casey sometimes seemed a little creepy, it shouldn't have come as a surprise to anyone."

Creepy? The Casey Fairfield/Starr I had met was the opposite of creepy. To the contrary, he'd been charming. Maybe even too charming. And the cats in his house looked perfectly fine, witness Snowball. Just as I was about to formulate my next question, the doorbell rang.

The real estate agent, right on time.

Chapter Twenty-seven

By the time I made it back to Scottsdale, the temperature was the Devil's favorite—one hundred-ten and climbing. The streets were deserted, the tourists hiding out in their air-conditioned hotels or slugging down ice colds at the Rusty Spur. Since my open Jeep didn't have air conditioning, I was not a happy camper.

I became even less of a happy camper when, after parking my Jeep in its covered space, I walked around the corner to my office and saw Frank Gunnerston, my wife-beating ex-client, about to open the door to Desert Investigations. The holster strapped to his thigh looked big enough to house a cannon.

He didn't see me come up behind him.

"Don't you just hate August, Frank?" I said, pressing the barrel of my .38 against his neck. "Heat. Humidity. Irritated private investigators."

When he tensed, I knew he was about to whirl around so I stepped back quickly and cocked the .38 before he could draw. I aimed. "Which ball do you like best, Frank. The right or the left? I'll let you keep one of them."

"Bitch!"

"I love you, too. Now let's go inside." As we went through the door to Desert Investigations, I eased the hammer back, but didn't holster my gun.

Jimmy was working so intently at his computer that he hadn't noticed the action outside. When he turned around he got a big surprise.

"Look who dropped by to visit us," I said.

My partner, slow to anger but quick on the uptake, was on the phone to 9-1-1 before the door closed behind me. Once he'd given our particulars, he hung up and said, "Mr. Gunnerston, are you aware that with your prior felony convictions, it is illegal for you to own a firearm?"

"Fuck you with a broom, Indian."

Jimmy ignored the insult. "Our records show that you pistol-whipped Mrs. Gunnerston, which is a Class Three felony, but because you had such a fine attorney, you only served six months. Add that to the fact that you are now carrying a handgun—loaded, I presume—and you've obviously entered our office with intent to cause bodily harm. That's a potential five to fifteen years."

Before Gunnerston could grow more agitated than he already was, I told him to lie down on the floor with his hands behind his back. Once he obeyed. I put my foot on his neck and pressed down. "Jimmy, would you be so kind as to get a pair of those plastic ties out of my lower desk drawer?" To Gunnerston, I said, "Looks like you're gonna be the one fucked with a broom, Frank. That's if you're lucky. From what I hear, you made some enemies among our red-wearing friends the last time you went down. Or was it the Crips? My memory isn't what it used to be."

"Whore."

I put a little weight on my foot. "Remind me to send you a copy of Emily Post's book on etiquette. You're sadly lacking in the manners department."

"Cunt."

"Don't have much a vocabulary either, do you? I recommend *Roget's Thesaurus* for that. Daily improvement, Frank, it's the path to a successful life."

Foot still on his neck, I took the plastic ties from Jimmy and secured Gunnerston's wrists. Then I relieved him of his firearm—a monster Beretta 96A1, for God's sake, and stepped away, re-aiming my comparatively itty-bitty .38 at his ass. I didn't want to kill him, just give him something to think about.

The wait wasn't long. The whoop-whoop of a siren and the glare of red and blue lights announced the arrival of friends. Two cars, this time. *Aren't I the popular girl?*

The first officers through the door were detectives Bob Grossman and Sylvie Perrins.

"Oh, looky, looky!" Sylvie crowed. "It's our old friend, Frank Gunnerston! Whatcha been doing, Frank? Disturbing the peace again?"

Upon her orders, the two uniformed officers who followed the detectives through the door yanked Gunnerston to his feet and hauled him and his whopper of a handgun out to their squad car.

Fun over, Sylvie settled herself into a chair while Bob remained standing.

"How's things up in Black Canyon City, Lena? They still partying hearty at that pie place?"

So she'd been keeping tabs on me. "The Dutch apple is as good as ever."

She snorted. "You old traditionalist, you. Myself, I go for the rhubarb crumble. More daring."

"Banana cream, here," Bob offered.

Sylvie pulled out a notebook. Seeing that, Bob lowered his big bulk into another chair, and Jimmy returned to typing.

"So," Sylvie said, her voice all business, "tell me what just went down here. You lure Gunnerston in with your feminine wiles, then have your way with him?"

There wasn't much to tell, but she kept interrupting my story with questions about my time in Black Canyon City.

"Hear you were shot at up there, too."

"Occupational hazard."

"We also hear that the gun used in the Norma Wycoff homicide was the same one that got cozy with you."

"That's what Ballistics said."

"Small world, isn't it, Lena?"

"Planes, trains, and automobiles. You can get anywhere these days. Besides, BCC's not much more than an hour's drive away."

"Report I read said the bullets never came closer than two feet from you. Shooter was a lousy shot, wasn't he?"

"Who said the shooter was a he?"

"Funny how sexism rears its ugly head in the simplest of sentences."

At this, Bob rolled his eyes. "Would you two get to the frickin' point?"

Sylvie turned to him. "Don't we still have a stash of porn magazines we took off that idiot kid over on Camelback? If you're bored, go read them." Then, to me, while Bob muttered darkly under his breath, "You never owned a .22 rifle in your life, did you, Lena?"

"Not after four years old. My memory's a bit hazy before that."

"There you go, then."

"Go then, what?"

"Then you can't be Norma Wycoff's killer." She grinned. "See ya at the submarine races." With that, she got up and left, Bob trailing behind her, still muttering.

From behind me, Jimmy said, "I feel sorry for Bob."

I laughed. "I do, too."

But something Sylvie had said made me think.

Once Gunnerston was driven off to the holding tank at the Scottsdale pokey, I got back to business, which in this case, was a drive to Queen Creek, yet another Phoenix suburb, this one south of Gilbert on the far southeast side. Once a series of dairy and produce farms, it was now headed down Subdivision Boulevard, with cookie-cutter homes all over the place.

It took me a while to find Daniel Shea, the retired fire captain of the Queen Creek Fire Department, but once I did, he delivered a gold mine of information.

"I'll never forget that Morris fire," he said. "It killed the mother and father and the eight-week-old baby sleeping in their room. Smoke inhalation, thank God for small favors. Three other kids made it out okay."

Shea had to be pushing eighty, if not already there, but he looked as fit as a tennis pro. Brown from work in the sun, and with a completely bald head and bushy white eyebrows, he looked like Mr. Clean's grandfather.

We were sitting in his kitchen in what had once been a farm-house but was now less than a hundred yards away from one of those cutesy suburban developments where all the houses mimic Tuscan farmhouses. The developer had tried to buy his land, Shea explained, but he'd been born in his house and planned to die in it, too. What land remained of the old Shea farm was still being put to use. A sorrel mare and a dappled gray gelding grazed in the pasture outside, while a palomino and her colt stared at us quizzically over the fence. All four looked in rough shape, which wasn't surprising. They were rescue horses, taken from their original owner because of neglect. Besides the horses, Shea's house was overrun by five dogs and what looked like a dozen cats. More rescues. Animals swarmed under our feet as we talked at the kitchen table.

After I turned down a cold beer, Shea served me up a tall glass of ice water and got busy with his memories. "Ever see a dead baby, Ms. Jones?"

There was no point in telling him I had seen several, so I said no.

"Awful thing, just awful. Oldest kid was a hero, though. Got the others out alive."

"That was Casey?"

He nodded. "Casey Fairfield. I'll never forget his name. Handsome boy. Quite the cool character for his age. He was about twelve then, maybe thirteen, wetted down a towel and tied it around his face. Led the other kids to safety."

"What caused the fire?"

He took another sip of his Bud. "The thing you have to understand is that we were an all-volunteer department back then. Sure, once we got the fire out we reached out to the sheriff's office, and they called in some arson investigator from Phoenix, but he came up with nothing. Case closed."

"No sign of accelerants?"

"Not that anyone found."

"Tell me about the kids Casey saved."

"Foster kids like him. Two boys and a girl. Those Morrises, they were great people. They'd been taking care of other people's kids for years."

"Was the baby, the one who perished, a foster, too?"

Shea shook his head. "No, the Morrises'. Kind of a surprise pregnancy because everybody, including Jessica Morris herself—beautiful woman, by the way, looked something like Sophia Vergara on a good day—thought she couldn't have kids. Say, you being a private investigator and all, do you happen to know where Casey wound up? I've always wondered. Brave boy like that, I'm betting he turned into something terrific."

I gave Shea a weak smile. "I have no idea where Casey Fairfield is."

Or who he really was.

I made it out of Queen Creek just in time for evening rush hour, which added to my bad mood. Stop-and-go traffic is lousy enough in the winter when the temps average in the sublime seventies, but in muggy August it means you eat fumes and sweat. By the time I arrived back at Desert Investigations, Jimmy had turned off the lights and locked up, so I bypassed the office and went upstairs.

Snowball acted thrilled to see me until I realized he was under the impression that a new scratching post had just walked through the door. I allowed him to claw his way up my once-black cargo pants to my thigh before lifting him by the scruff of the neck and cuddling him against my once-black tee shirt.

"See what you did?" I asked as he nuzzled my chin. "White fur all over me. Why can't you keep it to yourself?"

Maybe cats stopped shedding when they grew older. Or maybe not. Whichever, I certainly wasn't going to change out my entire wardrobe in order to co-exist with my newly acquired friend, which is why on my way home I'd stopped off at PetSmart and picked up an entire carton of Sticky Buddys. I made my way into the bedroom, where I plopped the bankers' box down at the foot of my floor-length mirror. Looking around, I noted with pleasure that Snowball hadn't destroyed my Roy Rogers and Trigger bedspread. In fact, the entire bedroom appeared untouched, except for the small stuffed rabbit I'd bought for him, which he'd deposited on Trigger's rump.

After feeding the little dervish, I nuked some ramen for myself, then set my laptop on the kitchen table and began transcribing my case notes. Before I'd entered the first paragraph, Snowball jumped onto my lap, turned around three times like a dog, then purred himself to sleep. He stayed there until I finished typing, then I cuddled him in my arms and carried him to the sofa.

"TV time," I told him, switching on the news.

It was the same old, same old. Muggings, shootings, and Kardashians. Bored, I eased Snowball off my lap and returned to my laptop. Something was nagging at me, but no matter how often I scrolled through my notes, I couldn't pinpoint it. In my business, if a statement didn't sound right, it wasn't. But who was the liar? The most flagrant contradictions in my notes were the statements concerning Casey Fairfield/Starr. Two people had described him as a budding psychopath. Another, as a hero.

But I also couldn't help remembering what Guy DeLucca, the social worker who'd placed the foster children with the Wycoffs, had said. "You've done the best of them all."

I read the notes again. And again. What was I missing?

The fifth time through, something struck me.

I grabbed my landline and called Jimmy's trailer.

He answered, sounding out of breath. "I'm in the middle of something, Lena."

"Hot date?" I teased.

"Very funny. Say what you called to say or I'm hanging up."

I bit back a retort and got down to it. "When you ran that backgrounder on Casey Starr-nee-Fairfield, did you check on his wife?"

"Why would I? She's not involved in this mess."

"Which means you didn't."

A sigh. "No, I did not check out Kay Starr."

"Most women change their names when they marry."

"I've noticed that."

"It shouldn't be too hard for you to find out her maiden name."

Another sigh.

"As soon as you find out, run the same kind of check on her that you ran on everyone else. When's the earliest you can get to it?"

"Tomorrow. At the office."

"Not tonight?"

"Lena, this may come as a surprise to you, but I do have a life."

Before he could cover the mouthpiece, a woman's voice in the background complained that he was taking too long.

"You have company!" I don't know why it bothered me to find out that Jimmy was entertaining a woman at his trailer, but it did.

"See you tomorrow, Lena."

He hung up.

Jimmy was right about two things. One, office hours were over. Two, he had a right to a personal life, and with whomever he chose. Judging from past history, the woman at his trailer would be crazy as a coot, but that wasn't my problem.

Something else was, if I could just put my finger on it.

Still bothered, I returned to the sofa to cuddle Snowball, but found no help there. The kitten was fast asleep. Disappointed, I set him/her down and stared at the wall.

I tried the deep breathing exercises that a long-ago yoga teacher had suggested. After several minutes—or an hour, I could no longer tell time—my breaths turned to gasps when I thought I felt spiders tiptoeing across my skin. The sensation became so intense I jumped up and ran to the full-length mirror hanging on my bathroom door only to discover that the spiders, metaphorically speaking, anyway, were all in my head.

I went back to the sofa. Could the Kardashians be any worse than this?

When I turned on the TV, I got my answer, so I turned it back off.

What? For God's sake, *what?*

It wasn't what someone had said, I finally realized, it was the look on someone's face when they'd said it.

Whose face had changed?

Well, there was no point in obsessing about the case notes again. Only rarely did I record someone's body language or facial expressions, only their statements. I glanced at my watch and was astounded to find that it was almost eleven. If I had any sense, I would forget the whole thing and go to bed, but given my insomnia, I knew I'd simply lie there staring at the ceiling until morning. The idea of another sleepless night didn't thrill me, but it was better than nightmares.

I looked over at my cat. "Snowball, purr or something."

When kittens sleep, they sleep deeply. No purrs were forthcoming.

A writer friend once told me she got her best ideas in the shower, so I left Snowball to his dreams and headed toward the bathroom again, this time at a slower pace.

Forty minutes later, my skin was as wrinkled as a prune's but I still hadn't figured anything out. Disgusted, I donned my usual nighttime apparel of pajamas bottoms and tee shirt and went to bed.

It took several moments for my still-asleep brain to realize someone was banging on my apartment door. I grabbed my .38 and ran to answer it.

"Would you please not stick that thing in my face?" Dusty said, when I opened the door.

I lowered my gun. "What the hell are you doing here in the middle of the night?"

"It's not the middle of the night. It's five in the morning. Aren't you going to invite me in?"

"If this is a booty call, cowboy, try elsewhere."

"Ah, Hon, still so cynical." That heart-breaking smile. "I come bearing gifts."

"Such as?"

"Such as coupons for a complementary two-hour trail ride up at Slim's."

Two-hour trail ride?

Slim Papadopolus, Dusty's ex-boss, owned the Happy Trails Dude Ranch in Carefree. Every now and then, especially when a case turned problematical, I rented a horse from him and took to the trails. I returned refreshed, often with the case sorted out. But it had been almost a year since I'd been up there, way too long.

"Dusty, I already told you no, remember?"

"I'm giving you another chance. If we leave now, you'll be back by the time Desert Investigations opens up."

Oh, what the hell. I stepped back and let him in.

An hour later we were riding through Tonto National Forest, me on a roan gelding named Storm, Dusty on a pinto mare named Esther. A horse's back being better than a psychiatrist's couch, I felt myself relaxing as we wound up the trail toward the ruins of an old Hohokam Indian village.

Despite many tourists' beliefs, most Indians hadn't lived in teepees. The Navajos used hogans; the Senecas lived in long-houses; the Hohokams, now extinct as a homogenous tribe, built centuries-standing pueblos. The pueblo above Carefree had been built more than eight hundred years ago, yet some rock walls remained upright, bearing witness to their skills. The residents also farmed, digging canals to irrigate the harsh desert climate, and today those canals could still be seen in satellite photos. The trail we were on had been used by the Hohokam people as they cared for their crops.

A couple of times I had ridden up here with Jimmy, whose Pima tribe was believed to be the direct descendants of the Hohokam. Part of me wished Jimmy was beside me today instead of my disloyal ex-boyfriend, but as they say, beggars can't be choosers, and I considered those coupons a gift from the Hohokam gods.

Thank you, Earth Doctor.

"What are you smiling about, Hon?"

"Just thinking about how beautiful this all is. The saguaros, the sage, the birds. Did you see the cardinal back there?"

"Saw two of them. Mr. Cardinal and his girlfriend."

I couldn't resist saying, "Sure hope she has better luck with him than I ever did with you."

"Oh, Hon, you wound me." That heart-breaking smile again. "Haven't I told you a hundred times that I've changed? Been to rehab, made my amends, cleaned up my act?"

The wind, as it wafted through the saguaros, seemed to whisper *Liar!* Due to the beauty of the day, I chose to ignore the warning, and concentrated instead on the sound of the horses' hooves against the fresh-smelling soil. Maybe Dusty was right, that life that turned me cynical. For certain, I had let myself become blind to life's frequent beauty. This soul-stirring day, for instance.

Two hours later we'd just finished putting our horses away when Slim, the ranch's owner, pulled me aside. "Got a horse I want you to meet, Lena."

I'd known Slim as long as I'd known Dusty, and if he wanted me to meet a horse, it would be a horse worth meeting. Dusty's temperamental opposite, Slim had honest gray eyes peering out of his dark Grecian face. An ex-jockey, he was little over five feet tall, which made me feel like a giant as I followed him to a corral behind the barn. Dusty remained behind in the tack room, explaining that one of the wranglers wanted to show him a hand-tooled saddle he might be interested in buying. Dusty liked flashy, thus his penchant for redheads.

However flashy that saddle was, it couldn't possibly compare to the mare romping and bucking her way around the corral. A half-Arab "leopard" Appaloosa, black spots the size of a silver dollar dotted her white body. Her dish-shaped face and narrow black nose authenticated her Arabian heritage. Her eyes, dark and wild, stared straight at me as I climbed the wooden rail fence and watched her caper.

I had never seen anything more magnificent.

"I let her out in the paddock an hour ago," Slim said, climbing up beside me. "It takes that long to get the kinks out of her system. Lots of fire in that girl."

"She's extraordinary."

"No lie there. Trouble is, she was owned by an idiot."

"Oh?"

The story Slim told me wasn't all that unusual. A newly arrived transplant from the East, having fallen in love with the West, decided to buy a green-broke horse. The problem was, the dude had never ridden before, and the first time up on the Appaloosa, she bucked him off and broke his leg.

"Probably had something to do with the fact that the ninny kept her in a stall for a month without letting her get any exercise."

I stared at him. "You allowed that?"

"Nah. I let her out myself every day, except for that last week. My sister, the one back in Hoboken, had a heart attack I flew back to see her. I was so shook up I forgot to tell one of the hands to see to her. When I got back, little Spot there had already done a number on him."

"He named her *Spot*?" I couldn't keep the outrage from my voice.

"Sure did. But that's not the worst. He was about to have her hauled off to the slaughterhouse, but I intervened. Paid him five hundred for her, a lot more than he'd get from those killers."

"You're an angel, Slim."

"Saint Slim, that's me. Here's the thing, Lena. I don't have time to mess around with a green-broke four-year-old, not even one that pretty, so I'm going to have to sell her on. I've got a couple more horses coming in next week on a long-term board so I don't have the room to keep her for long, either. There's a guy over in Cave Creek that's maybe interested in taking her on, but seeing as how you're here…" He let it trail off, knowing I would finish the sentence myself.

"You figured I might be interested."

The mare, as if sensing she was being talked about, stopped her antics and took a step toward us. Three of the leopard spots on her face ran so close together they formed a black blaze. As I admired her configuration, she moved even closer, flicking her ears back and forth.

"She seems to like people." I couldn't take my eyes off her.

"Some people, anyway. That girl has good judgment."

"Also known as horse sense."

Slim gave me a sidelong glance. "I'm not looking for a big profit here."

"And I'm not looking for a horse."

"Figured as much or you'd have already been up here, asking around."

"I don't have any place to keep her."

"You could keep her here until you make other arrangements."

"Thought you didn't have room?"

"A week in the paddock isn't going to kill her. I fact, it'll help her calm down some. I'll even put up a shelter to keep the sun off."

I didn't say anything for a few minutes, just watched her ears twitch back and forth. They were mirror-image crescent moons. As I sat there thinking, she reached the fence. Stuck out her narrow muzzle and smelled my riding boot. Looked up again. Met my eyes.

I surrendered.

"Jimmy's got a cousin over on the Rez who boards horses."

"What's that, a ten-minute drive from your office, fifteen? Hell, you could ride every morning before you started work. I can trailer her down for you."

"Figure she'll break my leg, too?"

"Nah, you two wild things were made for each other."

With that, we left the formerly named Spot to entertain herself in the paddock and headed to the office to take care of the paperwork.

First a cat, now a horse. What next?

I was still laughing at myself when I entered the tack room to tell Dusty what I'd just done.

Instead, I backed out of the tack room quietly enough that he never knew I was there.

After all, it's bad manners to interrupt a man in the middle of humping a big-breasted redhead.

Chapter Twenty-eight

Luckily we had taken my Jeep up to the stable, so I was able to make it back to Scottsdale, leaving Dusty to his own devices. Maybe the redhead had a car. Or a buckboard. Whatever. I didn't care.

Or at least I pretended not to care.

Walking into Desert Investigations, I announced, "I bought a horse!"

When Jimmy turned around, his smile faded into a frown. "Then why don't you look happier?"

"I'm ecstatic."

"Tell me another one. What's wrong with the horse?"

"Nothing a sensible woman can't fix."

The smile came back. "And that's you, I take it?"

"Yer durned tootin', pardner."

He laughed. "Your John Wayne impression needs a little work. Okay, so you bought a horse. Tell me all about him."

"Her."

I spent the next half hour showing him the pictures I'd taken on my phone, and extolling my new mare's virtues, which at this point were mainly her beauty. But I had spent enough time around horses to recognize a kindred spirit when I saw one, so I was confident that whatever problems she had could be worked through with a lot of love and even more patience.

Jimmy agreed. "And this business of keeping her at my cousin's, yeah, you could do that. He'd charge you a fair rate, too. But I have an even better idea."

"What could be better than that?"

"The secret I've been keeping about my construction project. I'm planning on buying a horse myself. In fact, I'm already halfway through fixing up a corral and sun shelter. That's what my cousin and I were working on when you called yesterday."

"Your 'cousin' sounded like a woman to me."

"You think women can't build things?" he scoffed. "I'll have you know Nita's handier with a hammer and nail than I ever thought of being, you sexist thing, you."

"Touché, Almost Brother. But do you think that corral will work for two? Sometimes horses can take a weird dislike to each other. Just like people.

He tried unsuccessfully to hide his smile. "Only if they're crowded. Right now, the paddock's already big enough for a small herd, but if you want, I'll divide it into two sections so your little App doesn't get her pretty hide bit. The water tank's supposed to be delivered around six tonight, and once it's in place, I'll start checking out the horses-for-sale ads. So what do you say?"

I thought about that for a moment, going over the pros and cons. The pros were obvious, a large—even private—space for my horse, close enough that I could almost jog to it. The con, though...

"You'd be my landlord!"

"You got a problem with an Indian landlord, Kemosabe?"

I burst out laughing.

Looking smug, he typed up a contract which I immediately signed. After slipping the contract into his jeans pocket, he said, "Welcome to the Rez. By the way, you said you were going to rename her. Any ideas yet?"

The perfect name had occurred to me during the drive from Carefree. "Adila," I said.

"Very pretty. What does it mean?"

"It's Arabic for *Equal*."

Okay, so maybe I was minus a boyfriend—not that I'd ever really *had* that bad boy—the trail ride had done two good things for me. One, I was now a horse owner. Two, being outdoors again had removed my memory block, so by noon I was knocking on the metal door of Richard Fairfield's trailer. I'd waited until his children were in school and his wife was well into her morning shift at the fast-food joint.

Fairfield wasn't happy to see me.

"What the hell do you want now?"

"Just a little chat."

"Chat, my ass."

"I can always come back when you're wife's here."

A sneer. "And that scares me because?"

"She doesn't know about Jacklyn Archerd."

"Aw, shit." He opened the door wider and stepped back enough to let me in.

Given Fairfield's record, I might have been more concerned about being alone with him in his trailer, but given his gimpy leg I figured I could handle him. If things got out of hand, there was always my favorite fallback: the .38 tucked into my pocket holster.

Without being asked, I settled myself on the sofa.

"You met Jacklyn at the Iron Cross?"

He laughed. "I'm no pussy but that place's too rough for me. Naw, I met her at that donut shop down the street from there. I was picking up a dozen to bring home and she was having coffee and we got to talking. You know how it goes."

An ex-con and a pretty woman. Yeah, I knew how it went. "You two still seeing each other?"

"Don't know if 'seeing each other' is what I'd call it, but naw, we flamed out something like a year ago."

I didn't bother asking him why he would risk his marriage over a fling with a woman he didn't seem to care about, because men are men, and that's the way they are. Some of them, anyway. "Did Jacklyn tell you about her son?"

"Stevie? Hell of a thing."

"She ever show you his room?"

He narrowed his eyes. "Why would she do a thing like that?"

"Answer the question."

"You're a nosy bitch."

"Not exactly breaking news."

He laughed again. "Okay, I saw the room. So what?"

"So did you decide to play knight in shining armor? Go hunting for the boy's abductor? Wreak vengeance on a different pedophile when you couldn't find him?"

He didn't respond right away, and when he did, no trace of laughter remained. His battered old face looked bereft. "My days as a knight in shining armor are long gone. Not that they were ever there in the first place."

Still feeling unsettled from my interview with Richard Fairfield, I headed back east to Scottsdale and the lair of Sean Beltran, Nicole's ex-husband.

His offices were in a steel-and-black-glass building abutting the Pima Reservation. The letters after his name on the door to his inner sanctum proclaimed him to be NCARB, AIA, LEED. When deciphered, the alphabet soup reinforced what I already knew, that he was an environmentally conscious hotshot architect. His corner office looked like he did: leathery and sleek. One floor-to-ceiling window faced the desert, the other the Pima end of the parking lot, naturally shaded by mature olive trees.

With his ruddy, weathered face, Beltran himself could have been half-Pima, but before making the appointment, I'd had Jimmy run him through the system. Beltran's parents both hailed from Connecticut.

In his early fifties and graying, Beltran remained slim and fit. My research showed that he had finished the Iron Man triathlon twice, and once made it almost to the summit of Everest before bad weather forced his party to return to base camp. He was giving it another try next year. In the meantime, he was keeping busy with weekly visits to the gun range with one of his many weapons even as his eco-friendly houses were going up all over the desert.

After a firm handshake, he said, "I have a client due in fifteen minutes, Ms. Jones, so let's make this as brief as possible. Unless you have news about my missing daughter." Brisk as he sounded, he couldn't keep the hope out of his eyes.

I shook my head. "I'm sorry, but no. When we talked I thought you understood that I'm looking into another case."

"Please don't tell me another little girl has been kidnapped."

"Not that I know of. Tell me, are you still a member of Parents of Missing Children?"

"I've given all that up, don't have time for it." He looked out of an eastern-facing window and pretended to be entranced by the sight of a mother javelina and her small brood rooting around in the brush.

"Your ex-wife remains a member."

Still watching the javelinas, he said, "That's her business, not mine."

Like his ex-wife had pointed out, people grieve differently. Women tended to join support groups, finding comfort by sharing their grief with others, but most men buried their grief under frenetic action. They organized searches, as I'd read Beltran had done in the early days of Candice's disappearance, or they doubled-down on work or a flurry of other activities. And then there were their marriages. When faced with tragedy, many marriages did not survive. The odds against them were even higher in the loss of a child, because you couldn't help seeing the child's features in the face of your spouse. It took a strong person to live with that kind of daily reminder.

Beltran finally tore his eyes away from the javelinas and looked at his watch. "Ten minutes, Ms. Jones, that's all that's left. Say what you need to say or ask, but that client's going to be here any minute, and I don't like to keep the Morgansterns waiting. They're good people and they care about the environment."

"Did you follow Brian Wycoff's trial?"

"Who's he?" Dead pan.

As I gave a brief summation of the case, his face remained immobile.

"Can't say I pay much attention to the news these days," Beltran finally said. "But it sounds like this Wycoff fellow got what was coming to him. Her, too, if she knew what was going on yet did nothing to help those children."

No pity, not even for a woman.

"You never felt an urge to, ah, exact revenge against Mr. Wcoff? Or his wife?"

"Be serious."

"You have a nice gun collection, I hear."

"I'm proud of it, yes. I even have the very Winchester John Wayne used in *The Searchers*. Ever see it?"

"Wonderful film. My favorite, even though that particular firearm wasn't manufactured until years after the period in which the action supposedly took place."

He looked pleased. "I like a woman who knows her firearms. You carrying now?"

"Nothing fancy, just an old snub-nosed Colt I'm particularly fond of. By the way, the article I read in *Phoenix Magazine* said you own quite the selection of .22 rifles."

"Same as most sport shooters in Arizona, except mine have a story behind them. My Smith & Wesson M&P 15, for instance, was once owned by Audie Murphy. Carved his name on the stock. Know who he was, Murphy?"

"Another actor. Won the Congressional Medal of Honor, among a slew of others."

Beltran liked that, too. "Why are you so interested in .22s? I'd figure a gun-savvy woman like you would be up for something more powerful."

"Just asking."

His happy expression vanished. "Oh, I get it. That Wycoff fellow and his wife? They were killed by .22LRs, right? And you came in here expecting to find some frothing-at-the-mouth vigilante. Sorry to disappoint you, but some time ago I decided to do something with my life other than obsess about what happened to…to…"

He swallowed. Searched for the javelina family again, but they had vanished over the ridge. Then he checked the north-facing window, where I saw a silver Mercedes angling into a space underneath an olive tree. In summer, smart Arizonans park in the shade, bird poop be damned.

"If you're looking for someone out for revenge, Ms. Jones, you should try…" He checked himself, took a deep breath, then began again, a note of finality in his voice. "Someone else. There's probably a long list of people who'd have been willing to do the honors for the Wycoffs. Now, if you'll excuse me, I see that the Morgansterns are here."

He stood up and escorted me out. As I crossed the parking lot, I saw a nicely dressed couple in their thirties exit the Mercedes. They had a little girl with them. She was about nine.

The same age I'd been when Brian Wycoff started hiding in my closet.

Chapter Twenty-nine

I arrived at Desert Investigations in a thoughtful mood. If someone hadn't shot at me, I wouldn't care who killed either of the Wycoffs. I had only begun my investigation because of my liking for Debbie Margules, proven innocent after the attempt on my own life. But the fact that the Wycoffs' killer had tried to kill me—and perhaps Nicole, too—meant that even after he or she had served his own brand of justice to those monsters, he was willing to kill the innocent.

Some poet once said, "After the first death, there is no other," and the meaning of that line has been debated by literary critics for years. I had my own interpretation because as a cop I'd seen it in action. After you'd killed one person, killing someone else came easy. For some people, it became downright addictive.

Then again, I had taken it for granted that only one killer was out there, but why couldn't there be two? Yes, I'd already dismissed the Agatha Christie solution of multiple killers as too fanciful. But killings committed by a couple weren't rare. Bonnie and Clyde, for instance, possibly the most famous lover/ outlaws of all. Then there was Charles Starkweather and Caril Ann Fugate, whose killing spree topped off at eleven bodies. Not to mention Raymond Fernandez and Martha Beck, who helped her lover romance vulnerable women, then robbed and killed twenty of them. Or David and Catherine Birnie, who together tortured and murdered five women. And Rosemary and Fred West, perpetrators of the torture killings of at least twelve women.

Maybe…

"Good grief, Lena, what are you thinking about?" Jimmy's voice pulled me out of my funk. "You look like you're about to kill someone."

"Who, me? I'm gentle as a lamb."

"Says the woman who a couple of days ago marched Frank Gunnerston in here at the point of a gun. You'd have shot him dead if he'd put up a fight, wouldn't you?"

"I don't like wife-beaters."

He gave me a pitying look. "How long has it been since you saw that shrink of yours?"

"A year, maybe. Two. Three. Hell, I don't remember."

"Now don't blow up at me, but you might give some consideration to going back."

"Don't be ridiculous. I'm fine."

"You're not fine."

"Says the computer expert moonlighting as a psychiatrist."

"When the Wycoffs were killed, I hoped that would be the end of it with you, that you'd be able to put the past behind you and live a normal life. Instead, this case has just dragged it all up again, just like I warned you it would. Leave it alone now, Lena. Norma and Brian Wycoff are dead. End of story. Drive back to Carefree and take a ride on that new horse of yours. Or go upstairs and pet your cat."

I actually considered his advice for a moment, but then I belatedly remembered something. I got up and headed for the door.

"Where are you going now?" he called after me.

"Glendale."

So many liars in the world, I thought as I knocked on Jacklyn Archerd's door, especially when you count lies of omission.

"What are you doing here?" Jacklyn said, opening the door just as I was about to knock again. Her hair was mussed and her lipstick smeared.

"Let me in and I'll tell you."

"I'm busy."

"Sure you are. Your boyfriend in there?"

"I don't have a boyfriend."

"Tell me another one."

She was getting ready to slam the door in my face when a familiar male voice called out, "Oh, go ahead and let her in. She apparently knows."

Resigned, she opened the door. When I walked through, I saw Richard Fairfield sitting on the sofa, a Budweiser in his hand. She'd planted so much lipstick on his face he looked like an Estee Lauder ad. Old cons, they just can't resist an adrenalin rush.

"While the cat's away the mice will play, eh, Richard?" I asked him.

"Why can't you mind your own business?" Jacklyn asked, taking her seat beside him. "We're not hurting anyone."

"Try telling that to his wife and kids. And, point of fact, when someone shoots at me, it becomes my business."

She crossed her arms across her chest. "Better lay off the weed, bitch. I never shot at you. If I had, you'd be planted in a cemetery somewhere."

Oddly enough, I believed her. Turning to Fairfield, I said, "How about you, Dick? Try any target practice lately?"

"I don't know what the hell you're talking about."

"Where were you last Thursday, say, around three-thirty?"

"Damned if I know. You think I keep a diary?"

Jacklyn gave him a look, then said, "He was here. With me."

Now that, I didn't believe. Ignoring Jacklyn, I said to Fairfield, "So you let your kids come home to an empty house."

He blinked. "Nah. That's something I'd never do. So I musta been there. I always am when they get home from school. You can ask them." Then he narrowed his eyes. "But you better not tell them why you're asking. Come to think of it, you stay the hell away from my kids in the first place. And my wife. You say anything to her about this and I'll..."

"You'll what?"

"Make you sorry."

I gave him a long look. Saw the truth in his eyes.

Couples.

You never know what's going on with them. Their relationship can look idyllic on the outside while they seethed with resentment inside. And yet if you threatened either one of them, the other would tear your head off.

On my way back to Scottsdale, I thought about the couples involved in the case, couples who despite their personal quarrels, might lie for one another. Jacklyn and Richard. Nicole and Sean Beltran, both still grieving the loss of their daughter. Casey and Kay Starr, although I'd not yet talked to her. Note to self: interview that woman. Then there was Cyril and Roseanne Sanders, two heartbroken people. Debbie and...No. Debbie was a widow. No man in the offing there. At least not as far as I could see.

Then again the word "couples" didn't always refer to the married or having-an-affair kind. They could be father and daughter, like Mario Genovese and Shana Genovese Ferris, both of whom had the motive and the spine to kill both Wycoffs.

Speaking of Mario Genovese, I remembered him telling me that for a brief time he and Debbie had been lovers. When I interviewed him at his house, I'd noticed a .22 rifle in his gun cabinet. Had the Yavapai County Sheriff's Office thought to run a ballistics test on the thing? Maybe not, because they were investigating a torture killing, not a shooting, and Norma Wycoff had been shot in Pima County, not Yavapai. As an ex-cop, I understood the gaps that can happen when different jurisdictions are involved in an investigation.

Roseanne Sanders had told me that while Mario had helped pour her drunken husband Cyril into the car the night Brian Wycoff was murdered, she'd never seen Shana. So Shana had lied about her actions that night. Because she'd been busy elsewhere, taking care of the threat to her children? I could easily imagine Shana shooting her uncle to death, but try as I might, I couldn't see her torturing him to death.

Torture takes a whole different level of hate.

During the drive back to Desert Investigations I received four calls from Dusty, but after listening to the oh-I'm-so-sorry-we've-got-to-talk message on the first call, I deleted the rest. One of the ranch hands must have seen me go into the tack room and had delighted in telling him.

Determined not to let the two-timing son of a bitch bother me again, I wiped him out of my mind by placing a call to Yavapai County Detective Yvonne Eastman. She wasn't in but I left a message on her voice mail: had a ballistics test been run on the .22 rifle in Mario Genovese's gun cabinet? Then I brought up my case notes and began going through them. I was puzzling over one discrepancy when Jimmy's voice cut through my mental fog.

"Lena, you need to see this."

Leaving the discrepancy problem for later, I walked over to Jimmy's desk, where I saw he'd pulled up a short newspaper article from the Reading, Pennsylvania *Eagle* on his computer. The article was an old one, dated twelve years back.

"What's that?" I asked.

"An obituary."

"What's so fascinating about the death of some engineer named Gordon Hazelit?"

He ran his finger along a sentence. "See here? 'Survived by spouse Kay Winston Hazlit.'"

"So?"

"Follow the magic cursor." He clicked out of that screen and brought up another obit, this one from the *Arizona Republic*, eight years earlier. Chiropractor Elias Mumford had died in a fall while hiking with his wife in the Superstition Mountains. Aloud, Jimmy read the obit's concluding sentence. "Survived by spouse Kay Winston Mumford."

What a coincidence. "Kay Winston, whoever she is, sure has bad luck when it comes to husbands."

He gave me a grim smile. "Remember yesterday, when you

asked me to look up Casey Starr's wife's maiden name. Guess what it is."

Light dawned. "You're going to tell me it's 'Winston,' aren't you?"

"Exactamundo, Kemosabe. Kay Winston, born in Pittsburgh, PA, only child of Jennifer and James Winston. She's a Scorpio, in case you're interested."

"Not." After taking a deep breath, I said, "Look, before we get all excited here, we need to know how her first husband, the unfortunate Gordon, died."

"I'm way ahead of you." Jimmy pulled up another *Reading Eagle* article, a two-incher on page three, which reported that Gordon Hazlit, an engineer for DiaCom Industries, had fallen in the bathtub, hit his head and drowned. After a brief investigation, his death was determined to be accidental.

"Looks like our Kay goes for guys who are unsteady on their feet," he said.

"What are the odds." It wasn't a question.

"Bet you're interested in the financials."

"Lay 'em on me, Almost Brother."

That grim smile again. "Kay inherited estates of mid-six figures from each husband, no great fortune, but…" He paused.

"People have killed for less."

I wondered what Casey Starr's business was worth. Somewhere in the millions, certainly. "Maybe she married for love this time around."

"Or as Scarlett O'Hara's father said to her in *Gone With the Wind*, 'Like marries like.'"

Not certain of my motive—former foster kids gotta stick together?—at the end of the day, I climbed into my Jeep and drove straight to Litchfield Park. Luck was with me. Casey Starr was home, but Kay was nowhere in sight. She didn't seem to spend much time with her husband.

Casey pretended to be glad to see me. Flashing a toothy grin, he asked, "Don't tell me you came back for another cat."

"Then I won't tell you." I looked around. "Where's your wife?"

The grin didn't dim. "Stuck in another meeting."

Husband Killers Anonymous, perhaps?

"Busy lady, isn't she?" I took the newspaper printouts from my tote and handed them over. Waited.

Casey was a good actor; most psychopaths are. He sounded perfectly normal when asking, "What made you think I'd be interested in this?" His eyes looked wary.

"A word to the wise. And, on second thought, I just might be interested in the rest of those kittens. And their mother. What kind of package deal can you give me?" Whatever was going to happen in this house—and something would—I wanted the cats safe. I'd worry about finding homes for them later.

Still smiling, smiling, smiling, Casey named a price so exorbitant I could have bought a racehorse with it.

Instead, I wrote out a check and walked to my Jeep, four felines richer.

After depositing Mama Snowball, Snowball No. 2, Snowball No. 3, and Snowball No. 4 in my apartment to help Snowball No. 1 finish tearing the place apart, I went downstairs to the office and pulled up the case notes again.

Scrolled down to the problem area.

Not that there was only one problem; there was a baker's dozen. As a crotchety TV doctor once said about his patients, "Everybody lies." That observation held true for murder suspects, too. People lied for so many reasons—fear, guilt, embarrassment—and every now and then, they lied to protect the innocent. Or even to protect the guilty.

Two evil people had been murdered. Norma Wycoff had died quickly, but Brian Wycoff only after a lengthy torture session. No one mourned either.

Certainly not me.

So I had to ask myself once again: why did I care? The world was surely a better place without those two monsters.

Squinting against the monitor's glare, I studied the problem area again.

Thought about it.

Read it again. Noticed what I'd not noticed the first time around, whether accidentally or accidentally-on-purpose. Then I logged onto the Internet and did some quick and dirty research that confirmed that my suspicions were right. Who knew? Certainly not me.

I thought about the situation some more.

Then I reread my research and reread my case notes. All of them, this time, starting with the first paragraph on the first page.

I should have spotted it earlier, but then again, I'm not a firearms expert—just an ex-cop who lugs around an old .38 out of misplaced sentimentality.

What the hell should I do now?

An hour later, after two Excedrin dulled the headache I had given myself, I realized the decision would be best left to someone else, so I typed up some information, printed it out, and made my way through the heat to my Jeep.

Sophia Ceballos, the fourth member of Parents of Missing Children had been released from the hospital a couple of days earlier. Unusual for a woman who was supposedly "in traction," as the other women at Debbie's Desert Oasis had claimed. She was still in a cast, but with the aid of a crutch, she was able to open the door at her north Scottsdale condo. She looked like hell, with a splint on her nose, a swollen jaw, and an eggplant-colored bruise covering the entire left side of her face. When I showed her my ID, the bruise darkened even further. She had to be at least in her fifties, but with an odd mercy the swelling on her face had smoothed out any incipient wrinkles.

"Debbie warned me about you," she said.

It's always nice to be greeted with joy. "May I come in? It's hot out here."

Sighing, she hobbled away, ushering me into a mostly-beige living room that smelled of antiseptic. A table next to the beige-and-beige sofa was heaped with vials of medication, a large box of tissues, and a carafe of what looked like iced tea. She didn't offer me any.

"Let's get this over with as quickly as possible. I just took another Oxycodone and I'll be nodding off in a couple minutes." She plopped down heavily on the sofa and folded her hands in her lap. A large bandage decorated her left arm.

The only things not-beige in the room were the framed photographs of young girl: girl with bright pink bougainvillea; girl with green bicycle; girl with red wagon; girl with golden retriever. Sophia's daughter, Trish, who had disappeared thirty-two years earlier when Brian Wycoff was still preying on the young and innocent. I felt a pang of guilt for the added misery I was about to inflict, but there was no avoiding it. I had to be sure, so without invitation, I sat down on a beige-on-beige chair.

"Your car's an automatic, right?"

"What's left of it, yeah."

"You've got a white Hyundai Elantra parked in your carport and it doesn't have a scratch on it."

"Rental."

"Been driving around, have you?"

"Somebody has to go to the grocery store and since I'm the only person living here, I won the coin toss."

Before I could ask another question, three fat Chihuahuas waddled into the room. The fattest of the trio took one look at me and growled.

"Poncho doesn't like you," Sophia warned, "so maybe you'd better leave."

"I'm used to not being liked. Haven't died of it yet."

While the other Chihuahuas settled themselves at her feet, Poncho waddled closer to me, the side of his lip sticking to a dry tooth. It made him look like he was sneering. Maybe he was.

I raised my feet off the beige carpet and tucked them under my butt. "Since you've been driving, maybe you drove over to Apache Junction."

"Bullshit."

"Then maybe, a couple days later, you took a trip up to Black Canyon City."

"More bullshit."

"Prove it."

"Since when do I have to prove a thing to you?"

I looked her up and down, noting the location of her injuries. "Your left side seems to have taken the brunt of the impact."

"Aren't you observant. Yeah, I got T-boned by a garbage truck. Good thing it took out the rear of my car, not the front, or I wouldn't be sitting here listening to bullshit."

"You're right-handed, I notice."

"Most people are."

Poncho growled again. Gee, Sophia and her dog were a barrel of laughs.

It had to be asked. "Did you kill Norma and Brian Wycoff?"

"I hear he died slowly and painfully." A smile tugged at her bruised lips.

"That he did. Mind answering the question?"

The smile segued into a smirk. "Yes, I do mind."

In a way, I admired her. After experiencing the greatest tragedy possible, she had survived with her spirit intact. Jimmy's research had revealed that she'd gone back to college—having originally dropped out when she became pregnant with Trish—and received her master's in psychology. Now a licensed grief counselor, she not only spent her free time volunteering at a no-kill animal shelter, but acted as a foster parent for hard-to-place dogs. Like nasty-tempered Chihuahuas. Yet here I was, cross-examining her.

"Okay, let's say you did kill them. What do you think your punishment should be?"

When she laughed, Poncho stopped growling. He gave her a yearning look, then rejoined the other dogs at her feet. I was surprised he didn't jump up in to her lap, but maybe the surly little pipsqueak couldn't reach it.

For some reason, Sophia Caballos decided to answer my last question. "What do I think my punishment should be if I killed those two? I think the Marine Corps Band should play 'Stars and Stripes Forever' as the President of the United States awarded me the Medal of Honor."

I smiled at her. "That's what I think, too."

Then I stood up and left.

The day not yet over, I briefly stopped at Desert Investigations. Upon checking my messages, I found one from Detective "*Maria*" Eastman, telling me, no, ballistics had not been run on any of Mario Genovese's firearms, and why should they? The victim in question had bled to death. If I had new information, call her ASAP.

I had also received several more phone messages from Dusty, delivering the standard begging and pleading. I erased them.

"What's wrong?" Jimmy asked.

"What do you mean, 'what's wrong'?"

"You don't look happy."

Jimmy had never been fond of Dusty, so there was no way I was going to let him know the cheating son of a bitch had snookered me again, so I just said, "You know what? I think I'm going to go upstairs, feed the cats, and take a cold shower. After all my driving around, I feel like I've got half the Sonoran Desert's dust on me."

Besides, now that I had talked to everyone involved in the Wycoff case, I had a major decision to make and a cold shower might help me think it through.

Ten minutes later I had reached my decision. I was dressed in fresh clothes and was giving Snowball No. 1, Snowball No. 2, Snowball No. 3, Snowball No. 4, and Mama Snowball an early dinner when I heard a polite tapping at my door.

I checked my Timex. Five o'clock on the dot. It was probably Jimmy, wanting to know if I needed anything before he headed home to await the arrival of his water tank. I smiled, looking forward to future days on my new horse. She might be only green-broke, but I was, too.

Equals.

Still smiling, I opened the door. "Maybe I'll have her trailered down tomorrow if…"

But it wasn't Jimmy.

It was Dusty.

Uninvited, the cheating son of a bitch rushed by me and plopped himself down on my sofa as if he belonged there.

"Get out."

He ignored my command. "But, Hon, it's not what it looked like." The man couldn't even deliver a plausible excuse.

"I saw your bare ass! And hers!"

"You don't understand."

"What's to understand? Hell, Dusty, this time you broke your own record for cheating. We were together for, what, three hours and you were already two-timing me. Just get out."

"But Hon…"

"Don't 'but Hon,' me. Go tell your sad story to Sexaholics Anonymous."

"I don't need…"

I heard someone coming up the stairs. I peeked around the open door and saw a furious Jimmy taking the steps two at a time. This mess was about to get messier.

"Lena, are you all right? I saw someone go by."

"I'm fine. Go see about your water tank."

He ignored me, too. Upon reaching the landing, he peeked around the door and saw Dusty. "Oh, for God's sake. What the hell's *he* doing here?"

I looked at him in shock. "I thought Indians never swore."

"Only when provoked. And I'm feeling pretty provoked right now."

"Not half as provoked as me," I muttered.

Jimmy strode into my apartment walked up to Dusty, and halted threateningly close. "Why can't you leave her alone? Doesn't she have enough trouble without you stirring up more?"

Face red, Dusty sprang to his feet. "My relationship with Lena is none of your business!"

I'd never known Dusty to get violent, but there was always a first time for everything, so I asserted myself.

"There is no relationship, Dusty. Now, both of you, get out!"

Menace hung in the air for a moment, then Dusty blinked. "Hon, I…"

"Out."

He stared at his boots for a moment, then stepped carefully around Jimmy and walked slowly to the door. Once there, he paused and gave it one last try.

"You sure this is what you want?"

"Never been surer of anything in my life."

He gave me a searching look. "Yeah. You're right. Maybe you need someone who's never hurt you."

He left.

One furious male gone, one more to go. I turned and faced Jimmy. "Since when is my personal life any of your business?"

"Since the rate of domestic homicide in Arizona shot to forty-five percent higher than the national average."

"You're quoting statistics at me?"

"I'd say statistics are pretty apropos right now."

"I can take care of myself."

A slight smile. "Who says you're the one I was worried about?"

I blinked. "You want me to believe you were worried about Dusty?"

"You're the one with the gun. Promise me you won't follow him to Black Canyon City and shoot him."

"Oh, Jimmy. I'm not going to shoot anyone."

"That's a relief."

Before I could stop him, he did something he'd never done before. Rapidly closing the distance between us, he put out his hand and caressed my cheek.

"You know where I live, Lena."

Then he walked out.

Chapter Thirty

Another rough night.

I played with Snowball No. 1, Snowball No. 2, Snowball No. 3, Snowball No. 4, and Mama Snowball for a while. Then I thought about Dusty. Then I thought about Jimmy. Then I drug the bankers' box from my storage unit into the bedroom and shut the door, confining the cats' havoc to the living room. I needed time alone with some photographs.

Moving the Vindicator aside, I took the picture of a child's bloodied dress out of the box. Looked at it. Laid it in my lap and folded my hands across it.

Let the memories come.

The shot.

My mother screaming.

Darkness descending as I lay on the pavement.

And earlier…

Running through the woods. More gunshots. Children screaming, dying.

My father falling. Dying.

My baby brother. Dying.

Jamie.

Oh, Jamie.

Chapter Thirty-one

The next morning Jimmy said nothing about last night's dust-up or his odd behavior afterwards, so the workday passed quickly. Yolanda Blanco and her daughter Inez stopped by Desert Investigations to say hi. Yolanda wanted to ask why her bill seemed so small. She didn't quite buy my explanation, but what expectant grandmother is going to argue about having an extra thousand dollars left in her pocket when that money can be used for baby clothes and a crib?

Bob Grossman and Sophie Perrins also dropped in to let me know that Frank Gunnerston had been bound over for trial, and that my name—as well as his ex-wife's—would appear on the witness list.

When I groaned, Sylvie sniped, "Maybe before you took his case, you shoulda first done due diligence."

"Guilty as charged. He get bail?"

Bob shook his head. "Judge Knopf just laughed when Gunnerston's defense attorney brought it up. Just between you, me, and the lamppost, word on the street is that the judge's granddaughter was stalked by an ex-boyfriend, got roughed up by him a few times, and fled the state before we could catch up with him. So Knopf is often sympathetic. Too bad there aren't more like her."

I expected Sylvie to add to the judge's accolades, but she didn't. She was probably thinking about other women, other crimes, endings that didn't turn out as well, killers that got away.

"I guess you can't catch them all," I said.

"Nope. You sure can't."

By the time the day was over, I'd finished the billing and taken on two new cases. Another runaway daughter and an elderly millionaire who wanted us to find out if his twenty-something fiancée loved him for himself or for his pocketbook.

Just another day at Desert Investigations.

But then the day ended, and I could no longer put off what had to be done. After going upstairs to give the cats enough food to last several days, I locked my apartment door and left.

Evenings, even in scorching August, are beautiful in Arizona. The skies are clear and spangled with stars. Rush hour long over, the streets were fairly quiet. I saw few joggers. As I neared Biltmore Fashion Square, traffic picked up and I found myself in the midst of a group of low-riders tooling down Camelback Road, their sound systems blaring out a mixture of mariachi and rap. I lost them when I hooked right on Twenty-fourth Street, only to find myself being tailgated by an orange Ferrari on its way to some big do at the nearby resort. Whoever was driving—I think it was a woman, but these days you can't always tell—was listening to One Direction, for God's sake. I lost the Ferrari two blocks before I made my turn on Bonadventure.

Guy DeLucca heard me drive up, and opened the door before I was halfway up the walk.

"What brings you out on this hot night?" he asked, as he ushered me into his monochromatic living room.

"For another go at that tea of yours. Most enjoyable I've had all week."

The old social worker smiled. "Then you must hang out in some pretty nasty places, because mine's instant."

"Say what you will about the taste, it's efficient."

"Then you've got a glass coming up. Sit, sit. I'll be right back."

I sat on the brown sofa, leaving the recliner for him. The sofa was surprisingly comfortable. The whole room, despite all its brown-ness, felt comfortable. I especially liked the military photographs, and the Civil War saber and the Walther PPK/S pistol hanging on the wall. If you're going to decorate, pick things that mean something to you.

When DeLucca returned to from the kitchen a few minutes later, he only carried one glass.

"Aren't you going to have any?" I asked, as he handed the glass to me. Several undissolved tea crystals floated on the surface. I didn't care. I was parched.

"This late in the day? Caffeine keeps me awake."

Not just the caffeine, I guessed. The memories of the seven children he had placed with the Wycoffs probably kept him up, too. As I chugged my bad tea, he eased himself into the recliner across from me.

"Why are you really here, Lena?" he asked.

"Making a delivery." I handed him the first page of the printout I'd made earlier.

He looked at it, frowned, then read aloud, "Lindsey Margules, nine. Steven Archerd, seven. Candice Beltran, nine. Trish Ceballos, eight." He looked back up at me. "What's this?"

"You're retired, in seemingly good health, and you have a lot of time on your hands. You're also resourceful, good at tracking people down. Finding out what happened to these kids would give you something constructive to do for a change."

The frown morphed into a faint smile. "Constructive?"

"As opposed to running around killing people."

"Ah. That."

He eased back in the recliner. "And here I thought I'd been so clever."

I eased back, too. "You sort of blew it when you made that fake attempt on my life up in Black Canyon City."

He had the grace to look contrite. "I hope I didn't scare you ladies too much, but when you told me Mrs. Margules had been arrested, I had to do something."

"So you made certain the authorities knew the killer was still out there, still in possession of the gun that killed Norma Wycoff. It worked, too. Mrs. Margules was released."

"None the worse for wear, I hope."

Remembering the delicious red velvet cake, I said, "The cops went out their way to be nice. You almost got by me, you know, until I remembered something odd about that Walther PPK—that it takes a .22 LR, a caliber usually associated with small game rifles." I motioned to the German pistol hanging on the wall. "Did your grandfather bring the Walther home from World War II?"

He nodded. "Been a family keepsake ever since."

"And it's unregistered."

The smile returned. "It was against regulations to bring commandeered firearms into the country, so he sort of smuggled it in."

There were two other things I'd already guessed but wanted confirmed. "Norma. You shot her in both eyes. Why?"

"Because she refused to see."

"That eighth burn on Wycoff's thigh. Who was it for?"

He glanced over at the photograph of him as a young man guarding the Tomb of the Unknown Soldier. "We don't always know their names."

I got it. "So the eighth burn was a symbol, too."

"We discussed the importance of symbols the last time you were here."

"Acetylene torch?"

He gestured toward his kitchen. "Culinary torch. I use it whenever I make crème brûlée."

"I saw your dessert cookbook but since your tea is so terrible I never thought of you as a foodie."

"Only when it comes to dessert. Speaking of terrible tea, want some more?"

The question, coming from left field, caught me by surprise. I looked at my empty glass. "That would be nice."

"Coming right up." He took the glass from me and went back to the kitchen. When he returned fully five minutes later, he wore a look of surprise on his face. "You still here? I thought you'd be halfway to the nearest police station by now."

"You thought wrong."

He handed me the tea. "After what I did, you're not afraid of me?"

"Why should I be?"

He was silent for a moment, then said, "You're right. I would never hurt you, Little Girl Doe."

"I'm a big girl now, Mr. DeLucca."

"When I look at you, I still see that scared nine-year-old I placed with the Wycoffs. And all the other children whose lives I ruined."

My memories were bad, but in a way, his were worse. None of mine included self-hate.

"This is it, then?" he said, sitting down. "You're not turning me in?"

Instead of answering, I opened my tote and removed the rest of the printout, all two hundred eighty-eight pages. "Here are the highlights of the investigations into the children's disappearances. Names, dates, alibis, etc. To my way of thinking, Brian Wycoff snatched Lindsey Margules and Trish Ceballos and killed them, but that's just a guess. You might find out otherwise. As for the other children, they're also cold cases. What with budget cuts and all, the detectives' caseloads are stretched pretty thin these days. So is Desert Investigations', although Jimmy and I will make time for you whenever you ask. One smart, resourceful man devoting himself full time to these disappearances might be able to make inroads where overburdened cops can't." I gave him a wry smile. "And unlike them, you wouldn't feel hampered by legalities, would you?"

He glanced at the Walther PPK hanging on the wall. "No. No I wouldn't."

Satisfied, I drained the awful tea and left.

Business accomplished, I aimed the Jeep north and drove through the warm night until I reached Black Canyon City. I passed by Coyote Corral, recognizing Mario's Chevy pickup and Shana's old Volvo. Despite the fact that it was only Tuesday, the parking lot was crowded.

Further along, I saw one light burning in the little yellow house at Debbie's Desert Oasis. All the guest trailers were in the dark, yet Debbie's small parking lot was crowded, too. There was something independent about a trailer—especially a trailer painted with horses or butterflies—that appealed to the nomad in all of us.

I continued on up the gravel road to the crest of the hill, then pulled off into a grove of scrub pine and stopped, looking down at the Genovese spread. Lit only by moonlight, the house sat in darkness. Brittany and Luke were asleep, maybe dreaming of new bikes and .22 varmint rifles. What did poor, confused Grace dream about, I wondered? Her dead brother?

If so, did she smile? Or did she scream?

For the rest of the night I sat there listening to the wind, the creek, the crickets, and the coyotes. Once I even thought I heard a baby cry but put that down to my imagination.

Oh, Jamie!

By the time the inky sky lightened into gray, then milky blue, the way forward had become clear. I turned my Jeep around and headed for the Pima Reservation.

To receive a free catalog of Poisoned Pen Press titles, please provide your name, address, and e-mail address in one of the following ways:

Phone: 1-800-421-3976
Facsimile: 1-480-949-1707
Email: info@poisonedpenpress.com
Website: www.poisonedpenpress.com

Poisoned Pen Press
6962 E. First Ave. Ste 103
Scottsdale, AZ 85251